A Fatal Ambition

A Fatal Ambition

Richard Haley

ROBERT HALE · LONDON

Robert Hale Limited
Clerkenwell House
Clerkenwell Green
London EC1R 0HT

www.halebooks.com

2 4 6 8 10 9 7 5 3 1

Dedicated to Barbara Nicholson

Typeset in 10/13pt New Century Schoolbook
Printed in Great Britain by MPG Books Group,
Bodmin and King's Lynn

O N E

The car drew off the road and into the car-park that was sited across from the entrance to the golf-links. Beyond the car-park was an area of grassland that gave way to a narrow valley known as Royds Cliff Gully. A vehicle had once been driven off the car-park and over the grassland and had then hurtled down into it. There had been three youths in the car; they'd all died. The car had been stolen and the assumption had been that the driver, who had no licence, had been fooling about and had lost control.

That incident had given the driver of the present car the idea. This car was now driven out of the car-park and on to the grassland, to a point halfway between car-park and gully. The driver applied the handbrake, but kept the engine running. The other person in the car was a woman in her twenties. She'd been drinking and the drinks had been spiked and she was in a heavy sleep. The petrol-tank's indicator showed that the car was close to running on empty. It was an older model and not fitted with airbags. The driver unbuckled the woman's seat-belt, gave a satisfied nod, then opened the door on the driver's side a little way, released the handbrake and began to drive as rapidly as possible over the uneven ground towards the gully. Within three yards of the edge, the driver pushed the door fully open and leapt out. The car shot cleanly over the edge and crashed down, rolling over several times. The driver stood for a couple of minutes as the early-hours' silence began to gather again, massaging the hip and thigh that had taken most of the impact in the leap from the fast-moving car. The driver then began to step carefully, using a small torch, down a rough footpath that cut though the scree and vegetation of the sloping terrain. A stream ran along the floor of the gully and the mangled wreckage of the car was half in it. The driver had to wade into the stream to be able, by checking a pulse point, to ensure that the woman in the wreckage was dead.

The woman was, very dead.

'I have an appointment with Mr Gillis. The name's Frank Crane.'

The receptionist pressed a key on a small switchboard. 'A Mr Crane to see you, John. He'll be along shortly, Mr Crane. Please take a seat.'

Crane sat down on a comfortable banquette that ran opposite the reception desk. A man approached him very soon. 'Mr Crane, how do you do. I'm John Gillis.' They shook hands. 'Come this way, please.'

Gillis led him from the reception area into a long office. Partitions enclosed what Crane took to be the different departments of the insurance broking set-up. There were a number of small, half-glazed offices to the left which would probably accommodate senior staff.

Gillis's space contained one large desk and one smaller one. A middle-aged woman occupied the smaller one. Gillis set a visitor's chair at the side of his own desk and both men sat down.

'Know much about insurance broking, Mr Crane?'

'Frank, please.'

'OK, I'm John. And the lady is Eunice and I'm hoping she'll make us some coffee.'

'Hello, sir,' she said, smiling. 'It's really John's turn to make the coffee, but I'll stretch a point. How do you like it?'

'Black, one sugar, Eunice, thanks.'

As she went off, he said to Gillis, 'The answer to your question is that I know as much about insurance broking as the man in the street.'

Gillis nodded. 'There's not much to know. We sniff out the best deals for our clients on any kind of insurance. It costs no more going through a broker than dealing direct with the insurance company. The insurance companies get more business and they don't have the hassle of getting the money in as the clients pay us and we settle with the insurers net of our brokerage.'

'Very succinctly put, John,' Crane said, smiling.

'Nearly all the people you saw as we came down the office sell insurance: buildings, contents, motor, life and so forth. My job is different. My work is all to do with claims. Ah, thank you, Eunice....'

The woman put down the cups of coffee and returned to her desk. 'I work on behalf of many of the insurers we deal with. They trust me to do my homework and deal with claims fairly. It all tends to be routine stuff and the insurer has the last word.'

He drank a little of his coffee. He was a big burly bear of a man. Everything about him looked heavy: great shoulders and large hands, a massive head of coarse black hair brushed straight back and bulging eyes that swam behind the strong lenses of horn-rimmed glasses. He was slightly flushed, as weighty men tended to be who worked hard under pressure, and his build gave the impression he liked to relax in the evening over a few pints.

'The reason I asked you to come, John, is because I've had a claim recently that looks just a bit iffy. I've had clearance to engage you by the insurers, assuming you're willing to take on the work. There's a million pounds involved that the insurers are liable for.'

'A lot of moolah.'

'The client was a woman and she took out a lot of term assurance just over a year ago. I daresay you know what term assurance is.'

'There's no pay-out unless you die between certain parameters of, say, age thirty to sixty.'

'Exactly. Men take it out to safeguard their wives if they should die in harness. It's fairly cheap, as men don't kick the bucket in harness too often these days. If they reach the end of the term still in one piece, of course, the insurers don't shell out a bean. For them it tends to be a win-win.'

'And this woman went and died on you?'

'You think fast. She dies young and her husband cops a million.'

'And that's where the iffy bit comes in?'

'More men than women take out term assurance and it's normally for much smaller amounts. Two hundred and fifty thousand top whack, rule of thumb.'

'Didn't it seem odd at the time it was taken out?'

Gillis smiled. 'I only get involved when a claim hits my desk. These young blades in the selling departments, they don't query the amount covered, the bigger the better as far as they're concerned. If the person in question can afford the premiums and gives evidence of good health the policy goes through.'

'How did the woman die?'

'We're at the golf-links beyond Heaton Woods. There's a car-park opposite the entrance. It isn't fenced and there's a grassy area beyond it which goes on to Royds Cliff Gully. Well, Lydia Glover, our client, crashed her car into that gully and died on impact. She'd taken sleeping tablets with alcohol and the police reckon she'd nodded off at the wheel. They have no explanation as to why she'd driven off the car-park and on to the grassland. The coroner had to leave the verdict open-ended.'

Crane said, 'I remember reading about the accident and I know the area well. No one has any idea what she was doing up there?'

Gillis shook his head and finished the last of his coffee. 'It was a total mystery; everything she did that night was out of character. It could have been suicide if she'd stayed awake long enough to drive herself deliberately over the edge. It was all gone into; she seems to have been in a stable marriage and the husband can't understand why she'd mixed drugs with booze and gone on driving. He can't understand either why she'd want to top herself, if that's what she really did.' He shrugged. 'Anyway, she always paid the premiums on the nail, she was in good health and even if it *was* suicide the insured sum will still be payable as the policy was over a year old.'

'But, as you say, it does seem iffy.'

'Frank, Eunice and I handle this stuff week in week out and we both had bad vibes about this one. Term assurance is cheap but not all that cheap when we're talking premiums to cover a million.'

'I've never known *anyone* take out such a large amount,' Eunice, who'd obviously been listening to their discussion as she worked, put in quietly. 'As John says, the limit tends to be a quarter of a million, enough to let the spouse pay off the mortgage and have some cash to sort herself out. Or himself in this case.'

Crane nodded. 'Have you met the husband?'

'He rang about a week or so after the death. I told him it would take a little while to process the claim and if there was a will it would have to go through probate. He said they'd both made wills and everything in each estate went to the other. He wasn't getting agitated about a pay-out.'

'How did he seem?'

'People react to the death of a spouse in different ways. Ken Glover didn't give me the impression he was overwhelmed by emotion. But he did sound, how can I put this, uneasy.'

'You don't think he could have had anything to do with the pills and the alcohol?'

'Well, I'm sure the police looked into all that, but the bloke just seemed edgy and I couldn't really see why, as he had every right to inform us officially of his wife's death and ask about the policy payout. Unless there was something dodgy about it all.'

Crane nodded again and thought for a few seconds. 'I'm not sure I can help you, John. The police have looked into the circumstances of a death that could be either an accident or suicide and all your paperwork's in order. It doesn't really give me too much to work on.'

'We thought long and hard before asking you in,' the big heavy man said, running a hand through his bushy hair. 'Both Eunice and I. But it all keeps coming back to such a large amount of term assurance, with only just over a year's premiums paid. And this woman had no apparent reason for taking her own life, if it was suicide, or simply driving round stoked up on drink and drugs.'

Crane said, 'I might bring you a big bill and no result. In fact I'd say that that was more than likely.'

'It's a chance I'm prepared to take. The insurers trust me to sort out their claims fairly and accurately, and something just bugs me about this one, though, as you say, all the boxes do look to have been ticked.'

Crane studied Gillis. He guessed he'd been in the insurance business most of his life to have built up such a grasp of the claims side. If he was unhappy about this particular claim it had to be based on a wealth of experience. 'All right, John,' he said, 'I'll see what I can do, though I'll promise nothing.'

'That's good enough for me.'

'Who gave you my name, by the way?'

'One of the police involved. And a DI Jones.'

Crane's old boss, still looking out for him.

'A CID man called DS Benson said the police were regarding the case as closed. There was nothing suspicious about it as far as they could see and they tended to lean towards the woman being depressed and suicidal. If that *was* the case she might have taken out such a lot of insurance to ensure her husband was well provided for. But if I had reservations about it he also suggested talking it over with you.'

'I'll spell out my charges.' Crane did so, with Gillis jotting down the figures in his desk diary. Crane didn't come cheap and people sometimes winced at the bottom line, but Gillis was a professional who accepted the figures as within budget. Crane took out his notebook. 'Well, if that's all satisfactory I'll take some details. The husband's address, what he does for a living and, if possible, his place of work. If I need any more information as I go along I'll contact you, if that's all right.'

'That's fine. Me and Eunice, we're always here.'

Crane pressed on steadily with routine work for the rest of the day: lifestyle checks, bad debt traces, some lunchtime surveillance of a wealthy man whose wife suspected, accurately, that he was having an affair. As he sat in his car patiently waiting for things to happen, his mind went back over his discussion with Gillis. He was still not sure he should have agreed to take on the case. There seemed to be little or no room for manoeuvre. A woman driving around erratically with drugs and drink inside her; well, it happened. And if you'd once been in the police force, as Crane had, you knew it happened quite a lot. He was inclined to take Ted Benson's view, that the woman was so depressed she'd reached a stage where death seemed like a blessed relief. Well, that happened too. And a million pounds was a colossal wedge to be insured for, but the premiums had clearly been accepted in good faith and in the insurance business the insurers sometimes lost out. That was the nature of the game.

Crane knew he'd taken on the case because there seemed to be nowhere to go with it. He guessed he'd lose sleep over it, trying to decide if John Gillis's instinct was reliable and, if so, if there *was* something dodgy about all the insurance Lydia Glover had taken out, how was he ever going to be able to prove it? He didn't know. He just knew that now and then he had to take on a case that seemed barely solvable, when nearly all his other cases could be walked through. He was like an actor, skilled, comfortably off, but stuck in a long-running soap, who pined for his agent to find him a really demanding role that would use every aspect of his talent. The type of role he'd dreamed of at RADA that would provide him with the kind of triumph that would renew his faith in his ability and would remind him why he'd been so driven to be an actor in the first place.

That evening, after an early dinner, he drove to a newish estate that angled from a road in Allerton called Crow Tree Lane. The Allerton and Heaton districts, which abutted, were generally considered to be among Bradford's better addresses, and Ken Glover's house on

Comstock Crescent, proved to be a good-sized detached, double-fronted and with well-designed gardens. A dark-blue BMW, two years old, stood in the drive. Comstock Crescent was a cul-de-sac and Crane parked in the square at the bottom among several other cars and began to do what he spent so much of his life doing; he waited. He wasn't going to wait longer than half an hour at most, to see if the dead woman's husband went anywhere.

He should be able to recognize him as he'd turned up the evening paper that had given a report on the tragedy. It had contained little that he didn't already know. The crashed car had been found by an elderly couple walking a dog along the gully, and they had alerted the police on their mobile. The police were pursuing their enquiries, but in the meantime were keeping an open mind as to why the accident had taken place. The details of the car's registration had shown that the car belonged to a Mrs Lydia Glover of Comstock Crescent. Ken Glover, her husband, had confirmed this and had identified the body as being that of his wife. Devastated by his loss, he'd been unable to throw any light on his wife's mental condition as she'd driven her car to her death.

A press photograph of Glover had accompanied the report, but there had been no photograph of his wife. That seemed a little odd to Crane, but maybe they'd been a couple who didn't do photographs. Lydia Glover had been a commissioning editor for a small Yorkshire publishing firm that specialized in ladies' romantic fiction with a strong local setting. She was regarded as a valued and focused member of staff who would be badly missed and very difficult to replace. Ken Glover was an estate agent who worked for a Bradford firm.

Crane was in luck. Glover left his house about twenty minutes later, got in his car and reversed out of the drive. He then drove into and up the steep Crow Tree Lane. Crane followed at a distance. Glover turned right at the top of Crow Tree Lane and took a road that led down to the city. His destination in the city was Bolton Road, where he parked in a car-park that was opposite a casino called Napoleon's. He crossed to this club and went in. Crane had been a member of this club since his days in the police force, when he and a few colleagues would drop in for an occasional drink or meal, though Crane had never had any interest in gambling.

A search of his wallet unearthed a discoloured membership card and he left his own car in the car-park and entered the club himself.

He checked out the bar and the restaurant but Glover was in neither, so he left the bar area for the gaming room. It was quiet as this was a Monday evening and only two of the roulette tables were operating. Then Crane spotted Glover. He was one of three people sitting at a curved blackjack table. He joined the group himself, as unobtrusively as possible, and changed a twenty for a handful of modest chips. Glover never looked up from his cards as Crane was dealt in, to Crane's relief, as he didn't want his to be a face that Glover might recognize later, though he could of course always disguise himself.

Play went on steadily for half an hour in the church-like silence casinos tended to have in the early evening, the only sounds the rattle of balls along the roulette wheels, the softly spoken requests for no further bets to be placed and the announcing of winning numbers. It was even quieter at the blackjack table, with the dealer flicking out cards from the shoe and when her own cards were played simply paying out any hands that beat hers.

It seemed to Crane that the preoccupation he saw at this early hour was that of compulsive gamblers. Not for them a leisurely meal, a glass or two of wine and then much later the evening rounded off enjoyably by a flutter at the tables. These men playing now had made straight for the rotating wheels and the flicked playing cards. It could be they earned plenty of money and could afford their addiction, but the people next to him didn't give that impression. The two men between him and Glover gave him a sense of barely contained desperation. They were youngish and wore business suits and perhaps the gaming tables made up for days of boredom in offices, providing them with the sorts of risks and excitement that other young men sought in the army or scaling mountains.

Glover reacted differently. He played with chips of high value, but took wins and losses with no change of expression. There was a sort of fatalism about him. When Crane had been in the force he'd known drug addicts to have that look. There was no longer any pleasure to be had from the hits, they simply needed the hits to be able to keep going, to feel half-normal. He wondered if there was something of that in the way Glover gambled. And could it be that Glover was locked into an expensive habit he couldn't really afford?

Crane, having broken more or less even, left the blackjack table and went back to his car. He decided he'd wait an hour to see if

Glover left the club. He wanted to check if he went directly home. He wondered how much he was going to lose this evening. He could, of course, come out ahead, but over a period the bank would be the winner, as the bank invariably was. Crane had not long ago worked on a case that had involved a casino and he knew only too well how very accurate the percentages were that a casino could expect to win by in the long term from the games they ran.

He had to bear two things in mind: how long had Glover been a gambler and how much money had he lost? And that Glover was now in line to receive a million pounds from his wife's insurers, which would enable him to clear off any debts his gambling habit might have incurred.

In which case his wife's death would have been very fortuitous. Very fortuitous indeed.

T W O

'Jason?'

'That's me.'

'Frank Crane, Jason. I've got a little job I'd like you to help me with.'

'Go ahead, guv.'

'A bloke called Glover. He works at Grant, Spooner, the estate agents. He lives at 19 Comstock Crescent, off Crow Tree Lane. I need a rundown: what he makes, state of his bank account, savings, if any, general background.'

'I've got you, guv. Leave it with me. I'll get back in forty-eight.'

'That'll do fine.'

Crane put down his phone. He was sitting in his little office, going through the desk diary with Maggie, a pensioner who did a couple of hours PA work a day for him. Their term for Jason was The Man with No Surname. Jason was one of those skilled people who are able to gather together almost any kind of information on almost anyone: unlisted phone numbers, bank account details, earnings, life-style. It was the sort of work Crane had learnt how to do for himself, but it took time and in these days of a full case load it was cost-effective to pay Jason to do it, who did little else and was completely reliable, despite his obsessive secrecy in keeping his own address under wraps and even his surname.

Crane explained to Maggie the details of the new case he'd taken on. She said, 'I read about Lydia Glover crashing the car. Covered for a *million*, that seems well over the top.'

'That's why Gillis has taken me on. He's convinced there's something dodgy about it.'

'And yet the death itself doesn't seem *too* unusual. Drink, drugs, depression, there's a lot of it about these days.'

Maggie, like Crane, had once been involved in the police force. She'd been a PA to a senior officer. She'd learnt a great deal over the years about the dark side of life.

'I agree, Maggie. It's just that Gillis is certain there's something wrong somewhere even though the police can't find anything suspicious about the death. I trust his instinct, I'd not have taken on the case otherwise.'

'And the husband gambles....'

'Quite. He doesn't sit at home weeping over a lock of hair.'

'On the other hand he might gamble to take his mind off his loss.'

'You're right, best not to read too much into it at this stage. A million is a lot, but we'll give him the benefit of the doubt and assume his wife meant a lot more to him than the money.'

'Yet gambling can be very addictive. With some people it's like alcoholism.'

'And he's only an estate agent. At the worst time to be one.'

'Exactly, an estate agent in the middle of the credit crunch. I read somewhere that they were lucky if they were selling one house a *week*.'

'That thought had crossed my own mind. How long can Grant, Spooner go on paying him if there's nothing coming through the front door but fresh air?'

'When he came out of the casino where did he go?'

'I waited an hour but he still hadn't come out. It looked as if he was going to make a long night of it.'

'It'll be interesting to see what The Man with No Surname comes up with.'

'We'll know soon enough....'

Grant, Spooner's premises were on Bank Street. Two large windows, one each side of the entrance, were filled with laminated cards giving details and showing photographs of the many properties on the firm's books, properties that no one appeared to have the remotest interest in. A youth, on the small side and neatly turned out in a grey suit, kept bobbing out from the reception area like a cuckoo in a clock the moment anyone so much as cast a glance at the cards. He was clearly attempting to inveigle them inside, where he'd be able to give them comprehensive details of any property they might be interested in, with an older person standing by to club them into submission with the hard sell. There'd probably be a nice cup of freshly percolated coffee too and a slice of almond cake, Crane thought, with a wry smile from across the road, where he strolled backwards and forwards, unobtrusive on the busy pavements. That morning he'd shadowed Glover from the Comstock Crescent house to get some kind of fix on his working day. But things were looking pretty desperate at his place of work if the office boy had been sent to all but drag people in off the street.

How things had changed from a time that seemed only yesterday when estate agents had had not too many properties on their books but too few. A time when every property they registered was gone within days, with mortgages of a hundred per cent absolutely no problem. Crane wondered how many of those houses, which had sold like ice cream in August, were now in negative equity.

Oddly enough, though unemployment was becoming a problem, Crane had more work than ever. When certain people began to feel the chill wind of a recession they began to act out of character. They stole stock from their employers; accounts people devised cunning ways of fiddling the books, and managers, aware that the firm they worked for was in difficulties, would conceal orders that they could use to ease their way into a more viable organization.

Crane wondered if the credit crunch, so-called, had preyed on Glover's mind, to the point where perhaps he couldn't get it out of his head how very much more his wife was worth dead than alive. At that moment, Glover emerged from the open doorway of Grant, Spooner's. He was a tall, lean man with naturally wavy blond hair which had a slightly metallic sheen and which he wore long at the back and sides. He had well-defined features though with a faintly petulant cast about the mouth, which Crane had noticed before occasionally in good-looking men. He was dressed in a lightweight, pale-blue suit, a white shirt and a maroon tie. He gave an indefinable impression of being rather pleased with his trim, well-cared-for appearance.

He stopped to have a word with the youth, who still doggedly bobbed in and out of the reception area. The youth began to make the sort of gestures that seemed to indicate that he wanted to accompany Glover, but Glover firmly warded off the suggestion, if that's what it was, though with a pleasant smile and a reassuring pat to the youth's arm. The youth returned the smile, but thinly.

Both Glover and Crane's cars were parked in a street that angled off Bank Street, where parking was permitted if you could get there early enough; Glover had been there at 8.15. He now led Crane into Manor Row and along Manningham Lane, from which he turned left at Lister Park and drove up Oak Lane and then Toller Lane, finally slowing in Haworth Road and turning into the drive of an old, well-maintained semi. The house had a Grant, Spooner FOR SALE board displayed just inside the garden wall. As it was now five to eleven it looked as if Glover had an appointment to show someone round. Crane drove on past the house then took a left into Heights Lane. He was able to turn his car round in the parking area of a small block of shops, drive back on to Haworth Road and park diagonally opposite the house for sale. Glover was now standing at the side of his car in shirt sleeves and he glanced at his watch as Crane looked on.

At 11.05 a small, black Fiat pulled into the drive of the semi behind Glover's BMW. A woman got out who looked to be in her late twenties. She was auburn-haired and shapely. She was wearing a white top and a cotton button-through skirt in a muted floral pattern, which greatly added to her attraction on what was now a fine summer morning.

She and Glover exchanged warm smiles. There was a lingering quality about them that made them seem to Crane a good bit more than the routine friendly smiles that would pass between an estate agent and a client. They didn't shake hands either, though they might already have met at the Bank Street premises earlier. Yet Crane was given a strong impression they were quite well known to each other and could now be putting on some kind of an act in case neighbours' curtains were twitching. Glover led the woman to the front door, which he unlocked and pushed open for her to enter.

That meant the owners had given Glover permission to show people round in their absence. Perhaps they were away, sorting out the details of a house they were buying. They might even have completed on the next house. Some people could afford to do that even though up to then not having been able to sell their own. If that was the case, he wondered if the furniture was still in place in this house.

He knew that estate agents weren't keen on showing people houses with bare walls and empty rooms. Pictures and pieces of furniture could be strategically placed to conceal flaws best kept hidden from a prospective buyer.

Would the beds then still be *in situ*? It seemed to Crane that the couple were both wearing the sort of clothes they could be out of in seconds. The woman might even have deliberately selected the button-through skirt. Crane's cynicism occasionally depressed him, but it was securely based on the work he did. It seemed to him the pair were anxious to give the impression Glover was simply showing a client round a house, but what if it was a clever way of hitting the duvet together? Though if that was the case why didn't Glover simply take the woman to his own house? Could it be that he didn't want the neighbours to see him doing that so soon after the death of his wife in tragic circumstances when he was supposed to be in deep mourning? Not that Crane had seen much evidence of that.

Extending that theory, perhaps Glover couldn't go to the woman's place for the same reason: neighbours. Maybe the woman had a husband or partner she was anxious not to alert. These days that was often the case. And if there *was* something going on, Glover couldn't have had a better set-up for it. He had access to a number of houses and knew exactly when the owners wouldn't be in them. And even if an owner should come back unexpectedly, Glover, rapidly back in his trousers, was simply showing a punter the house and had got as far as the main bedroom. Crane wondered if he was being too cynical by half. Perhaps everything was exactly as it seemed, Glover being extremely charming to an attractive woman but whose bottom line was a house he was anxious, possibly desperate, to sell.

But Glover and the woman didn't leave the house for the best part of an hour. It seemed a very long time to look over a three-bed semi. Crane put small powerful binoculars to his eyes again. The pair were now chatting and looking over the exterior of the house. But what was the body language telling him? Was that a tender look he seemed to detect in the woman's face as from time to time she gazed up at Glover? He noticed also that Glover's tie was missing and his shirt collar left open. No doubt he'd replace his tie before going back to the office, but, if the house viewing had been genuine, wouldn't it have been unbusinesslike to have removed it in the first place?

The pair got into their cars, reversed out of the drive and drove off. Another tryst artfully arranged? Crane was now convinced something was going on. And if it was it would mean that Glover, apart from having a recently dead wife, a gambling habit and a job in the wrong business, also had a lover.

How long had he had a lover? He might have picked up the woman since his wife had died, but the affair could go back a long time. And could possibly have made Lydia Glover so unhappy and depressed that she'd take her own life. Or had been helped to take it because her dead body would be lying on a million.

Crane was too busy to devote any more time to Glover's daytime activities, but he kept an eye on the Comstock Crescent house on the following two evenings. On the first evening Glover went to the casino again, though this time Crane simply noted it and returned home. It gave him further proof, if any were needed, that Glover really did have a serious gambling habit. On the second evening Glover led him to a detached house on Brankdale Avenue in Heaton. It was quite late and becoming dusky. Lamps had been lit in the front room of the house and the curtains not yet drawn. Crane parked a short distance away then strolled back past the house. He was now able to see that Glover was now with a woman in the lit room. They were both standing and, as he moved past in the falling light, he saw them embrace. It was the same woman of the meeting at the house for sale on Haworth Road.

That seemed very odd. If the woman had a house that appeared to be available for lovemaking, why had they met at the Haworth Road house and given the impression she was looking it over? Was this one of the days when her husband or partner, if there was one, was away from home? If so, wasn't she playing a dangerous game? What if this man returned unexpectedly? In his work, Crane had been provided with a good deal of information about the consequences that arose out of partners of both sexes returning unexpectedly. Perhaps she liked living dangerously. Some people did. She could, of course, be single or separated. But the house seemed rather big and expensive to be maintained by a woman of her age in either case. And if the house *was* hers, wouldn't it make her trysts with Glover in other people's places seem even more bizarre?

Crane walked on as far as the main road, then went back to his car. As he passed the woman's house again she was now drawing the curtains of the front room. If he waited long enough he was pretty sure he'd see the lights go on in an upper room, but knowing they were definitely lovers was all the information he needed at this stage.

He got back in his car in a thoughtful mood. As he did so his mobile began to ring. 'Frank Crane.'

'Jason, guv. Your Ken Glover ...'

'Go ahead, Jase.'

'He's sailing close to the wind.'

'I thought he might be.'

'He's on a basic salary with Grant, Spooner, plus a commission on each house he moves. I reckon his basic's about twenty-five grand. He was quids in when properties were flying off the books before you could get them in the window, but he still managed to spend every sov he made. Well, with no bugger buying houses any more and the building societies not shovelling money out like mad hatters, he's existing on an overdraft and a raft of credit cards.'

'As bad as that?'

'I'd say he was in line for a repo this side of Christmas.'

'He must be one worried man. I daresay your researches have given you a background to the case.'

'About his missus banjoing her car up by the North Cliffe golf-links?'

'She was insured for big moolah, Jase, very big moolah. The police have ruled out anything suspicious about the crash itself. She'd mixed booze with sleeping tablets and then gone for a drive. The bogies reckon she was in a state of depression and could have deliberately topped herself.'

'And Glover can account for where *he* was the night her motor went flying through the air?'

'They'll have checked him out, Jase, you can be sure of that, but it's something I intend to look into myself.'

'He comes with a bit of form, guv. Nothing official.'

'Does he now?'

'I happen to have a contact in the estate agency business. These people know what goes on in the game that people like you and me don't get to hear about. Glover was once involved in a selling scam. Not at Grant, Spooner, this was an earlier firm. It was the old favourite, where the agent sweet-talks a little old widow-woman, keen to down-size fast, into accepting a valuation on the house that's well below its real worth. A mate of his then comes along and says he'll give her cash on the mantelpiece, no chain, if she'll knock five grand off even the phoney price. She accepts and the con artists then sell it on at maybe twenty grand plus more and split the difference. Well, one little old lady who'd got all her chairs at home had her house independently valued and reported the scam to the boss of Glover's agency, who was genuinely in the dark. He gives the old lady a hefty back-hander so she'll not go to the police and give his firm a bad name, and the same day he gives Glover the welly.'

'Well done, Jase, that rounds out the picture nicely, because what I'm learning about the beggar doesn't get any better. Just by the way, why do you suppose Grant, Spooner took him on? They must have known he was bad news.'

'They'll have turned a blind eye. It's a great profession for not seeing any ships. Glover will have the gift of the blarney and they'll have warned him that if they took him on he'd better keep his nose clean.'

'I'm sure you're right. He looks every inch the smooth-talking bastard. Well set up, too. I've been keeping an eye on him.'

'Are we thinking on the same lines, guv?'

'I'm sure we are. A crook who's managed to move into a bigger league, though I'll have my work cut out proving it. Well, thanks a lot, Jase. What do I owe you?'

'Three hours, usual rate. If you could drop by the Fox Friday evening, early doors. It'll be a doll called Babs.'

Grinning, Crane cleared his phone. It was always payment in notes in a brown envelope with The Man with No Surname and slipped to one of his rather rough-looking but not unattractive girl-friends. Presumably Jason guarded the details of his exact income as carefully from HMRC as he guarded his address and surname from the people who used his highly skilled if dubious services.

Crane turned on Classic FM and thought some more in the purpling dusk of a clear summer sky. So Glover had form and gave every impression he'd been involved for quite a long time with the woman he liked to give one to in other people's houses. On top of that he was in such a critical financial state that Jason was convinced the repo man would be round before very long to slap a compulsory purchase order on the nice Allerton house.

And Gillis had a hair-trigger instinct for a dodgy insurance claim. So, if Glover was in there somewhere, how had he managed to pull it off?

THREE

On the morning of the following day, Crane rang the central police station and asked to be put through to Detective Inspector Jones. 'Morning, Terry, can you spare me a few minutes?'

'How're you doing, Frank?'

'Fine. It's about Ken Glover whose wife was killed when her car went into Royds Cliff Gully. You gave my name to a bloke called John Gillis at the insurance brokers TD Russell.'

'The case is still fresh in my mind. Ted did the legwork.'

'Gillis doesn't like the smell of the amount of insurance that was on Lydia Glover's life.'

'We didn't like the smell of the car crash itself, but Ted checked it out every which way – you know what he's like – and it all seemed straightforward. The lady was loaded with pills and booze. One theory is that she might have been driving round in a state, gone into the car-park maybe to sleep it off and then for some reason kept on rolling. Could have been suicide, of course. The coroner's only option was to leave it open.'

'It would be Glover who ID'd the body?'

'It was.'

'I'd be interested to know how he reacted.'

'I'll get Ted to give you a bell.'

'Thanks, Terry. Look, I'm checking Glover out. He's already seeing some other woman. He's also got a serious gambling habit, he's flat broke and he was once involved in a house-buying scam. His boss at the time had to use a fistful of money to keep it away from the police and the papers. He then had Glover out through the door.'

'You have been doing your homework.'

'Do you think he ought to be given a pull?'

Jones was silent for a few seconds. 'I've got to admit it doesn't look good, not with him standing to be quids in with the insurance just when he's in big financial trouble. But the thing is, Frank, we see people in rocky marriages every day of the week. All right, he's got his bit on the side, but maybe she had too. And the guy's flat broke, but so's half the country the way the economy's been buggered about with all the banks running on empty. Maybe he was gambling to try and recoup his losses, but how many times have we seen *that* kind of stupid behaviour? And you've found out he's been a bad lad in the past. The trouble is none of it gives us anything we can act on. Maybe the sod doctored her booze, but it was a lot of booze and she shouldn't have been driving a car in any case. And we know about his fancy woman, by the way, because she was his alibi. He was with her the night his wife died.'

Jones paused, sighed. 'Frank, we've never liked the look of that car crash, but there's absolutely nothing about it we can prove seems dodgy. Now if you can turn up anything strong enough to let us take another official look we'll do just that.'

'All right, Terry, I understand. I didn't hold out much hope to Gillis, but he talked me into taking it on and so I'll just have to do the best I can. I must say I was hoping Glover wouldn't have *quite* such a good alibi for that night. Who is the totty anyway?'

'Can't just remember the name. Ted'll know. It seems Glover was a bit jumpy about letting on about her. Didn't want it to get in the papers, the way it would look, didn't want the partners knowing at the firm he works for. They don't like the staff having affairs apparently; they want the firm to have this ultra-respectable image. Anyway the woman confirmed he'd been with her, though Ted said she was edgy too.'

'There seems to be a lot of it about, edginess. Gillis told me Glover was very nervy when he rang in about his wife's death and the insurance. Well, thanks a lot, Terry. This referral you got me to Gillis, I might not be able to sort out anything for him in this case, but it could get me more insurance work.'

'Fancy a noggin at the Toll Gate one evening soon?'

'Any day to suit you.'

Crane put down his office phone. Jones wasn't making an empty gesture about meeting for a drink and a chat. Before Crane had had to leave the police force Jones had been his boss. He'd pulled a good many strings to help set him up as a PI. They'd got a lot of time for each other.

Later, Ted Benson rang him on his car phone. 'Terry asked me to give you a call. Lydia Glover, the ID.'

'How did Glover seem, Ted?'

'Putting it on, you ask me. It's not too difficult to spot the difference between someone who's genuinely shattered and someone who's doing a Laurence Olivier.'

'You don't surprise me. The woman he was with the night his wife died, know much about her?'

'Mrs Pam Draper. Divorced. I suppose you know Glover's an estate agent. He gave out some bilge she was really a client and he was advising her on selling her house. He knew I didn't believe a word of it.'

'She lives on Brankdale Avenue, yes?'

'How do you know?'

'I'm keeping the guy under obbo. Him and Pam have been up to quite a lot that has sod-all to do with buying and selling houses.'

'I had a strong impression his wife's death came as something of a relief behind the long face and the dabbing of the eyes.'

'I'm sure you're right, especially as he stands to trouser a million.'

'Christ, as much as that!'

'Ted, you know all the circumstances, what's your gut feeling?'

'That the sod was involved in her death. Can't begin to figure it out. We spent a long time talking to him. Why was she driving round pissed and drugged? No idea, he tells us, they lived a happy enough life on the whole and she liked her work at the publishing place. He said she did have occasional depressions. She'd had a miscarriage and couldn't seem to get pregnant again. It had put her through a bad patch, but that was a long time ago.'

'She might have been depressed the night she died because she'd cottoned he had another woman on the go, though I reckon Glover wouldn't need any lessons when it came to keeping his love life and his home life a good many yards apart.'

'That's about all I can tell you, Frank. And, as I say, he was putting on the stricken looks and the broken voice at the ID and he did it very well, but it still came across as Central Casting.'

'They develop useful acting skills as a breed, estate agents.'

'Tell me about it....'

Crane drove on. There was no question of him and Benson getting together over a drink. Benson had once been his closest friend, right up to the point when Crane had been dismissed from the force. After that nothing had been the same. Benson owed him for the massive good turn he'd done him, but, as Crane's mother had once told him many years ago, you should never do anyone a favour that they may not be in a position one day to return, as they'd never forgive you. And that had been the kind of favour Crane had done Benson.

When he got home that night he made himself a simple if nutritious meal of baked cod and broccoli with a side salad, which he ate with a glass of white Burgundy. He thought over the evening that had passed and what to make of it. He had first checked out Glover's movements. He'd gone to the casino again. Knowing he'd be settled for the night, Crane had driven on to the house in Brankdale Avenue where Pam Draper lived. He'd thought long and hard about taking this approach and with misgivings, but in the end he'd decided it seemed the only way to get the case moving, and even so it would be a very long shot. But he had to have some input from someone.

He rang the front door bell of the detached. A few seconds later the door was opened a little way and she looked out. 'Yes?'

'Mrs Draper, my name's Frank Crane. I'm a private investigator and I'm working for the insurers of the late Mrs Lydia Glover.'

'What's that got to do with me?' she said quickly, but reddening.

'I ... think you know *Mr* Glover rather well, Mrs Draper.'

'What ... what makes you think that?'

'As I said, I'm a PI. People engage me to find things out. And one of the things I've found out is that you see Mr Glover fairly regularly.'

She was still flushed. 'I don't think it's any of your damned business *who* I see. I'm going to close the door—'

'Mrs Draper, I work closely with the CID. I used to be a CID man myself. There are just a couple of matters we're anxious to clear up regarding Mrs Glover's tragic death.'

'So you work for the police, do you?' she snapped. 'Well, what if I were to ring the police right away and tell them I'm being stalked by a total stranger who's now wanting to ask me personal questions?'

'I can give you the home numbers of DS Benson and DI Jones. I believe you've had dealings with them. They were involved in investigating the details of Mrs Glover's car crash.'

She watched him for some time in silence, then gave a heavy sigh. 'What can you *possibly* want from me, Mr whatever your name is?'

'Crane. Frank Crane.'

'All right, I *do* know Ken Glover. We're trying to be discreet because it doesn't look very nice being seen together so soon after the accident.'

The colour was beginning to leave her face.

'A couple of questions is all I need to ask. I really won't take up much of your time. It ... would be helpful if we could talk inside.'

She began to watch him again, very carefully. He couldn't blame her, she didn't know him from the meter-reader. But it was summer and still light and Crane had the sort of nondescript features that somehow inspired confidence, and he was well turned out in a cotton sports shirt, chinos and a linen jacket.

'All right,' she said grudgingly, 'but I really don't think I'm in a position to help.'

She led him through to the lounge. It was comfortably and expensively furnished: a modern suite, a plasma television, bookshelves to each side of the fireplace that held books that looked as if they were actually read, a patterned rug over a dark-green carpet, a drinks tray on a side table, fashionable prints on the walls.

She waved him to an armchair and sat down herself at the end of a long sofa. 'Now, Mr Crane.'

'Frank, please. Perhaps I can call you Pam?'

'Very well ... Frank, but ... but what *is* all this?' she said in exasperation. 'What can you imagine I can possibly tell you about Mrs Glover's *accident*?'

Crane hesitated. He had to accept that what passed between them could be relayed to Glover himself, but he'd taken that into account. What if it did and what if Glover really was involved in his wife's death? Well, that could be all to the good. If Glover did have something to hide and began to think he was under suspicion, it might mean he could panic and make a wrong move.

'Look, Pam,' he said, in a friendly tone, 'Lydia Glover was insured for a very great deal of money and the insurers can't quite understand why. The type of insurance she had, people take it out to see their spouses clear of any financial worries should they die prematurely. I've been told that a quarter of a million would tend to be the top of the scale in an area like this.'

'If the insurers thought she was taking out too much insurance why didn't they query it in the first place?'

'It's a good question. Well, insurers tend to take the money and run. They only begin to ask the searching questions when someone dies in unusual circumstances. They should admittedly have asked the question in the first place.'

'I can't see what any of this has got to do with me.'

'Pam, the police checked that Ken was here with you on the night Lydia died—'

'My God, you can't believe that *Ken*—'

'No; I'm simply going through the details to get it all quite clear in my own mind.'

'The police said it was just ... just a routine query that they did in all ... in all cases of a death in unusual circumstances.'

She was beginning to colour again and kept having to catch her breath.

'That's true,' he said, continuing to talk in the same calm and friendly tone, 'it was a strange death and the police would be trying to find out how Lydia came to be driving with drugs and alcohol in her system. I'm afraid their first port of call is invariably the next of kin. They *have* to ask the spouse or partner first if they can throw any light on the circumstances and need to rule out that spouse or partner of any involvement, of course, before they go any further. Well, as I said, I'm an old CID man and I tend to tick the same boxes.'

'I ... I think I need a drink,' she said, still with a tremor in her voice. 'How about you?'

'Thank you. A G and T, if I may.'

She went to the drinks table. His chair faced towards it and he watched her in declining sunlight. She was a woman who took care of herself. She was wearing a turquoise v-neck T-shirt above an abstract-print skirt of a similar shade. When she'd led him into the house he'd caught a hint of a very delicate scent and her long hair had also received a good deal of attention, with muted blonde streaks lifting its coppery colour. Her face was square and well balanced and she had eyes of an almost luminous pale-blue. Her nose was rather too long, but it was the type of flaw that somehow enhanced the looks of an attractive woman if anything.

She put down his drink on a small table near his chair and sat down again at the end of the sofa. Her eyes had not lost an uneasy look since they'd first talked at the door. She took a big sip of her drink. She really did look as if she needed it. 'You can't think that Ken,' she said in a tone that was almost a whisper, 'you *can't* ...'

'Look,' he said gently, 'let's get this out of the way and then you'll never see me again. Ken was definitely with you that night?'

'Yes, definitely, yes, yes!'

'What time did he leave?'

'Late.'

'The death crash was estimated to be in the early hours of the morning. Was he still here so late?'

'He was here all *night*!' Her voice had taken on a shrill note.

'A married man?'

'They went their separate ways. It was an *open* marriage!'

'Did you ... tell the police he was here all night?'

'He didn't want the police to know. He knew it would look bad if it came out, Ken here and her driving round in such a terrible state.'

Crane had to conceal his disappointment carefully. Had Glover spent only part of the night here there'd still have been time for him somehow to have been involved in his wife's death. But if he'd been here all night that put the lid on it. His wife might have been in a state because of her husband's affair, but as far as the crash went he had to be in the clear.

'Well, Pam, I'm very sorry to have troubled you and I hope I've given no offence. I'm just doing a job. If Ken was here all night he's completely above suspicion. I shall pursue my investigations elsewhere about why Lydia was so heavily insured. Thank you very much for your patience and co-operation.'

She flopped against the back of the sofa in a sort of reflex action but her luminous eyes still seemed uneasy and watchful. He'd expected her to look relieved. First the police and then a PI had homed in on Glover as a man who needed to be carefully checked on, but now her man was completely out of the loop. She took another large sip of her drink. 'It was so very upsetting that you should all think a decent type like Ken could ... could ...' The words trailed off.

'I know,' he said. 'It can be very distressing for people who are on the receiving end like you. The husbands and wives always come in for special attention in cases like this, as I said. I really don't wish to give the impression I'm trying to implicate Ken in anything. My brief is simply to try and pin down why Lydia had taken out all this cover on her life. And it would help, of course, if I could pin down why she was driving round in the state she was in.'

She began to nod, as if finding his words placatory. 'How did you *know* about Ken and me?'

'I shadowed him from the estate agents the morning you met up with him at the house in Haworth Road. I guessed you were using one of his for sale houses to get together.'

Her eyes moved away from his. 'We didn't want to meet at Ken's place. The neighbours …'

Smiling, Crane said, 'What puzzles me, not that it's any business of mine, is why you needed to meet in empty houses. Why not meet here, as you did last night?'

He found the way the colour kept rising in her cheeks rather endearing in its youthful almost girlish quality. 'I'm … I'm a translator,' she said. 'French, German, Dutch and Danish. I work very much to deadlines. If I know there's a rush job coming through on the Internet that means I'll have to work through the afternoon and evening. I sometimes meet up with Ken in what spare time I have available. He can combine meeting me with doing his work. Of course, in time, when we have an open relationship….'

Crane wanted to smile again, but didn't. Glover had sorted out the leg-over situation with great skill but he did have the look of a man who had the sort of sex drive that required regular maintenance. Maybe the sex really was spiced up by an owner arriving home early, or even someone from the estate agents themselves, checking up on him because of his past record. He suspected that Pam went along with it, but would very much prefer either to be in her own bed or Glover's when lovemaking was on their minds. But Glover was a good-looking and clearly charming and charismatic man, yet with that slightly petulant cast about his mouth now and then, which probably meant he usually got his way.

'I'm divorced,' she told him. 'I trained as a translator so that I'd be able to work from home when the babies we were planning came along. But just as I was about to stop taking the pill Matthew went and found someone he preferred to me.'

She looked down into her almost empty glass. She sounded sad, but not bitter. From experience, Crane had found that real bitterness only seemed to kick in when the babies had actually arrived and the husband had discovered he couldn't after all cope with motherhood and apple pie, not when the narrow-waisted twenty-year-old with the sleek blonde hair in Production Planning kept gazing at him with her full moist lips slightly apart.

'I'm sorry,' he said.

'To be fair Matt was genuinely contrite. He did his very best for me. This house came out of the settlement. When I was looking at houses I met Ken. It was, you know, we clicked straight off. I was lonely and very miserable. He did such a lot to help me regain confidence in myself. He admitted right away he was married but that they lived their own lives.'

He nodded with a sympathetic smile but it struck him that Pam must have seemed desirable in every way to Glover, not just in her looks. She owned her own well-furnished house and possibly, as another part of the divorce settlement, also received a living allowance. She'd be making good money too from her translation work. Maybe Glover, having thought along the same lines, had decided he was on to a winner. If Pam had a few bob on one side and no mortgage, and he talked her into letting him live with her, it would certainly help to relieve the strain on his own dire financial situation. It would, of course, all be academic when the insurers paid out.

If they paid out.

He wished he could warn her of the position Glover was in: a compulsive gambler, flat broke, just as likely to throw all his money away – and hers too – even if he did inherit a million. He got up. 'I'll not take up any more of your time, Pam. Thanks for your help.'

'That's all right. I'm so glad we've sorted things out. And my time's my own this evening as Ken's working and I'm between jobs. Can I offer you another drink?'

He detected an encouraging note in her voice now, as if she really wanted him to stay. But his work here was now finished, he didn't think he could learn any more that would be of use. 'Thanks, but I'd better be getting along. I've not eaten yet and I'll need to put a meal together when I get home.'

'You live alone too?'

'A relationship wouldn't be a good idea, the sort of life I lead. I have a girlfriend, but we only meet up about once a week, sometimes not even that. Like me, she works silly hours.'

She also got up. 'This … this money. The insurance money. It was on Lydia's life and you say there was an awful lot. The premiums would be very high, wouldn't they?'

She still looked uneasy, even vulnerable. He wondered why. He said, 'It wasn't an endowment policy, it was simply term assurance, no pay-out if you live beyond an agreed age. Even so, yes, the premiums wouldn't be cheap.'

'Why would she *do* that?'

'Presumably she wanted Ken to be in a good financial position if anything should happen to her.'

'But, Ken has a good job and there were no children. Did Ken take out a similar policy if anything should happen to him?'

'That I don't know.'

But it was a good question. Could Glover have made a reciprocal arrangement? It seemed unlikely the way his finances stood.

'I'll see you out, Frank, if I can't persuade you to have another drink.'

He put a hand lightly on her arm. 'I wish you all the best for your future. You deserve a little happiness and I hope you can now sort out your life.'

'That's very kind of you...'

Crane poured himself a second glass of wine and cleared the small kitchen table of his dinner things, still thinking over the discussion with Pam. Had Glover *really* stayed the night at her place the night Lydia had died, or was she just saying he had? She had been very nervy about it all. Why had she been so nervy if she was telling the truth? When Crane had been in the CID he'd heard the same alibi a dozen times from men who'd had a record as long as your arm, 'Ask the girlfriend if you don't believe me, I was with her ...' The trouble was, the girlfriends were usually as case-hardened as their boyfriends and could lie with total confidence. No nerves, no hesitation, eyes that stayed unblinkingly on yours. It was the decent, middle-class women who found it hard to lie for their men. They gave exactly the same impression that Pam had given, that they just might be being economical with the truth.

He sighed. It didn't make a scrap of difference one way or the other. Whether she was lying or not she'd confirmed that Glover had been with her all night and so that was that.

The wall-mounted phone began to ring. 'Frank Crane.'

'John Gillis, Frank. I'm sorry to trouble you in your leisure time. One of those days when I've never had a moment to ring you from the office.'

'I don't really do leisure time, John, so don't worry about that. How can I help?'

'It's the Glover carry-on. As you know, the lady was insured through us for a million. Well, I have friends in the insurance business. We can natter to each other in confidence. You're not going to believe this, but I just happened to mention to one of them that it looked as if I might be arranging one of the biggest pay-outs I'd ever seen on term assurance, and damn me the bloke says he's got a claim going through for the same *amount*.'

'Not on Lydia Glover's life?'

'On Lydia Glover's life!'

Another million coming Glover's way. Crane stood for a few seconds in stunned silence. 'I can't begin to get this together.'

'That makes two of us.'

'Didn't your friend find it odd, a policy for such a high figure?'

'He works directly for an insurance company, not a broker. He says the firm has a number of high-flying companies on its book where the chief exec is covered for a tidy sum with term assurance in case he kicks the bucket early and they need a good quality replacement sharpish. They're used to high insured amounts. He reckons Lydia Glover slipped under the radar.'

'So long as she could give proof of good health and paid the premiums.'

'Exactly. Anyway, this chap was very interested to know we'd engaged you to look into it and reckons his firm will share your costs, as they'll be very keen not to pay out a million if they can help it. Frank, I know you've not had much time, but have you got anywhere at all?'

'There's only one suspect, John. Glover's got big debts and a gambling habit and he's in the estate agency business when everyone's making do with the house they have. And he was having an affair when Lydia died, an affair he's anxious to keep very quiet. Now his girlfriend says he was with her the night Lydia died, but I'm not sure I believe her, though she comes across as a very respectable type.'

'My word, you're not just sitting there, are you?' Gillis said, on a note of admiration. 'And you think Glover...?'

'I was certain he had to be involved. And if he was I reckoned he'd have had to do certain things on the night Lydia died, things he'd have no alibi for. But he had an alibi and it seems watertight. Even so, I'm certain the guy's in there somewhere.'

'I've handed you a tough one.'

'I'll keep plugging away. Do you know if Glover ever covered *himself* with term assurance?'

'No, I looked that up right at the beginning.'

'Could you confirm who actually *paid* the premiums on Lydia's insurance?'

'Lydia herself. I checked that too. The cheques were from her account and it wasn't a joint account.'

'All right, John, that might help. The minute I feel I'm getting anywhere I'll get back to you.'

Crane hung up the phone. So now there were £2 million on the go. He gave a wry smile. With all the colossal sums being bandied about in the banking crisis that had engulfed the country, a couple of million was beginning to look like car-park money; in fact, one of the economics pundits had said that billions were now the new millions, and even trillion was beginning to sidle its way in as a political buzz-word.

Even so, £2 million would come in very handy to a man who seemed not to be in a position to lay his hands on £200.

FOUR

Pam mixed herself another drink. Normally, she had only one when she was alone, but this evening she needed a second one. She wished Frank Crane had stayed, he was such an easy man to have around. There was something very reassuring about him: he had the manner of a man you could trust. No looks to speak of, but tall and strong-looking. She wondered why he didn't have a wife or a proper partner; there had to be a story there.

She took her glass to the window and gazed out over her neatly tended front garden. She paid a man to look after it. He had spent his days looking after gardens since losing his job in the recession. The recession seemed not to have affected her translation agency so far, she had a big Dutch piece of work coming through in the morning that would take several days but which wasn't urgent.

It was almost dusk. On a clear summer evening the darkness seemed to filter across a blue sky like a deeper shade of blue ink. She loved to watch the slow transformation from day to night, to see the lights igniting in windows, like woodcuts against their shadowy backgrounds.

It had been the same at Wilsden, the village on the grassy outskirts of the Bradford area, where they'd lived in a big house on a new development. She'd also gazed out of the windows there to see the spring and summer light falling. Matt would often join her and they'd stand there together over a drink while the evening meal cooked. That was when he was at home. He worked for a chemical company and though he'd had first-class technical skills it had soon become clear that his special talent was for selling. And so he travelled extensively on the successful sales trips that provided him with expensive motors and large comfortable houses in pleasant surroundings.

She sighed. Matt had been so good with people. He always had the ready word and the warm smile, always had an amusing anecdote from his latest trip that would have the table rocking with laughter. It was the way he told them, as one of the comedians used to say. So many tables, so many tasty meals, so many good friends. She'd read somewhere that women tended to prize a sense of humour in a man well above looks. Well, Matt had had both and she'd seemed to surf on the crest of a permanent wave: going to dinner, or having people in, being whisked off to London to see the latest show, weekends in Paris, fortnights in Tuscany, shopping trips to New York. She'd thought it would never end, not even when they began to think of babies, as there'd always be money for nannies or au pairs.

She knew now she'd not allowed herself to think he might possibly be having affairs when he was away from home, even though she could never quite get out of her mind the admiring glances from so many of the women they met in the life they led. One Sunday evening he packed rather a large bag. She'd supposed he was going for a long trip. How right she'd been: it was a trip he'd never come back from, and neither had the wife of one of his best friends.

That had been a bad year, the worst she'd ever known. They'd spoken on the phone, she'd wept uncontrollably, but though he'd been penitent and apologetic, he hadn't concealed the distressing truth that he simply couldn't live without the other woman. It couldn't be explained, it had just happened, even though he'd not wanted it to happen. He'd made the divorce as stress free as possible. Not only had he bought her this house, he'd provided her with an allowance. Combined with her own earnings this had made her comfortably off, if lonely and depressed.

She wondered if she'd lacked ambition – not worked herself up the ladder in some firm or other, like several of his friends' wives, some of them even combining motherhood with a demanding job; having it all, in the jargon. And yet he'd always said he preferred her to be at home when he got back from his travels. But she couldn't help reflecting that the woman he'd gone off with had been a high flier.

It was quite dark outside now and she drew the curtains. She knew that, looking back, she'd not thought realistically about what was obviously going on in her cosy little world. It was her very worst fault, striving always to conceal an unpalatable truth from herself, assuring herself that things would work out, there was no real problem. It had been totally apparent, at those many dinners, that Matt was spending too much time talking to Imogen and that Imogen was looking far too starry-eyed. She should have reacted to it, challenged him about it, had it out with him. She knew it wouldn't have made any difference to the outcome, but the separation wouldn't have given her quite such a frightful blow.

She gave another sigh. And now she was doing it again. Not seeing her relationship with Ken in quite a true light. She had to ask herself why, when one charming and witty man had walked out on her, she was taking up with another who had many of the same traits. And she did know the answer in some part of her mind, that as usual she didn't want to examine too closely. Ken was a substitute for Matt, but though he, too, was charismatic and fun to be with, he didn't really have the other qualities Matt had.

She found herself wishing she could meet up with a man like Crane. He was nothing like Matt or Ken and yet he was attractive in his unassuming way. He didn't smile much, but when he did it was a very engaging smile and gave you a feeling he was a really sound bloke. She reddened again, even though she was alone, to think that Crane might be thinking she'd not been able to wait to take off her knickers for Ken in one of his for sale houses. In fact, the truth was that she sometimes went to those houses with no knickers *on*. But she didn't want Crane to think she was an easy lay, even if she was. She'd had a marvellous sex life with Matt and she'd not had a man in her bed for a long, long time.

She shook her head, went to the drinks table again, but stopped herself pouring another. Alcohol was just too helpful in getting you to see things in too comforting a light. She knew she had to think candidly about Ken. It wasn't easy because he'd brought such a lot of happiness into her life at a time when her self-esteem had hit the buffers and she'd begun to feel herself a total failure, doomed to a lonely and colourless future. Her life had changed overnight on meeting Ken. He was so attentive, so outgoing, such good company over a dinner table. She'd begun to feel a lightness of spirit she'd not known since meeting Matt at uni. She'd begun to sing to herself as she tidied the house, had started to actually enjoy getting up in the morning, delighted to embark on a new day. And meeting up with him in those deserted houses, in between her translation deadlines, had been so exciting as he was such a skilled and virile lover.

She went from the lounge to the kitchen to remove herself from the temptation of the drinks table. She knew she mustn't give in to her old habits of modifying the truth. And the truth was that Ken was just a little too charming, had taken up with her in a way that was just a little too accomplished. And though his bedroom skills had given her such intense pleasure she'd really been able to tell, now she was forcing herself to admit it, that it could only be because he must have had such a lot of experience with other women. She also knew that in a dozen subtle ways, he'd contrived to get out of her things she should have been more circumspect about: her financial position, ownership of this house and the sort of return she made from her translating work. He'd then begun to hint that it would be the best thing all round if he made a clean break with Lydia and came to live with Pam. And now that she was forcing herself to be scrupulously honest she had to remember that when she'd not instantly agreed to the idea of sharing her house with him his lips had set in that disturbing little moue of discontent that she'd noticed more than once recently if things weren't going quite as he wanted them to.

Pam was uneasy. She'd been uneasy ever since Frank had stood outside the front door. A policeman, a PI, both asking the same question: had Ken been with her the night his wife had died? She was quite certain in her own mind that Ken had had nothing to do with Lydia's death. But there was one final truth she had to take out of that place in her mind where she tried to bury unwelcome thoughts and carefully examine: she'd not been completely honest with Frank. Or the police.

Maggie rang him on his car phone. 'Frank, I've had a call from a woman who wants to see you about a mis-per. I told her you were very busy and might not be able to take it on and had she contacted the police. She said she had but they hadn't been very helpful.'

'The mis-per must be over sixteen.'

'She is, well into her twenties. I explained that the police concentrated on missing persons who were under sixteen, but depending on the circumstances of the case they'd certainly make routine enquiries.'

'Where does she live, Maggie, the woman who rang?'

'In one of those large terraces just before you get to Lister Park. Walbank Villas. Flat-land.'

'Did the mis-per also live in Walbank Villas?'

'She did.'

That was why the police weren't showing too much interest. People drifted in and out of that area, taking flats on short-term leases, sometimes leaving with rent outstanding. If someone went missing from that corner of the city, well, it happened all the time.

'I'll think about it,' Crane said. 'Give me the details.'

She gave him the house and flat number. 'She's called Tracey Sharp.'

'I'll let you know what I decide to do.'

'I'd do nothing, you want my opinion ...'

Crane was on his way back from Sheffield where he'd just made someone very happy. It was to do with a will involving a considerable estate. The wealthy woman who'd left it had died, in her nineties. She'd outlived the handful of people who would have benefited from the will except for a last relation who'd barely known she existed. Crane had tracked her down for the solicitor concerned. She was a woman in her thirties, struggling to bring up two small children on her own and working part-time as a physiotherapist. The tough life she was living had shown in her face and it had been a pleasant duty for Crane to bring her such good news. He'd not known the amount of the bequest, only that it was substantial; enough, he'd been able to tell her, to enable her to lead a much easier life.

He drove rapidly along the M1. It was only rarely he could make someone as happy as he'd made that weary-looking woman in her stained apron. It was invariably a legatee. Someone who would beam and gasp with pleasure, taking his hand and vigorously shaking it as if he were the man from the National Lottery. He pulled into a service area where he could have a sandwich and a coffee. When he'd eaten he put in a call to the woman called Tracey Sharp.

'Frank Crane here. You rang my office about a missing person.'

'Thank you for returning my call, Mr Crane. Could you come and see me?'

'I'm on the M1 at the moment, but I'll shortly be back in Bradford. Are you in all afternoon?'

'Yes, I am.'

'Would three o'clock be convenient? I'm not sure I'll be able to help.'

'I'd be pleased if we could talk it over.'

'I'll be with you at three then. Who gave you my name, by the way?'

'I found it in the Yellow Pages.'

The bulk of his work came through referrals, but he was pleased the rather expensive display advert also seemed to work. He walked out to his car and opened the doors for a minute to release the heat build-up of a sunny day. Mispers could be time-consuming and right now he hadn't got much time to spare. Yet he never liked turning work away. He couldn't forget the early days of building up his agency following the well-paid position he'd had to leave in the police force. Not that he was badly placed financially these days due to the lucky break he'd had with the Reliance Security case. But the instinct was always to take the work.

Tracey Sharp had a very attractive voice, one of the nicest he'd heard over a phone. Well-modulated, velvety and yet clear. He wondered if the looks went with the voice, but they very often didn't. If they did he could think of several firms who'd be pleased to have Tracey's as the first voice you heard when you were ringing in to place an order, or book a service, or reserve a table for dinner. It was the sort of agreeable voice that gave an indefinable impression you'd be in good hands. He wondered if she had such a job. He wondered why she was at home on a week day. He wondered why a woman with such a pleasant voice lived in flat-land.

He drove on, his endlessly shifting mind inevitably going back to the Glover case. He really couldn't decide the next step to take. He was now totally convinced that Glover had pulled some kind of a scam. What possible reason could there have been otherwise for Lydia to have taken out all that insurance? And how had she been able to afford it, when it looked as if the bulk of her earnings must have gone towards the upkeep of the house on Comstock Crescent if all the money Glover earned went across gambling tables?

It stank. He knew it; Terry Jones knew it; Ted Benson knew it. But if the car crash had been an accident, or even suicide, and the police couldn't turn up anything suspicious about the circumstances, there'd be no reason why the insurance pay-out couldn't go ahead. To Ken Glover, who'd been with Pam Draper the night his wife had died.

Walbank Villas was a row of tall well-built houses that went back to the early part of the twentieth century. They weren't very far from the city centre and would one day have been occupied by mill managers, senior office staff, solicitors, doctors, accountants. Those kinds of people had moved out to the grassy uplands after the Second World War and the villas had begun to have that look defined as shabby genteel. Young married couples and respectable work people had begun to occupy the flats they'd mainly been converted to. One of the buildings had become a boarding-house and another a hotel. Finally, they'd become faintly disreputable, a home to the sorts of people who drifted into Bradford in search of temporary unskilled work and wanted somewhere cheap to stay for a few months.

Crane drew on to the pot-holed crescent of a small private road. The houses were screened from the ceaseless traffic on Manningham Lane by a stand of sycamores, once kept well pruned but now abandoned to grow as they would. He went up the front doorsteps of the number he'd been given and pressed the bell to flat three. It was opened seconds later by a woman with short dark hair and dressed in jeans and a lilac-coloured T-shirt.

'It's Frank Crane. And you are Tracey Sharp?'

'That's me. How do you do.' She offered him her hand. 'Please come up.'

He followed her into a wide hallway, carpeted in worn and elderly dark-brown rubber-back, and up stairs which had banisters that had many scrapes and scuffs, probably from the frequent passage of furniture manhandled by people who lacked professional removal skills.

But her flat was quite decently furnished. There was a *chaise-longue* in beige with matching tub chairs, a persian-patterned rug over a woollen carpet in dark-blue. There were well-fitted damask curtains and in front of the window stood a compact dining suite, the table covered in a clean cloth. Overhead lamps had Tiffany-style pendants and there was a bookcase filled mainly with paperbacks. A vase of fresh flowers stood on the mantelpiece of a gas-fire and the walls were hung with several Vettriano beach scenes.

'Sit down, please, Mr Crane. Can I get you anything ... tea, coffee?'

'I'm OK thanks, Tracey. Call me Frank.'

They sat on the tub chairs. The looks did go with the voice. Her bobbed dark hair was styled and cared for and she was pretty, with very clear green eyes, well-defined features and flawless teeth. She was of middle height, slender and shapely, and she made Crane wonder again what an attractive woman who spoke so well was doing in flat-land.

She said, 'I do hope you'll be able to look for my friend, Frank.'

'How long has she been gone?'

'Just over two weeks.'

'From one of these houses?'

'She has a flat in the next house but one.'

'You don't think she's just decided to move on?'

'She'd not do that without telling me. She's my best friend. We spend all our free time together.'

'Does she have a job?'

The colour rose in her cheeks and her eyes fell from his. 'Does it … does it really matter what she does for a living?' she said hesitantly.

'It might have some bearing on her disappearance.'

'She … she was … is … a prostitute.'

He nodded, but the question then seemed to hang unspoken in the air: why did a woman as well presented as Tracey have a prostitute for a best friend? Her eyes came slowly back to his and he knew what she was thinking.

'We're both on the game,' she said in a low voice. 'Libby … she worked on Lumb Lane and I'm what's known as a call girl.'

'I see.'

'That's why the police aren't very interested,' she said quickly. 'And that's why the other private detective didn't want the work. You're the second I've tried, I'm sorry. And … and if you don't want the work it would be better if you said so before we go any further and—'

'Now go steady, Tracey,' he said in a calm tone. 'I've got a completely open mind about the way you and your friend make a living. But you have to try and see it from the police's point of view. Thousands of people go missing every year for all sorts of reasons and the police are so stretched they have to concentrate on the under sixteens or people in very stable partnerships.'

'Libby … she could be lying dead in North Cliffe Woods.'

'I'm afraid they're not going to search any woods on the off-chance. Did Libby go missing when she was working?'

'I don't know for sure. But the girls all look out for each other and take car numbers if any ... if any new men want to pick them up. She would have got back to the street safely, or they'd have raised the alarm.'

'Have you tried talking to any of the other girls?'

She nodded, her mouth going down at the corners. 'They'd not tell me anything. I think they thought I was a police officer in ordinary clothes trying to get information about one of their men. The men often push gear apart from ... from minding the girls.'

And if she'd said she was a friend of Libby's they'd not have believed that either, it seemed to Crane, a well-spoken woman like Tracey mixing with a woman who worked the pavements.

'I miss her so much, Frank,' she said in a voice almost a whisper. 'We were very close. She just wouldn't go off without telling me.'

The self-possessed woman he'd met at the door had now been replaced by someone whose face was crumpling in distress. He wondered what the basis of the relationship had really been. A call girl who had the looks to pick and choose her clients and was probably highly paid, and a woman who sold herself in Lumb Lane for the best price she could get. Maybe it was the sort of relationship Toulouse-Lautrec had pinned down so accurately in his comprehensive experience of Paris brothels: that of women who sold their bodies and lived in a loveless world, except for the love they could find among themselves. Perhaps the only genuine love Tracey and Libby had ever really known had been for each other.

'She might come back, Tracey,' he said gently.

'I just can't understand it. Her flat's as it was, her clothes ... there's really nothing missing.'

'How do you know?'

'I have a spare key. I've checked with the owner. He says she said nothing to him about leaving and she doesn't owe any rent.'

'Was she with anyone round about the last day she *was* at home, apart from you?'

'Only the tract woman.'

'Tract woman?'

'She hands out what she calls tracts to the Lumb Lane girls. About Jesus and finding the true path and giving up a sinful life, all that. The girls just throw them away, but Libby would keep hers. The woman homed in on her, followed her to her flat. Libby had quite a lot of time for her.'

'Why was that, do you think?'

'Libby ... Libby ... well she wanted to come off the game. We ... we both do. We'd have a couple of drinks and try to plan how we'd do it. Well, it's easy to get in, not so easy getting out.'

She was still flushed, still finding it hard to meet his eyes.

'Do you know where the tract woman lives? Her name?'

'I'm afraid not. I really didn't want to get involved with her.'

'Have you ever seen her?'

'Just once. She looked to be into her thirties. Tallish. Brown hair in a bun. Grubby pink jerkin over a long skirt.'

'Do you think Libby going off might have had something to do with her?'

She shook her head. 'She knew the tract woman was a nutter really. A nutter, but harmless. But Libby ... well, she'd had a Catholic upbringing. There was something inside her that I think really wanted the religious talk.'

And it could have given her hope, Crane thought, could have given her the idea that perhaps she *could* break away from the dismal streets and the braking cars and the words that must have been seared into her brain: 'How much, darling?' How much, how much, how much? Perhaps the tract woman, even though possibly not entirely right in the head, had given her the idea there was a definite chance to live some kind of a normal life, a thought that probably wouldn't find favour with Tracey, who was trying in her own way to do exactly the same for her best friend.

Crane really wasn't keen to take on the case. With his wide knowledge of people and motives, his gut instinct was that the tract woman really *had* persuaded Libby to take the plunge and pack in the kerb life. And maybe Libby had decided a clean break was the only way, even to the point of abandoning her flat and possessions and not saying goodbye to Tracey, who would perhaps be too much of a reminder of the life she'd lived.

But Tracey was hurting. She was very young, perhaps too young to be able to accept that people did sometimes act as Libby might have acted. That she'd found the only way to make a new start was to abruptly leave the villas, the area, even the drinks and the shared confidences, and possibly a bed, with the woman who'd been closest to her. Crane had a feeling he'd not find it too difficult to trace Libby. And if his instinct was right and she was with the tract woman and making a new life for herself then at least Tracey would know her friend was safe, if not much else.

There was almost a pleading look on the young woman's face in the short silence as he thought rapidly through the situation and his options. 'All right, Tracey,' he said then, 'I'll do what I can.'

'Oh, would you, Frank, would you really?' Her shoulders sagged a little in relief.

'Have you got a photo of her?'

She shook her head. 'She'd not have a photo wearing her working clothes. She hated those. Too tarty. I said one day when she'd changed into her nice clothes I'd take one then, but we never got round to it.'

'It doesn't matter too much. The methods I'll be using won't depend on a photo. How would you describe her?'

'Shorter than me. Nice figure on the plump side. Medium-length fair wavy hair. She had rather unusual pale-grey eyes, round face, small nose. Attractive, though she never thought so herself, poor kid.'

'That helps a lot,' Crane said, jotting down the details in his notebook. He then went carefully through his charges and possible expenses with her. She seemed almost indifferent, casually nodding when he'd finished.

'That's all fine, Frank. You'll be wanting a, what do you call it, a retainer? I can make it cheque or cash. Or … if you—'

She abruptly broke off, her eyes sliding past his again. He could have got it very wrong but he had the slightest impression she might have been prepared to offer payment in kind as a retainer, in place of cheque or cash, the sort of kind he could have had right here on the *chaise-longue*. It could be that she settled other of her bills in this way and if she was in the business, why not?

He smiled. 'I don't need a retainer, Tracey, not from people I can trust. All I ask is that you meet a weekly bill which I'll keep as reasonable as possible.'

She gave him a peculiarly endearing smile then, like a little girl standing in sunlight. 'Thank you so much. What else can I tell you?'

'Her full name. Any relations who might live in Bradford.'

'Libby Dawson. She had a very poor start in life. Her mother was a hopeless case, she had Libby and her brother by different men and couldn't cope. Her brother was adopted, Libby was brought up by her grandparents. She was happy with them, they gave her the Catholic upbringing. But they both died when she was still in her teens and she rather went to pieces she was so unhappy. She had quite a good job as a dental receptionist, but she took one of these flats and, because she needed more money, she drifted on to the game.'

'And that's when you met her?'

'You must think it's a bit strange, me in my line and Libby in hers.'

How right she was. He shrugged. 'I suppose I did think ... you being at the Rolls Royce end and Libby among the Ladas ...'

She nodded with a wry grin. 'It was Libby as a person, I suppose. She was so sad and lonely. She's attractive, but she has so little confidence, and you need confidence *and* looks to do what I do. I took her under my wing, I suppose. She's such a sweetie, funny, kind, generous. We both want to come off the game, truly. I told her I was sure we'd be able to find normal work if we gave our minds to it.'

'I'm sure *you* could,' Crane told her. 'With your looks and that excellent voice.'

It seemed he couldn't have said anything that could have pleased her more. 'You like my voice? I'm so pleased. It was what I was born with but when I got into this business I booked lessons with a voice coach. She ironed out the glottal stops and got me sounding my aitches and rounding off my words. I ... knew if I wanted to attract the right types I had to speak properly and not sound like one of the *Coronation Street* machine-shop girls.'

Crane was impressed. She'd gone into an unsavoury business, but she'd thought it through very professionally. The sort of men he felt she wanted to attract would be middle-class types in well-paid jobs and she'd figured that she had to sound and seem like them to charge the sort of prices that went with the superior article. He guessed also that she would give very good value for money lying naked on or under duvets. He was certain now he could have offset his costs to her for excellent sex, but if he had the relationship would then have altered in a way he'd not have wanted.

She sighed. 'The trouble is, Frank, I probably *could* get some kind of a decent job, but I left school too soon and I've no qualifications and no training. Maybe my looks could get me in somewhere, but in Bradford ... when it got out what I'd been doing, and it *would* get out, then the men would all begin hanging about, trying to get my knickers off. I'd not want any of that, this part of my life would be over.'

'You could try moving away.'

'We were talking all these things through and then ... and then Libby goes AWOL. I don't mind telling you that these past few years I've made a lot of money, enough to put a very good deposit on a decent house. The big scheme was that Libby and I could live in it together, find work, maybe find the sort of blokes we could settle down with. But ... well ... everything's on hold till I know where she *is*.'

Her eyes were moist and he could see she was near to tears. He'd been with her only a short time, but he'd begun to like her a lot, had begun to sense a peculiarly protective urge in himself towards her.

'I have to be going now, Tracey,' he said, 'but I'll do the very best I can for you.'

When he'd gone she dabbed her eyes carefully with a tissue. She'd been near to tears again as so often recently. But she had to keep her eyes looking good, no traces of bloodshot in the whites. She glanced at her watch. Time to make a start. She liked to give herself plenty of time to make herself look her very best for the evening.

What to wear? It was a hot sunny day. She made a decision on the champagne-coloured satin blouse, the white soft-line trousers and the sling-backs. All easy to get out of and back into gracefully she thought, with a crooked grin. But then the grin faded when she remembered being on the point of offering Frank sex as an option against a cash retainer. She'd done it several times in the past so that she could save as much money as possible. She'd got a good discount on her last car by taking the salesman to bed. She'd done well, too, with the slim-line telly.

But Frank was different and she was glad she'd stopped herself dropping the hint in the nick of time. There was something really warm and friendly about Frank, something almost fatherly. How often had she longed for a father who'd stayed? Hers had cleared off when she was small, as fathers so often seemed to do. And later her mother had taken up with the reptile. Just the *thought* of him made her shudder. Home had not been a good place to be.

Frank had been complimentary about her voice. That had really, really pleased her. He was the only man who ever had. She'd had plenty of compliments about her looks and her skills in the bedroom, but never any about the way she spoke, which had been the hardest-won skill of all.

She sighed, went into the bathroom and set the bath taps running. Call girls had to be very clean and smell very fresh. She had an idea Frank might have thought she and Libby could be lesbians. If so, he couldn't have been more wrong. They made their living from sex, they certainly didn't need it from each other. What they *had* needed was a loving friendship in a loveless world of endless lovemaking. She took off her clothes and stepped into the delicately scented water.

She lay back in the bath, thinking of Derek. It all went back to him really. Gift of the gab and made her laugh. His boss, he'd told her, would love an hour of her company and was a very generous bloke. It had seemed a lot of fun and she'd been up for it. His boss had taken out a wallet stuffed with fifties, not just tens and twenties.

That man had been the first. She'd packed in the dead-end job and started on this way of life almost overnight. Derek's boss had put her in touch with other well-heeled contacts. The money had come in easily and there was a lot of it. She got out of the bath and began to dab herself down with a soft thick towel. Too much money. It was going to be very difficult to find any sort of a job she'd be any good at and it wouldn't be easy to cope with the dramatic drop in earnings. But she was determined to try.

She went into the bedroom and began to lay out the clothes she'd decided on. She studied her naked body in the full-length glass as she did every day. She still looked good: firm breasts, narrow waist, well-shaped bottom. But how long had she got left anyway in this kind of life? Five, maybe ten years at best.

She dressed carefully and began on her make-up. She was so skilled now in its application that she knew exactly how to give her face that subtle glowing look while appearing not to wear any make-up at all. She had once thought that one or other of her younger clients, who looked to be going somewhere, might be so taken with her he'd want to make her his permanent partner, but that had never happened. To them she was still a prostitute even if she came out of the top drawer. And Derek had gone in the end too, though he'd been the one who'd eased her pathway into the easy money. He'd married a woman from a good family who'd not slept around.

But, as time had passed, she'd begun to realize that not only did she want to leave escort work, but also that she wanted to meet a man one day she could love for himself, not just for his money or his prospects, though if he had those things it would be a bonus of course. A man she could settle down and have babies with.

She sighed again. 'Oh, Libby, come back. I can't make a new start without you.'

F I V E

'Frank Crane.'

'Hello, Frank, it's Pam Draper. I need to speak to you. Could you call in sometime? Or I could come to your office.'

'I could make it this evening, about seven. Would that be OK?'

'That would be fine as long as I'm not putting you out.'

Her smile, when she opened the door to him, seemed to be one of relief. She took him through to the lounge, waved him to a chair. 'You'll have a drink. G and T?'

'Thanks, yes.'

He studied her as she dealt with the gin and mixers at the drinks table. She looked a little jaded as if she'd not slept well, though it could have been the intense humidity of a day of heavy cloud. She put down his drink and sat at the end of the long sofa as before. She was wearing a slightly crumpled sleeveless pale-green T-shirt and fawn jeans. They gave an impression of having been the first clothes to come to hand. Her coppery hair too hadn't been given its usual attention.

'I have a confession to make.'

'Go ahead, Pam.'

'I should have been honest with you,' she said in a low voice. 'You and the police.'

'About Ken *not* staying with you all night?'

Her mouth fell open. 'How did you know? How could you *possibly* have known?'

'I just had the feeling you were doing your best to give him an alibi but were finding it hard to bend the truth.'

She watched him in silence for several seconds. 'He...he was never here,' she said, her voice almost a whisper. 'When ... when Lydia was found in the crashed car and the police contacted him he

49

told me he'd said he was with me because he had no witnesses for where he really was that night.'

'And where was he really?'

'He said at home. He said he didn't think the police would believe him with Lydia dying like that. He just felt the questioning would drag on and on, and if the papers got hold of it it would be bad for his image as a respectable estate agent.'

'I see.' He spoke calmly, but it wasn't easy to control the effect of that frisson of intense satisfaction her words had given him. This was the breakthrough he'd been searching for. This could be the key to that intricate puzzle that would reveal just how Glover came to be standing in line to get so much money on the death of his wife.

She drank from her glass. The hand that held it was trembling. 'What should I do, Frank? About the police? I can't stop thinking about it. Won't they say I've, what do they call it, perverted justice?'

'Perverted the *course* of justice,' he corrected gently. 'The police won't want to get into any of that, not now you're prepared to admit how it really was. Leave it with me. DI Jones is a good friend of mine. I'll explain exactly why you covered for him. He'll understand, it's happened many times before. But they'll probably want to speak to you again at some stage.'

'Thank you so much. It helps put my mind at rest. But I'm worried, Frank, so worried. You don't really think Ken had anything to do with...?' The words were left dangling.

Crane was certain the CID would be able to box Glover into a corner, that they'd be able to force the details out of him of how he'd really spent the night his wife had died. But he had to bear in mind that Pam was in love with Glover and he needed to find the right words to leave her optimistic, at least for the present. 'These enquiries are all very routine, Pam,' he told her in the blandest tone he could muster. 'Ken was worried about his image, well, it was silly to lie about being with you but his motive was understandable. The police, all they want to do is to eliminate him from their enquiries and move on, it's as simple as that.'

She got up and moved restlessly to the drinks table, where she turned back to him, grasping the edge of the table behind her. 'But it's the money though. The insurance money. I can't stop thinking about that too.'

'It seems odd, I agree. But there may be a perfectly reasonable explanation why Lydia took it out. She could simply have wanted

Ken to be in a good situation if she died. And we need to remember that the coroner returned an open verdict. In other words the crash could have been an accident or ... well, suicide. Maybe we'll never know the answer to these things but if, as he says, he was really at home, well, there's nothing to worry about.'

'But if he *was* at home surely he'd know how Lydia got herself into the state she did.'

'They were living separate lives though, weren't they? Maybe they'd reached the stage where they simply didn't involve themselves in what the other was doing.'

Crane was beginning to feel as if the weasel words were sticking in his throat like stale bread. However anodyne he tried to make the situation seem, Glover still came over as three different kinds of a shit. And it was becoming obvious he wasn't really bringing her much comfort anyway.

She moved back to the sofa, unable, it seemed, to stay still. 'I'll be completely honest with you, Frank, I'm really very fond of Ken. When Lydia as alive he was talking about an amicable divorce and he and I setting up together. I thought that was what I wanted as he really was helping me to get over Matt. But ... but with everything that's happened: you coming along, not just the police, and then all this money Lydia was insured for ...'

She held a hand briefly against the side of her face. 'Ken ... he'll be wanting to come and see me soon ... or ... or want me to meet him in one of his houses. I just feel I need to be alone for the time being. It will be very difficult, but until things are sorted out ...'

Crane nodded and thought for a short time. 'Could you not say you've got this very long complicated job and you're on a tight deadline? Give yourself a week. That should give the police time to go over it all again.'

'I really think that might be best. I simply can't believe Ken could possibly be involved in anything ... anything shady, but I think I'd better put him off.'

They both got up. Crane put a hand lightly on her arm. 'I'm sure the police will be able to clear it up very quickly, Pam, and eventually I'll be able to find some straightforward reason why Lydia insured herself as she did.'

'You'll keep in touch, Frank? I'm finding it difficult to sleep.'

'I'll ring you every evening. And if you need me I'll be at the end of a line: home, office, car-phone, mobile. They're all on this card....'

*

'Terry Jones.'

'It's Frank, Terry.'

'How're you doing, Frank?'

'Fine. Terry, the Lydia Glover case.'

'Keep talking, old son.'

'I've been to see Pam Draper again, Glover's girlfriend. She's admitted Glover *wasn't* with her the night Lydia crashed the car. Glover asked her to tell you people he was with her as he had no witnesses to confirm *where* he was. He told her he was at home but feels you might not have believed him.'

'That's one thing he's definitely got right. Good work, Frank. Ted'll be throwing his cap in the air; he's totally convinced the smarmy sod was lying. We could have the bugger in the frame any day now.'

'You'll go easy on Pam, Terry? I've just about managed to convince her you'll not be banging her up for trying to pervert the course of justice.'

Jones chuckled. 'If Glover denies he was lying then we'll be needing to ask her for a statement. If he doesn't we'll not take it any further. How's she taking all this?'

'She's very fond of Glover, but I think he's using her. She's a nicely placed divorcee and has a lot to offer a bloke who couldn't find a tuppenny piece to scratch his arse with.'

'If he says he was at home that night she must think it very odd he didn't know his wife was tanking up on pills and booze.'

'I reckon she's beginning to think why is she choking on all this smoke if there's really no fire.'

'We'll have him in in the morning, ready to nail him to the wall. You've done good, Frank.'

'She'd have owned up to you and Ted in the end. She's a decent type; she couldn't live with the lie, not like certain women in this city.'

'She could have agonized for weeks though. But one look at that kindly nice-guy mug of yours and she coughs overnight. Have I ever told you I wished you were back?'

Jones had, several times. But it always made Crane's day to hear the words.

*

'John Gillis.'

'Frank Crane, John. I can report a little progress.'

'Very pleased to hear it, Frank.'

'I've been able to prove that Glover wasn't where he says he was on the night his wife died. In confidence, the police are getting him back in the morning. Jones and Benson are two very able CID men and I'm certain that they'll be able to wring the truth out of him.'

'This is very good news. Any idea what the truth might be?'

'That the car accident might not have been an accident.'

'You've made my day.'

'A couple of caveats. I've not met Glover, but I get the impression he might be a shady beggar. And if they can charge him with anything it'll take a long time before anything's resolved. And in the end there's a possibility he might be cleared.'

'Well, it would mean I could at least hold up any claim on the insurance until the investigations are complete.'

'I think you're looking at a fair chance the claim need never be paid.'

'Good hunting, Frank. I'll hope for the best. Or the worst from where Glover's standing.'

Crane put down the phone. He'd not wanted to get Gillis *too* excited though he himself was ninety per cent certain that by the end of the week Glover would be charged with somehow causing his wife's death.

'Hello,' she said, trying not to sound as nervous as she felt.

'*Hello*, darling. OK if I come round tonight? I could bring a take-away to save you having to cook.'

'Oh, I'm … I'm sorry, Ken, I'm snowed under with work, all on deadlines. We'll have to leave it for a few days.' She tried to control her breathing. She knew she was speaking too quickly.

'Oh, come on, honey. Surely you can take a break in the evening.'

'I really am sorry, Ken, but I've got yards of Dutch legal work to translate. I can barely find time to eat at all. The trouble is, if I don't take the work it'll go elsewhere and then I might end up getting none.'

'Oh, Pam, just a couple of hours. I've not fondled those lovely breasts for three *days*.'

'It can't be done, Ken, truly. Just give me a few days and then—'

'You sound odd. You've never done this to me before. At least meet me for an hour in one of my houses.'

'I've never had such a long complicated job—'

'There's something wrong, isn't there? Something to do with you and me. Why are you stalling?' There was an edge of curtness in his tone.

'I'm *not* stalling. All I ask is a few clear days.' She knew he'd detected the note of unease she was unable to keep out of her voice.

'What's going on, Pam? Why are you putting me off?'

'I'm *not*! I'll ring you when I'm *free*!'

'Look—'

'Sorry, Ken, but I've got to get on. See you later.' She put down the phone. It began to ring again in a few seconds but she didn't answer.

It had been a mixed day for weather but the evening sky was more settled and Crane drove along Lumb Lane in declining sunlight. He'd already driven along it three times and the woman he'd finally selected stood at the edge of the pavement in a pink sleeveless T-shirt and a short floral skirt, both garments clean if not very new. She had the indefinably shop-worn looks most of them had and he guessed she was on drugs, but she didn't look too spaced. He keyed down his window and held out a twenty. She looked at it scornfully.

'What's that, a down-payment?'

'It's yours if you'll just answer a couple of questions.'

'You a bogey?'

'Private detective. Do you know the lady they call the tract woman?'

'Who doesn't?'

'Does she still come round here?'

'Funny you should ask. Haven't seen her for a couple of weeks or so. But she'll be back. Tract women, the Sally Army, the bogies, they all come back sooner or later to stop us bad-lassing, know what I'm saying?'

'The last time the tract woman was here, can you remember if she went off with the girl called Libby Dawson?'

The woman thought about this, reaching for the twenty-pound note, but Crane wouldn't release it until he had an answer.

'I think she did, you know. I remember thinking it was a funny carry-on. But Libby was a bit funny anyway. She used to *keep* the tracts. Can you believe it?'

'Do you know where the tract woman lives?'

'In a caravan park, you ask me.'

'Do you know where Libby is?'

'They come, they go on the Lane. You get as you don't ask. Why, what's she done?' But the woman glanced to the rear of Crane's car and said, 'Look, mister, there's a bloke slowing down behind you who'll be wanting a bit more than a chat about the tract woman.'

'OK, love.' He let her take the note and released the hand-brake. As he pulled away he saw the other car draw up and the woman get in. Trade looked to be brisk. Maybe the living was easy in summertime, as the old song said.

'Thank you for coming in, Mr Glover. Take a seat.'

Glover sat down at the plain, metal office table. The oblong table and chairs were all the small room contained, apart from recording equipment standing against a wall. 'What is all this? I hope that thing isn't going.'

'No, this is just an informal chat. I think you know Detective-Sergeant Benson. The situation is that our enquiries are still ongoing into your wife's death. Now then, you told us you were at the house of a Mrs Pam Draper on the night your wife died, but we have reason to believe that that may not be the case.'

The look of slight discontent that Glover had come into the room with intensified, but nothing else changed in his face. Jones had to take into account that the work Glover did had been good practice in concealing his emotions. 'Of course I was at Pam's,' Glover said. 'You checked it out with her.'

'I … think she was just being helpful because of your relationship. You may have asked her to confirm it because you had no one to verify where you really were that night, or what you were doing.'

'Has Pam told you this?'

'We shall be speaking to her about it in due course, but our own enquiries have led us to believe you were never there.'

'I don't understand. If she *says* I was there—'

'She'll confirm our version, Mr Glover, we're quite certain of that,' Jones said heavily.

'But you've not spoken to her directly?'

'Let's not mess about, Mr Glover,' Benson said. 'We're quite sure of our facts. Now, so we can try to clear up this matter of your wife drugged, drunk and dead at the bottom of Royds Cliff Gully we need to know *exactly* where you were that night.'

'So we can eliminate you from our enquiries,' Jones added.

Glover's wary glance passed from one to the other of the two men sitting opposite. He was clearly thinking hard. After a prolonged silence he gave a heavy sigh. 'All right, I was at Napoleon's. The casino. It just looked bad, me being there when my wife crashed the car. I didn't want it getting in the papers and I didn't want endless complications about not being able to admit where I was that night. But I look to be getting them anyway.'

He looked across the table again into two sceptical faces. Jones said. 'Can anyone at Napoleon's confirm this?'

'It could be. I spend a lot of time there.'

'If you'd told us this right at the start someone might have remembered you being there. All this time later their memories will be uncertain,' Benson said irritably.

Another silence. Glover passed a hand over his rather metallic-looking blond hair. 'I ... do believe I may have had a meal there that night. If I did I'd have paid by credit card. They should have a copy docket. Ah ... I remember now, I also bought some gambling chips later on with the same card. Why not check with them?'

'Oh, we will,' Benson said. 'You can be sure of that.'

'And it won't get in the papers?'

'If you have no involvement in the circumstances of your wife's death nothing will go anywhere.'

'What involvement *could* I have had?'

'At the very least, Mr Glover, surely you must have had some idea of the fragile state of your wife's mind for her to go driving around with alcohol and sleeping tablets in her system.'

'I explained all this before. We lived virtually separate lives.'

'So separate you didn't notice that your wife was in a state of what could have been chronic depression?' Benson demanded, scepticism tinged now with contempt. 'Her own doctor said he'd treated her for depression in the past.'

'A quarter of the women in England must be treated for depression at some time or other,' Glover said. 'That was a while ago. She'd got over it and up to the day she died she looked to be fine. If she'd *seemed* to be in a state, of course, I'd have asked her about it. We've gone into all these things before. I can't understand why you don't let the matter drop.'

Jones's eyes met Benson's. It was a look that said the matter wouldn't be dropped until the big insurance pay-out that was coming Glover's way was explained to their satisfaction. Jones wished he could tackle him about that pay-out but the information at this stage was still unofficial. Benson said, in a more even tone, 'We thought you'd be pleased we're still giving so much time and attention to this case, Mr Glover. Surely you must be anxious to know the truth about your wife's death, if that's going to be possible, even if you *did* live separate lives.'

Glover watched them in silence again with the same guarded look he'd had before. 'Well, yes,' he said at last, 'I don't want to appear callous. We got on well enough. The marriage didn't work but we stayed good friends. I'm just finding it hard to live *with* her death, and all the reminders ...' The words dangled and he tried to arrange his features into a look of distress that didn't quite come off.

'You can go, Mr Glover,' Jones said flatly. 'Thanks for your time. I'm sorry we have to keep troubling you like this, but once we have a clear picture of your movements that night we shall be able to move on. We'll keep you fully informed if our investigations take us anywhere.'

Glover got up and they walked him through to the reception area. When he'd gone, Jones said, 'Off you go to Napoleon's, Ted, quick-sticks, on a docket-hunt.'

'A fiver says I'll find none.'

Jones gave a thin smile. 'You know me, Ted, have I ever bet against a sure thing?'

They were both as certain as Crane that they'd called Glover's bluff and they now had him in a corner.

When she opened the door there was a look of hope in her eyes. '*Hello*, Frank. Come on in.'

He went into her clean tidy flat. 'Please sit down. Can I get you anything?' she said, in her polite well-spoken way.

'No thanks, Tracey,' he said, sitting on one of the tub chairs. 'I just needed to go over a couple of things with you.'

The light seemed to flicker out in her clear green eyes and she shrugged. 'I suppose I thought ... with you coming back so quickly....'

'It could take a little time, Tracey, but I've got a line to work on.'

'You have!'

She was dressed as before, in jeans and a neatly ironed T-shirt, her soft dark hair falling into a natural wave, her face clear of the make-up that he guessed she put on carefully and took off carefully when her call girl activities were completed.

'I was in Lumb Lane last evening,' he told her. 'I managed to get a little information from one of the street girls.'

She gave a wry smile. 'You had more luck than I did.'

'She thought I was a bobby, but when I said I was only a PI she told me what she could. She was able to confirm that Libby went off with the tract woman the night she went missing.'

She watched him wide-eyed, her mouth falling open. 'Did she? Did she really? I can't get that together. I knew she got on quite well with the woman, even had her in her flat, but to go *off* with her ... I mean she *knew* she was a gallon short of a full tank.'

'I'm pretty sure it was a religious thing. You told me Libby was brought up a Catholic. I've heard it said that once a Catholic always a Catholic, even if you lapse.'

Tracey nodded slowly. 'She did get very upset now and then about not being able to go to mass and something called communion. She said she couldn't go because she wasn't in a state of grace, whatever that is. She was very upset last Christmas because she couldn't go to midnight mass and hear the singing.'

'Have you ever been a churchgoer?'

She shook her head. 'We weren't religious people. In my family it never came up. Why do you ask, Frank?'

'How did you react when Libby was telling you how upset she was about being lost to the faith?'

She watched him for a short time in silence. 'I ... I tried to be kind when she took it so badly, but ... well, to be honest, when we were having a couple of drinks and a bit of a laugh and chatting about this and that, and she suddenly started on about missing mass and so on, I suppose I did get a bit bored.'

'Now look, Tracey, this is absolutely no reflection on the way you tended to react, but perhaps ... just perhaps Libby saw in the tract woman someone who was really on her wavelength about her longing to return to the faith.'

'But ... but you don't think she might still be *with* her?'

'Could be. Could very well be. The tract woman might not have been the full shilling, but maybe she could provide the right atmosphere for Libby to break away from Lumb Lane and go back to the church.'

'Do you really think that might be what happened,' she said sadly, 'that she could go off without a word?'

'I'm just kicking ideas around. PIs do a lot of that. But if she *is* with the woman I'm sure she'll be back in the end. If she has returned to the faith I'm certain she'll want to come back to someone who's been so kind to her.'

She began to look relieved. 'Oh, Frank, I do hope you're right. Perhaps she did need to get right away for a while so she could concentrate on making a completely new start. I really can't believe she'd want to walk away from a friendship like the one we had.'

'Whatever happens, the tract woman will show up again sooner or later. The girl I spoke to is certain of it. Maybe she's suspended her handing out of tracts while she concentrates on a Libby make-over. But if Libby *isn't* with her I'm sure she'll know where she is.'

'You've given me such a lot of hope,' she said, her smile widening.

'I'll not stop looking. The tract woman has a high profile among the street girls. When she came to Libby's flat that time did she have a car, would you know?'

'Yes, she did. It was a dark-blue Clio.'

'I'll look out for it.'

'Thanks for everything you're doing. And keeping me in the picture like this.'

Crane knew he hadn't really needed to make this call. He could have had the discussion over the phone. But he'd been drawn to seeing her again. When she smiled there was something about the slight wrinkling round her nose that made her seem very young, in fact gave him a kind of impression of the captivating little girl she must once have been. The way she smiled could be a big turn-on for the men who were her clients; for Crane it made her seem somehow like a younger sister, not that he'd had one. But if he had had one he felt certain she'd have aroused in him both affection and an urge to protect, and it was these feelings, as strong as they were difficult to account for, that he now felt for Tracey Sharp.

'Tell me,' he said, 'have you thought any more about getting out of the call-girl business?'

'I think about it all the time, but I can't quite think how to go about it. No quals, no experience. I don't think I could face stacking shelves.'

'Had you thought about reception work? You've certainly got the looks and the voice.'

'I've never done anything like that before. Wouldn't you have to know about switchboards and computers?'

He smiled. 'I think they'd be prepared to train someone who looks like you. And you could enrol in a basic computer course, there are plenty on offer.'

'I'm not as young as I was, Frank.'

'Plenty young enough to make a new start. I had to make one a few years back. It's hard at first, but it gets easier.'

She was beginning to have a slight look of awe as they talked about these things. He wondered if it was something to do with the many men she'd provided services for. Maybe it was because none of them had ever talked to her of anything other than themselves, or what they'd like her to do for them. Maybe this was a first, a man actually talking about *her*.

'It's this thing about not working in Bradford,' she said. 'If it got out what I'd been ...'

'My job takes me all over Yorkshire. I've worked for a number of firms where they like to have a good presence in the reception area. If you like I can ring around to see if any of them are looking to fill that kind of position.'

'Would you really?' she said, the eager light back in her eyes that had been there when she'd opened the door to him. 'And not in Bradford?'

'Anywhere but Bradford.'

'But what could I say I'd been doing these past years?'

'We could cobble you a CV. I don't think they'd ask too many questions. And they'd trust my word.'

'Oh, this is really, really good of you, Frank!'

'If you've set your mind on making a new life for yourself, Tracey, I'll give you all the help I can.'

'But why, you hardly know me?'

'Because I think you're worth a lot more than the life you've got.'

Tracey watched from her window as he went out to his car. She still felt as if she couldn't quite get her mind round it, a man doing something for her and not wanting anything in return. She knew to the pound how attractive she was. Every day of her life she saw men who gave her the sort of looks that told her how much they wished they could take her out, touch her, kiss her, sleep with her. The only men who didn't look at her in that way were gays. Or Frank Crane. And she knew he wasn't gay. She could always tell; she was now an expert in male orientation. And yet she knew he didn't want to sleep with her. He just seemed to like being here. And she certainly liked having him around. It was as if he wanted to look after her. It gave her such a lovely warm feeling. She was so glad sex hadn't got in the way. It had certainly got in the way in the past with the few men she'd gone out with who hadn't been clients. It would be great if Frank was going to be a true friend. He'd be the only one she'd ever really had apart from Libby. She knew Libby would like Frank. When he found her.

She glanced at her watch. Time to lay out her clothes, take her bath, do her make-up. She sighed. She *would* make a new start. It had gone on the back burner with Libby going off, but if Frank could find her an opening she might as well make the new start now and then help sort out Libby when she did turn up. The big man had filled her with such *optimism*. She began to sing as she went in the bathroom, something she couldn't remember doing in months. If at all.

Crane's next job was to get confirmation, through his long-focus lens, that the wife of a supermarket manager was having an afternoon affair. It was rather unusual as it was normally the other way about. Men tended not to be as acute as women about the possibility of their partners leading a double life. He parked on a road in Wibsey where the woman lived and began to do what he spent so much of his time doing: he waited.

He couldn't stop thinking about Tracey. He still wasn't sure why but he couldn't get her off his mind as a sort of cute kid sister. He knew nothing of her background but guessed it must have been dysfunctional for her to have become a call girl. The biological father had probably cleared off early as so many of them did these days.

Such a waste. If she'd had the sort of loving and caring parents Crane had had where might she have been now? She was bright and she was intelligent; surely with the right encouragement it would have been A-levels and the university, the networking and the degree. She'd have gone from strength to strength given the breaks. With her looks and voice reading the news on television would surely have been just one of many options.

The hunger was there, he'd sensed it. She still had a good many years she could have counted on as a call girl, but she had the determination to get out early despite all the money she could make.

She'd not be able to make that kind of money in the sort of job he might be able to get for her, but he had the feeling somehow that once started she'd get on. He just wished the good fairies had been able to arrange to provide her with a worthwhile upbringing.

Pam was in the back garden. It was a warm evening and she'd felt the need for some fresh air. She'd been sitting at a computer screen most of the day. The borders were in fine shape as the recession victim who looked after her garden had a good touch with seasonal flowers. She drifted about the lawn, enjoying the declining sunlight. She thought she might have a drink out here, sitting at the little table on the patio. It was too late now for anyone to be offering her work and if they did the answer-phone would record the message. The little screen on her phone's hand-set told her who was on the line and if it was Ken she wouldn't answer.

He'd tried a number of times to get through to her though the calls had now dropped off. She supposed she'd have to see him eventually. She was very much tempted to bring the relationship to an end and yet she really would miss him. He was so lean and good-looking, had such presence and charm. And so good in bed. She badly missed the sensations that that body of his could arouse in hers.

But following the last meeting with Frank she'd found herself giving a great deal of thought to her situation with Ken. She had to remember that when Lydia had died she'd been shocked, of course, but had had to admit that she'd been so taken with Ken that there'd been relief there as well. It meant there'd be no problems, no lengthy divorce proceedings to stand in the way of she and Ken becoming partners.

Ken, too, had been very shocked, or had appeared to be, when Lydia's body was found. She supposed she couldn't have expected him to be upset for too long, as he'd always insisted that he and Lydia lived separate lives, and he also was pleased there were now no obstacles to him and Pam setting up together.

She knew it had been Frank coming into her life that had made her begin to think more carefully about Lydia's death. She realized she'd been up to her old tricks of putting out of her mind things she didn't want to dwell on. She had to accept that Ken should have had some idea of the state Lydia had been in to do what she did. She now found herself having waves of pity for that poor woman, a feeling of genuine compassion, even though she was dead, even though she'd never known her. And the trouble was she couldn't really convince herself that Ken felt anything much at all for a woman he must once have loved so deeply that he'd wanted to spend the rest of his life with her.

And then all that insurance on her life. It still gave her broken nights. She really did hope Frank could find a satisfactory solution to these things, but even so she was beginning to wonder if she truly did want to continue a relationship with a man like Ken. If the one with his wife had ended with them leading separate lives could that mean the same fate might overtake her?

She went back in the house and made the preparations for a tuna salad and a crusty roll that would be her evening meal. Then she mixed herself a gin and tonic with lemon and plenty of ice and stepped out into the garden again. She put down her drink on the little wooden table and was about to sit on one of the wicker armchairs when she suddenly became aware of a long shadow thrown by the setting sun.

'Good timing, Pam, I'll join you. After a day like this I could murder a large G and T.'

Her heart lurched. It was Ken.

S I X

'Frank Crane.'

'It's Terry, Frank.' He sounded dispirited. 'The news is not good. We had Glover in and asked him where he'd really been the night Lydia died, no bull-shitting. He finally gives out he'd been at Napoleon's. Hadn't wanted it to get out he'd been gambling while his wife was totalling herself.'

'That's just another lie, Terry. He goes there a lot, but I'll bet the house and car he wasn't there that night.'

'We were just as certain as you were,' Jones said heavily, 'but it looks as if the bugger *was* there—'

'But who could definitely remember him *being* there after all this time?'

'He had dinner there. He bought gambling chips later from the cashier. Casinos keep careful records and they could turn up copy dockets for both the meal and the chips. Both showing that bloody *date!*'

'I can't get this together.'

'Neither could Ted. He even checked out the record of bookings for meals. *And* the signing-in register. Everything showed him being there.'

'It's all just too pat, Terry.'

'Exactly what Ted says.'

'Glover's a compulsive gambler, for God's sake. Compulsive gamblers don't *do* dinner, they get straight into the action. And getting chips from the cashier, he could have done that at the table.'

'We're all agreed, he's covered his arse. God knows how he pulled it off, the car crash, but there's nothing we can do about it.'

'He's in there somewhere, he's got to be.'

'It's looking like the end of the line, old son. I can't see there's anywhere else we can go.'

Crane cleared his phone, stunned. The sense of simmering elation he'd had since Pam had changed her story about Glover had completely evaporated. He couldn't begin to guess how Glover had pulled it off, he seemed to be covered now for the entire evening, even for the period when Lydia could have been washing down the sedatives with alcohol. His alibi was now set in pre-stressed concrete, but the stronger the alibis became the more convinced he was that Glover had somehow engineered his wife's death. He stood in the kitchen as his dinner cooked, staring dismally into space, his mind a blank.

She felt chilled in the balmy evening warmth. 'Hello, Ken.' It was an effort to get the words out and she could tell her voice sounded strained. It had been a mistake coming outside.

'I thought you'd be crouched over your computer with that big job you've got, on a deadline.' He spoke in his usual pleasant way but there was a sarcastic edge to his tone.

'I ... I've only broken off to eat. I'll be back to it when I've eaten.'

'But you've found time for a drink too.'

'You ... you shouldn't have come, Ken,' she said uneasily. 'I told you I couldn't break off.'

'Not even for an hour? Not even to pick up the phone?'

She turned from him and went back in the house. It was instinctive. She was a private person and if he was going to make a scene she didn't want neighbours to hear who might be on their own patios beyond the hedges. Voices carried on quiet, still evenings like this. But then she began to wonder if this was the wrong decision too.

In the lounge, with hands that shook a little, she mixed him a gin and tonic.

'What's going on, Pam?' he said, in a blunt tone she'd not heard before.

She handed him the drink. 'My *work*. Once this big job's over—'

'Come off it. You've never had a job before that came ahead of a good bonk.'

She watched him, unable to find words. His blond hair was caught in angled sunlight and his mouth had the slight peevish cast she'd seen before only rarely. He was wearing chinos, a short-sleeved checked shirt and espadrilles, and she suddenly found herself longing for the old Ken to be back, the one before Lydia had died, with his engaging manner and his sense of humour and his sexual expertise.

'What have you been telling the police about me, Pam?'

It handed her a big shock. She felt herself paling. 'What can you mean?' she cried. 'What can you possibly *mean*?'

'The police know I *wasn't* here the night Lydia had the accident. They could only have known that from you.'

'I haven't *spoken* to the police. Not ... not since that first time. They must have found out in some other way.'

'The police couldn't possibly have found out unless it came from *you*.' He drank half his gin and tonic in a single gulp and slammed down the tumbler on the drinks table at which they still stood. 'I'm not leaving this place till I know who you spoke to and why,' he said, his voice now so harsh it was hardly possible to connect it to the one she'd always heard before. Her hands were shaking badly she was so frightened. It *had* been a mistake not to have stayed outside.

'I haven't spoken to the *police*!'

He grasped her by the wrists then and twisted them so that she gave a yelp of pain. 'Who did you speak to and why?'

'Let me go, let me *go*! Take your hands off me. I don't know *how* the police found out.'

He continued twisting her wrists, the pain was unbearable. 'You'll break my arms!'

'That's up to you. If you don't tell me the truth I probably will.'

She could hardly breathe she was in such pain. She knew she'd have to admit to something if she didn't want a broken limb. But even with the pain she knew she couldn't let Frank's name slip, though she almost had done. 'It was the *inspector*!' she screamed. 'The one called Jones. Now let me *go*!'

'They had you down to the station?'

'No! He rang me. He said ... he said ... was it the truth ... that you were here? He ... he said if I wasn't being honest I could make it very difficult for myself. What ... what could I do? I was frightened. I was *frightened* ...'

'You stupid *bitch*! You only had to stick to the story we'd agreed. They'd never have been able to prove anything different.' But his powerful grip loosened on her wrists and she tore her hands away, her body so limp with relief she felt she could hardly stand. He stood with a face so angry and brooding he seemed not to be the same man. But she could tell he believed her. 'Do you know what it means?' he went on, his voice low but still harsh. 'Do you? It means they're beginning to think I'm somehow involved in Lydia's death.'

She struggled to get her breathing under control, while massaging her throbbing wrists. She spoke then without thinking, as it would have been wiser to say nothing, to get him out of the house as soon as she could. 'Where were you anyway, the night she died?'

It was some time before he replied. 'We're trying to lease an office property on Well Street to an MD. I took him for dinner at a club caller Napoleon's.'

'Why didn't you tell the police that at the start?'

'I didn't want any comebacks. This man was one of the big people and the negotiations had reached a delicate stage. I didn't want him being quizzed by the police for confirmation I was with him. I needed to keep Lydia's death as low-key as possible as obviously it didn't reflect well on me.'

She couldn't tell why but she was certain he was lying.

'I'm sorry, darling,' he said then, 'I really didn't mean to hurt you. I can't think what came over me. It's beginning to really get me down, the police digging it all up again about the car accident and somehow implying I was involved. Can I top up my glass? Shall I pour you one? Can I stay for a meal? Anything will do, an omelette, beans on toast ...'

It seemed scarcely credible, but he had the gleam in his eye she knew only too well and which had once made her insides flutter. He was thinking in terms of a couple of drinks, a meal and then a session in her bed. She was appalled. After the pain he'd put her through. She was certain he'd have broken something had she not lied about speaking to Inspector Jones. Maybe he got off on it, putting himself in a state of arousal by causing a woman pain. She'd learnt more about the man he really was in fifteen minutes than in all the time she'd known him. She wondered if that cruel streak had had anything to do with what had happened to Lydia.

'You'd better go,' she said flatly. 'I still can't get it together you wanting to hurt me so badly. Just go.'

'Oh, come on, Pam. I'm very, very sorry. I really don't know what got into me. I was so angry, thinking the police might have poisoned your mind about me. Please forgive me. Come on, let's sit down with a drink.'

He put his hands on her shoulders. Her body tensed instinctively, as if she were going to be hurt again.

'Please go, Ken. I need time to get over this.'

She caught in his face a brief shadow of the peevishness she'd seen earlier before it was replaced by the tender smile that had been such a draw when she'd first known him. It was clear he was confident he'd be able to talk her into letting him stay. 'Oh, come on, honey, let me get you another drink.'

'I need time on my own and I need it *now*,' she said firmly.

The smile faded. She could tell he was taken aback that his near-indestructible charm didn't seem to be working for once. He watched her in a lengthy and reproachful silence. 'Well,' he said at last, 'if you feel you must. But I really am very sorry. All right, have some time out, darling, and think things through. I'll come back tomorrow.'

She felt she barely knew him. She couldn't believe he still felt himself to be in with a chance. In twenty-four hours he seemed confident she'd be keen to have him back again: over drinks, over a meal, in her bed. Things he seemed convinced would clear from her mind the intense pain he'd inflicted on her. But she felt she had to tread carefully. 'Just give me some space to get over this, Ken, it's given me a bad shock. I'll ring you later.'

'That's a promise?'

'That's ... a promise.'

'Can I kiss you?'

She let him. It was a very brief kiss, not one of the lingering ones she'd always given him before, her body again automatically tensing. He drew away from her. He seemed bemused that she'd not melted, her body language telling him that of course he could stay, after all. She caught one last almost subliminal glance of the tell-tale peevishness that seemed to mean he simply couldn't believe his attraction, his way with a woman, was getting him nowhere. There was a childishness about it. She felt she could see for a moment the infant he must have been: winning, lovable, but spoilt, demanding, given to tantrums when he was refused a third piece of chocolate cake.

'Frank Crane.'

'It's me, Frank, Pam.'

She told him everything that had happened that evening.

'This isn't good, Pam. He's showing all the signs of a man starting to lose control. Look, if he turns up just give me a ring and I'll be round myself. Keep your doors locked and don't let him catch you in the garden again.'

'Why do you think he's behaving like this?'

'I'm sorry to have to tell you, but I think you should know. Jones, Benson and me, we're all convinced now that Ken was definitely involved in some way in Lydia's death.'

'Oh, *Frank*! He ... he *says* he was really at a place called Napoleon's that night.'

'I know. Ted Benson checked it out. There's firm evidence he was there until late.'

'He said he was entertaining an important client.'

'He'd not take an important client there, Pam, Napoleon's is a gambling casino. Apart from anything else, Ken has a serious gambling habit. He's also on the verge of bankruptcy and that's another reason why he's under suspicion.'

'I never knew. I really never knew, Frank.' Her voice was faint with shock. 'I'd no idea of any of this. Are you sure? He never gave any impression he was hard-up.'

'I have a totally reliable source. He'd not have wanted you to know, he'd want to give the impression he was a going concern. Who'd want to take on a penniless gambler?'

'I ... I almost did,' she said, her voice close to a whisper. 'I've learnt more about him today than I ever wanted to know.'

'I'm sorry about this, I really am. I don't like giving a dog a bad name. He might be completely innocent of anything in spite of what it seems. We've all been wrong before. But for the time being you must take care. And, if you ever feel you're in the slightest danger, ring me.'

'Thank you so much. I shan't see him again. It's not just the gambling and being broke and the lies he's told, I simply can't believe any decent man would hurt a woman the way he hurt me. I've learnt too much about the man he really is beneath all the charm.'

'I've always distrusted charm. Maybe it's a Yorkshire trait, preferring to see people in their unvarnished condition. I think it was Barrie who wrote something about if you have charm you don't need anything else.'

'That seems to fit Ken,' she said sadly. 'I don't really think he *has* got anything else.'

'It's me, Polly.'

'Yes, Ken?'

'There's been a kind of hitch.'

'Do go on.'

'It's the police. They're trying to stitch me up. They're beginning to think the crash is down to me.'

'Why should they think that?'

'They've had me in the station, going on about where I was that night.'

'You can prove where you were.'

'I *told* them I was with my stupid cow of a girlfriend. They started putting the squeeze on her and got it out of her I wasn't there.'

'But you were supposed to be at Napoleon's.'

'Everything *proves* I was at Napoleon's.'

'Why this other story then?'

'To keep this kind of heat off. I knew if she stuck to the story I was with her it would knock any other enquiries on the head.'

'Do they know about the insurance?'

'I don't think so. But they'll pick up on it. That's the reason I wanted to keep everything low-key. When it comes out about the insurance they'll start feeling my collar again. They're already starting to think I'm half in the frame.'

'But if it's watertight about you spending the night at Napoleon's, there's nothing they can do about the insurance, even if there is rather a lot of it.'

'I can do without it though, this aggro from the police. It doesn't look good at the office and with this silly bitch I'm going around with.'

'She doesn't *know* anything?'

'Not a thing.'

'Shall you end it with her?'

'No. I had to throw a scare into her for blabbing her mouth off but she'll come round. They always do.'

'What's the attraction?'

'She owns her own house, she gets an allowance from an ex, she's on a decent earner and she's not bad in bed. It'll help me sort out a few short-term problems.'

'See here, Ken, don't worry about the insurance. Nothing at all can be proved about that, however it might seem. And if you're covered for the night in question there's nowhere for the police or anyone else to go. Once the insurers pay out it'll all start to go quiet, I'm certain of that.'

'I suppose you're right. It just threw me, the police getting restive.'

'Just sit tight and lead your normal life. It'll all work out.'

'All right, Polly. I'll let you go.'

'I'm glad you rang though. There's just one final matter that really needs attending to rather soon.'

'There *can't* be!'

'Even the best laid plans don't always work with total precision.'

'What's the problem?'

She gave him the details and he reluctantly agreed to do as she asked. 'It might get them going again,' he said uneasily.

'But once again they'll not be able to *prove* anything. That's all that matters, Ken....'

Polly went back in the drawing-room and poured herself another glass of wine. It was best if Jane didn't hear these discussions. There was no secret about them, it was just that Jane's nerves weren't as robust as Polly's.

'It was Ken,' she told her. 'He was a bit agitated because the police had questioned him again about his movements that night. But he can prove exactly where he was. I told him to stop worrying. It put his mind at rest. Are you ready for another?'

Jane held out her glass. She loved the early evenings: the ceremonial opening of the bottle of chilled white wine, chatting with Polly about the day that had gone, going over their plans for the future. And in the background there'd be some of the music that Polly liked so much: Wagner, or Beethoven, or Mahler. In half an hour they'd have dinner and then later they'd stroll to the Mayfield for drinks with the boys. They always called them the boys but they were really mature men, nearly all businessmen or professionals. These were the types Polly liked to attract and Jane had never known anyone as skilful as Polly in doing that. Polly was, of course, very sexy and each night they stood in the centre of a little circle of admirers.

'Well, old girl, two or three weeks, a month at the most, and the money should be in my account. Probating wills is always a slow business.'

'And we'll be ready.'

'And we'll be ready. We'll make an immediate start on this place, but we'll marry it in with the other work. And inside three months we'll have more work than we can handle, you'll see.'

'You don't miss London too much?'

'I did at first. I was doing very well up there, as you know, but I just hankered for my own set-up and no one would bankroll me, let alone Brain-dead. But I'm glad to be back. I'd not realized how much the family name meant to me. To be able to make something of it again perhaps – that's why I reverted to my name as a singleton.'

'I'm sure you will, Polly. It means such a lot to you.'

'I couldn't ask for a better colleague. What tremendous luck, we two meeting in town like that. We couldn't possibly have seen where it was all going to go, all the doors it was going to open.'

Jane still found difficulty in absorbing it all. After these last four or five awful years to be living such a different life, such an *exciting* life, with Polly. How could she have imagined, when she was a teenager at school, that Polly would one day be not just a colleague but her closest friend?

Because in those days Polly had simply not noticed her. She'd moved around with half-a-dozen girls who all had a wild streak, none as wild as Polly's. Polly had been the natural leader. All her life Polly had been the one in charge. She'd almost been expelled because of the smoking and the vodka-sipping in the school grounds, and her attitude to certain teachers who she knew, correctly, didn't know as much about a subject as she knew herself. But her father, still a big name in the City despite the reduced circumstances, had talked the headmistress out of it and made a donation to school funds. That anyway had been the rumour. Not that it had stopped Polly going to all-night raves and sleeping with the promising football player and smoking cannabis in the pub where the landlord turned a blind eye.

And Jane had gazed on, wishing she were an exciting person, the sort of girl boys wanted to take out in their mothers' motors.

'Any more ideas on what we should call ourselves?'

'Something simple that says it all. Polly and Jane Design perhaps.'

*

'Hello, Frank!' Her eyes gleamed in a welcoming smile. 'How nice to see you again.'

'I need to say right off it's not about Libby.'

'I didn't really think it would be. You did say it could take a while. Come on in. Please let me get you something this time: tea, coffee, a drop of the hard stuff?'

'Coffee would be fine.'

'Sit down, I'll be back in a tick.'

Instead of sitting down he moved over to the little bookcase with its shelves crammed with paperbacks. A lot of them were chick-lit, but here and there were copies of several classical novels that had been filmed or televised by such writers as Hardy and Dickens and Jane Austen. He drew out *Emma* and *Far From the Madding Crowd*. Their condition gave clear signs they'd been handled and read. He wondered if that was another aspect of the person she wanted to be, a woman who read good books and now longed to break away from the call-girl life and perhaps simply mix with men who'd never know she'd once been able to be bought.

There was a framed photograph of her on the table that held the vase of flowers. He wished he could have a print of it. He still couldn't quite understand why she drew him so strongly in a non-sexual way. Perhaps there was no point in thinking about it too rationally. For him it was something about her that seemed to bypass the obvious attraction of her face and figure; it was a sort of youthful, ingenuous, almost virginal quality that seemed to remain intact and unscathed by the years of marketing her body. It aroused in him that peculiarly familial affection and protective urge. He wanted to stroke her hair and pat her cheek, wanted to give her copies of other books she might enjoy, take her to a good restaurant for a meal, help guide her footsteps in that new life she wanted.

She came back into the room with a cafetière, cups and saucers, and some expensive-looking biscuits on a tray. 'I've been trying to guess why you're here if it's nothing to do with Libby. Though there doesn't *have* to be a reason. I'm always pleased to see you.'

He believed her. He wondered if she too was conscious of the bond that seemed to be growing between them.

'How do you like your coffee, Frank?'

'Black, one sugar, thanks. I'll not keep you in suspense. I've been ringing one or two firms I've worked for in the past. One of them is in Harrogate, it's a head-hunting set-up. They have a very high-grade office suite. Their receptionist is taking maternity leave but the feeling is she'll not be back. I told one of the partners about you. I said you'd done reception work in the past, that you looked good, were well-spoken and could probably start right away. He'd like you to go for an interview.'

'Oh, Frank,' she gasped, wide-eyed. 'That's wonderful, just *wonderful!*'

'He said if you were prepared to do some VDU work that would be all to the good. The present woman would give you training.'

'I can't believe you've found something so *quickly*.'

'Just luck.'

'You must have spent such a lot of time ringing round. You must charge me for it.'

'No need, Tracey. I spend a lot of time sitting in my car, just waiting for things to happen. I was able to ring round while I was sitting there.'

'Oh, *Frank!*' Her voice was high-pitched and gleeful. 'What should I say I've been doing these past years?'

'It might be best to say you've been living in London. Maybe with a partner and it fell through. You did temping work for the agencies.'

'That's a good idea. I actually did live in London for a short time three years ago; Fulham. So I could fill in the background if I was asked.'

'Good.' He tore a sheet from his notebook. 'These are the details. With your looks and manner I don't think they'll want to go too closely into your past. And this man trusts me. You do realize the money will seem like loose change to what you make now?'

'I don't care. I really don't care. I've put by most of what I've made. I'm watching what the papers say about the housing market and when it really hits bottom I'll buy a place of my own. I should only need a smallish mortgage.'

'You're a clever girl. Just use that kind of thinking in your new job and you'll get on very well.'

'I'm so *pleased!* Look, I've forgotten to pour the coffee.' She did so now, passed Crane a fragrant cup and held out to him the plate of biscuits. 'I do hope you can trace Libby soon. We can look at houses together then and I can perhaps help her to find work too.'

'I'll not give in. I just need a sighting of the tract woman.'

'You're not a man who gives in much about anything, are you?'

'Maybe I recognized that in you.'

'But it would have been *so* difficult without your help. Libby and I, we've been talking about a different life for months, but we couldn't decide how to go about it. We just wanted to be normal. Normal women living a normal life. It was one of the things that drew us together. Well, once I can get her into a place of our own and she sees me working in a proper job ... that's if I *get* the job.'

'My contact is so keen to fill the job with someone like you I think it could safely be regarded as yours for the asking.'

'What do you think I should wear? What should I say I do in my leisure time? Should I say I'm looking to settle in Harrogate? Can you tell me how these head-hunter people operate?'

She was as excited as a child going to a Christmas party. For the next quarter of an hour Crane answered all her questions patiently and as well as he could, pleased that she wanted to do her home-work. He felt certain that any of the head-hunters' clients approaching a reception desk where Tracey sat, warmly smiling in a crisply ironed blouse and elegant skirt, would think that she herself had been head-hunted.

He put down his cup and saucer. 'I'll have to be moving on, Tracey. Give that chap a call after lunch, he'll be expecting one. And good luck. Let me know how you go on.'

As he got up she jumped to her feet and threw her arms round him. 'Oh, Frank, thank you, thank you, thank you. Let me give you a big kiss.'

She did so and Crane got his wish, to be able to put a hand over her smooth cap of hair and pat her cheek.

'If I get the job will you come and have a meal with me, as a proper thank you? I *can* cook, you know, I'm not just a bird who takes her clothes off.'

'I'd love to, I really would.'

'Frank Crane.'

'It's Gillis, Frank.'

'Hello, John. How can I help?'

'Frank, I had the solicitor on this morning who's handling Lydia Glover's will. He was asking when he could expect the settlement of the insurance claim on her life. I said I'd go into it with the insurers and get back to him. Then I said, "Ken Glover's going to be on easy street when the will's probated with all the loot that's coming his way". I don't know if you've met Jeremy Green but he's the sort of legal man you can have a bit of a joke with.'

'I know him well. I've done a lot of work for him, tracking down legatees and so forth. You're right, he does have a relaxed attitude.'

'Thing is, Frank, this time he didn't hang on. He went quiet and then changed the subject. Well, with a chap like Jeremy a silence can often mean more than words.'

'What are we saying, John, or what do you think Jeremy might be implying?'

'Well, if Glover really is coming into a bunch of money I reckon Jeremy would have come back with a bit of repartee of his own. But all I got was the sound of silence.'

'You don't think there's some sort of possibility Glover *isn't* going to collect?'

'Makes you wonder.'

'That's very odd. If for some reason Glover isn't in line for the pay-out, who is? And why would he have any involvement in his wife's death? That's the way all our minds have been working.'

'I could have it wrong. It was just an impression I had.'

'I don't suppose we'll know for sure till the will's probated. And presumably that can't happen until you OK the claim.'

'By the way, any more news on where Glover really was on the night Lydia died?'

Crane sighed. 'I was intending to speak to you about that. There is news, but it's not good. Glover has unshakeable proof he was actually at Napoleon's casino all that night.'

'What rotten luck. You were all so sure you had him against the wall, weren't you?'

'Thought we had him on toast, John. And in the short term there seems nowhere else to go. Do you want me to carry on?'

'Yes. The question I'd still like answers to, if at all possible, is why she took out all that insurance in the first place.'

Tracey was so excited she couldn't stop pacing up and down her living-room. She'd spoken to Colin Sykes at the head-hunting firm and he'd asked to see her in the morning. He'd sounded so positive, so keen. He'd told her that if she came with Frank Crane's recommendation she was in with an excellent chance. And the fact that she was in a position to start next Monday was a feather in her cap.

She went in the bathroom and set her bath running. Darling

Frank, he'd become such a good friend in the short time she'd known him. She was so glad sex hadn't come into it, it would have been such a complication. She'd not have been able to rid herself of the idea that he was only giving her a helping hand so that she'd go to bed with him. But she was convinced now that he just wanted to look after her and it was a great feeling. She couldn't remember any other man in her life who'd reacted to her the way he had. Patting her head so gently like that, as if she were about ten, encouraging her with her plans for a new life, giving her such sound advice. Yes, she was so glad he'd not wanted sex. But she hoped that one day she might meet someone like him, someone who'd realize she had dreams and ambitions of her own and not just see her as a woman who was good in bed.

She stepped into her bath. She was working this evening. She lay back smiling in the scented water. All at once it had hit her that she'd not been as happy as this in years. Depending on her interview in the morning this could be her very last job as a call girl. It was a house on Fox Ridge. From memory, they were rather large and isolated. She didn't know the client, just that he was safe. She'd always been very careful about checking clients out. This one came spoken for by a man named Ken Glover, someone she could trust. He was a womanizer, but when he was between girlfriends he'd sometimes book an hour with Tracey. He was funny and charming and so skilled in bed he'd once or twice suggested she gave him a substantial discount, as if she was expected to pay *him*! She'd refused of course, she was simply a working girl who went to bed for a living, but on being turned down he'd had that funny little look around his mouth, something her mother had always used to call a 'petted lip'.

But he was reliable and she could take his word that the man she'd be seeing this evening was risk-free. She'd always warned herself that you could not be too careful even at this end of the game. She got out of the bath and dried herself. Then she padded into her bedroom, glancing at herself as usual in the full-length looking-glass for any signs, however minor, of wear and tear. She smiled once more. She might never again have to give her body this scrupulous attention. Nor would she need to spend half an hour on her face to give it that glowing look. She'd not have time for all this stuff anyway, not if she had to be in Harrogate for a day that started at nine. That would be the only downside, not being able to linger in bed in the mornings. But she couldn't wait for her new life to begin.

And she was sure this was going to be her last evening for being paid to take off her clothes.

'Thanks for seeing me, Jeremy, I know how busy you are.'

'I seem to spend half my time talking to young chaps who want to train for the profession now they've lost their high-rolling jobs in the banks.'

'Things have never been this bad.'

'Not in our lifetime anyway. How can I help, Frank?'

'It's a delicate matter.'

'Try me.'

'I don't know if John Gillis has told you but he's very uneasy about all the money Lydia Glover was insured for. I'm working for him to see if I can turn up any reason why she took all the insurance out. I know you're handling the will. What I really need to know is if all this insurance money is willed to Ken Glover.'

Green watched him in silence for several seconds. 'All right, seeing as it's you. I know I can trust you with the information.'

'You have my word, Jeremy. And between you and me Glover comes over as a decidedly dodgy character.'

'Lydia did seem to be over-insured. And then the car crash. The circumstances do seem odd. Well, to begin with her entire estate was willed to Glover, but she suddenly changed her will. The actual insurance pay-out now goes to a woman called Polly Manning.'

'Is that so? Where does she fit in?'

'I really don't know. Lydia gave me the new instructions and I just drew up a codicil.'

'Does Glover know this?'

'Again, I couldn't say.'

'I can't get this together. The thing is, I don't like the look of the car accident and neither do the police. We thought Glover might have had some involvement, but what you tell me puts it in a new light. Do you know anything about this Polly Manning?'

'As it happens, yes. Her old man was a big wheel in textiles.'

'One of *those* Mannings.'

'The family owned the big mill over in Little Horton. Fleece wool went in at one end and fine suiting cloth and household fabrics came out the other. What they call a vertical operation. But the industry was dying and they needed either to adapt or close down. Wilfred Manning did neither and had to close down in the end on the worst possible terms. He was left in very reduced circumstances.

'Polly was the daughter. There was enough money left to send her to Bradford Girls' and live a bit longer in the big house. But she was a wild one. Ran with a fast crowd. I used to see her around, we're about the same age. She was a tough nut too. If she didn't get her own way in everything, any boyfriends were through the door. She once went out with a young footballer, said to have a dazzling future in the beautiful game. The story goes that he called at The Hall one night when Polly was at home alone. She wouldn't answer the door. She opened her bedroom window and said if he wanted her he'd have to climb up to her on some kind of trellis affair. The fool was crazy about her and he had a go. The trellis gave way and he fell and broke his leg and badly injured his pelvis. He never played footer again, and in the end had to walk with a stick because of a limp. At which point Polly gave him the heave-ho, saying there was no place in her life for a cripple.'

'Seems to have had a way with words by the sound of it. What happened after the father stopped being wealthy?

'She took up with a man who worked in a bank, married him and disappeared from view. Then suddenly she was back, single, and reverting to the family name.'

'And now she's in line for a hefty inheritance. It must strike you as very odd, Jeremy.'

The other man shrugged. 'People do funny things with their estates, it happens a lot more than you might think. At least she didn't leave it to a donkey sanctuary. Not that I've anything against donkeys, but I tend to take the old-fashioned view that people come first.'

Tracey drove up to the garage and got out of her car. It was an old detached house but well maintained. There was a FOR SALE board near the gate under the name of the estate agents Ken Glover worked for. He'd mentioned that the man she'd be seeing was aiming to sell up. It had a very private atmosphere. There were tall hedges and the windows were hung with Venetian blinds set at an angle that made it difficult to see inside. She rang the doorbell but there was no response. Ken had told her if no one answered to go straight in as the door wouldn't be locked; the client was a busy man and might be a few minutes late. She opened the door and went into a large hall. It was rather shadowy but she liked it. The walls were half-panelled in dark oak and there were some nice watercolours of the Aire Valley in the changing seasons. There was a coat-stand with a looking glass and she automatically checked her appearance. She looked good. She wore a white cotton crinkle jacket over a simple top and a fawn skirt with a leaf pattern design. She was lucky with her hair, it was soft but with body and the short style brought out the best in it. Her face had rarely looked better, but the glow it had this evening wasn't just down to the make-up, the extra hint of animation was there because she was so pleased with life. Pleased that she might be getting away from all this: the meetings in hotel rooms or apartments or expensive houses like this, the banknotes in envelopes, the absolute necessity to be a fun person, to smile and laugh a lot, however bad a day you'd had.

And then the big act in the bedroom, the legs that writhed in apparent bliss, the fingers that fondled, the buttocks that wildly gyrated, the obligatory gasps of breath, the little yelps of delight. And finally the abandoned convulsions of her body when she laid on her endlessly rehearsed impression of scarcely being able to cope with an orgasm of such overwhelming intensity it almost pitched her off the bed.

She smiled. She'd learnt two valuable lessons as a call girl. The first was that if you couldn't rapidly develop superior acting skills you'd not build up a worthwhile clientele. The second was that *all* men, in their hearts, never really believed you were acting. They were convinced it was all down to them, the intense pleasure you appeared to revel in, could never bring themselves to doubt that they were genuinely turning you on. And when they took you to your car and you flopped into it with a sigh, giving every impression that their virility had exhausted you into a state of delicious languor, they simply could not believe that you might be driving home for a quick shower and rapid repairs to hair and make-up, before driving on to give the next client his turn.

She pushed open doors. One led to a big airy kitchen, another to a dining-room with a long table and elegant chairs. She then pushed open a door to what she guessed would be called a sitting-room. It had table lamps and deep armchairs and bookshelves in alcoves. There were dozens of books, all in hard covers, some in sets by Evelyn Waugh and Anthony Powell and Somerset Maugham. There was a lovely old-style fireplace with a screen in front of it on which was a flower pattern that looked to be hand painted. There was a lovely rug, old but with rich colours in an attractive design; she was fairly sure it was either Turkish or Chinese. There were more paintings on the walls, this time of sea-scapes that reminded her of the resorts on the East Coast. She'd sometimes gone to those with a client who'd just received his bonus and was in a position to pay for an entire weekend of her time and acting skills.

The room did things for her. She ran a finger along the books on the shelves, some of which were even leather-bound. She smelt the flowers in their pretty vases, switched lamps on and off to see the effect of their ruched or pleated shades, listened with delight to the soft chiming of an ornate wooden clock that stood on a sideboard next to a silver tray which held decanters. She felt that one day she had to have a house like this with a room like this. It would be something to aim for. Surely she'd meet a man eventually who'd like these sorts of things too.

She gazed through a window which overlooked a lengthy back garden. There were wickerwork chairs and a table with a parasol on a patio. In her mind she could see a trampoline and a doll's house and a little paddling pool. Broody, that's what she was getting to be, on top of everything else. But she had to smile again, in anticipation of that day when—

She was so lost in her thoughts that she was unaware that someone had entered the room and footsteps made no sound over the thick carpet. She turned just as the baseball bat swung with great force against her head. It kept on swinging until her skull was smashed and she was quite dead.

Tracey's instinct had been sound: it *had* been the last evening she would ever spend as a call girl.

SEVEN

'Frank Crane.'

'It's Colin Sykes, Frank. This young lady you put me on to, Tracey Sharp. I arranged to see her at ten this morning. She never showed.'

It handed Crane a shock. She'd been so delighted about the opening. If she got the job it was to be the start of a new life. She'd not been able to thank him enough. He couldn't believe she'd lost her confidence.

'I'm … very sorry, Colin. I really can't understand. She seemed so very pleased you wanted to see her.'

'Not to worry. She may have been held up in some way. She sounded good and certainly seemed to have the manner. Perhaps you could contact her and we could make another appointment. There's no reply from her landline, by the way. I don't have a mobile number.'

'I'll call in at her flat, Colin. I hope she's not had some kind of an accident. She's normally a very reliable type.'

Crane drove on uneasily. It had to be something serious to have kept her from that interview. Could she have had a motor accident? Maybe she was in an A & E right now. A sudden illness? She'd looked to be in the peak of health yesterday. Had she been with a client last night? Been involved in a session that had turned abusive? He dismissed the thought. She controlled every aspect of her life very carefully; she simply wouldn't go to a client she'd not checked out. And the clients themselves, if they could afford a woman like Tracey, would be respectable middle-class men.

He drove on to the little crescent that ran in front of Walbank Villas. Her car wasn't there; perhaps she *had* been involved in an accident. He knew now to go straight in through the front door. The landlord occupied the ground-floor flat and left the front door unlocked until six o'clock. Crane ran up the stairs to Tracey's flat and knocked on the door. He knew she'd not be in. Very agitated now, he went back to his own car and checked out St Luke's Hospital and Bradford Royal Infirmary to see if she'd been admitted to either. She hadn't. He tried to decide what to do next. The trouble was she lived alone, gave the impression of not being in touch with any members of her family, and her best friend, who'd once lived next door, was also missing.

He put through a call to Terry Jones. 'Terry, it's Frank. Could you spare me a couple of minutes?'

'Are we talking Ken Glover, Frank?'

'No, something completely different. I've taken on a job for a woman called Tracey Sharp. She's a call girl. Her best friend went missing and she wanted me to try and find her. Well, Tracey herself has gone missing now.'

'How long for?'

'Only since last night, but—'

'She's a call girl and she's been missing half a day?'

'It's not like that, Terry.'

He briefly explained the circumstances. 'She's really keen to get off the game, but she never made it to the appointment. She's not in her flat. I can't raise her on her mobile and she doesn't seem to have been in an accident.'

Jones was silent for a short time. 'All right, Frank, I trust your take on the lady. I'll ask to be kept in the loop here about anything that means there might be a young woman in any kind of trouble. Leave it with me.'

'Thanks, Terry, I appreciate it.'

When Crane couldn't get this kind of worry off his mind he found that the only answer was to keep soldiering on. In fact, work was the only answer to most things in his life. He turned once again to the problem of Lydia Glover's insurance. Jeremy Green had given him the address of Polly Manning's house and he now drove over to the Eccleshill area to have a look at it. It was a very old house on an estate of modern detached houses off the Harrogate road. It stood isolated from the estate itself and gave an impression of being a decaying tooth set against teeth that were clean and cared for. It seemed odd that it hadn't been demolished along with all the other elderly buildings that must have stood on the land before the new estate was built.

It had been badly neglected but would once have been an imposing residence. It was gabled and had chimneys and rosemary tiling, but the roof needed a good deal of attention. Several of the window frames were rotting and the whole place needed a coat of paint. The garden though had had a great deal of work put into it. Ornamental trees had been expertly pruned and laburnums, flowering apples and cherries were heavy with blossom. The lawns too were weed-free and perfectly cut, with skilfully designed beds filled with seasonal flowers and not a dead head in sight. Polly Manning appeared to be a dedicated gardener.

He recalled Jeremy Green's words about her. Daughter of a mill owner who'd later lost much of his wealth. She'd married a banker but they'd split up. Crane wondered if a divorce settlement had provided her with the means to buy either a modest modern house, or a big old house that needed renovation. Maybe she'd hankered for a house similar perhaps to the one she'd lived in in her youth.

He was parked on the road that passed through the centre of the small estate. There were other cars dotted about and he wasn't conspicuous. The road ran up to the old house and ended there, the house itself standing face on to the estate houses and appearing to dominate them. He sat there for half an hour, pretending to study papers, but no one came out of the house in that time. He decided to return that evening and see if Polly Manning emerged then. One way or another he needed to get some kind of a fix on her movements and way of life.

It was mid-afternoon when Terry Jones rang him. 'Frank,' he said gravely, 'a house on Fox Ridge. They've found the body of a young woman with severe head injuries. She had a handbag but there was nothing in it to identify her. But there was a car in the drive that checked out as belonging to a Tracey Sharp.'

Crane had a sensation as if the nape of his neck had been touched by cold steel. 'Who ... who found her, Terry?'

'The middle-aged couple who own the house. They'd been in the Lakes looking for a retirement property. They got back this lunchtime.'

'The Fox Ridge house was on the market?'

'It was. And the selling agents were Grant, Spooner. And, as we both know only too well, that's where Glover works.'

'Was he selling it?'

'That's something we'll have to go into. Look, Frank, the SOCOs are up there now. Ted's handling it. Would you go too? We need ID though I'm afraid it's certain to be Tracey. We'll have to sort out next of kin later for a formal one, but you had recent dealings with her and it'll save a lot of time.'

'I'll go,' Crane said, given a sudden wave of nausea. 'Look ... Ken Glover ... we know he took women to empty houses for sex.'

'But this Tracey, you say she was a professional.'

'Pam Draper's broken off with Glover. Maybe he was making do with call girls.'

'Why might he *kill* a call girl?'

For a few seconds Crane found it difficult to speak. He could see her as she was yesterday, so happy, her eyes shining, throwing her arms round him and kissing him again and again. 'I ... I don't know, Terry,' he said shakily. 'He ... he had a violent streak, that's why Pam stopped seeing him, but ... but *murder* ... it doesn't add up.'

'Are you all right, Frank?'

'It's ... it's just given me the hell of a shock. I hadn't known her very long, but I'd got to like her a lot. She was a nice kid. She should never have been on the game.'

Jones wondered if he'd been sleeping with her. Women had a lot of time for him though he hadn't much in the way of looks or charm-school talk. The way Jones's mind was working, though he was not going to say this to Frank, was that if they couldn't nail Glover for involvement in his wife's death maybe they now had a chance of getting him for the topping of a prostitute. 'Look, Frank,' he said, 'if this is going to be too upsetting for you we could hang on till some relative comes forward.'

'No, you're right, Terry. The sooner we're sure it's her the sooner you can act. I'd like to see this through.'

'All right, old son. Thanks a lot and I'm sorry about this.'

Crane drove to Fox Ridge in a state of acute depression. How *could* the kid have got involved with someone who'd smash her head in? She'd simply not have gone to a place like the Fox Ridge house without being sure of the status of the man she was going to meet. He was certain she'd never in the past been in the slightest danger. And where did Glover fit into all this? He had sex with women in empty houses but what could possibly be his motive for killing a call girl, if it had been him? He didn't yet know about the change his wife had made to her will so would be certain he was in line for a small fortune. Why mess everything up by leaving a woman dead in a house that was almost certainly on his list? It made no sense.

A woman police officer stood outside the door of the house on Fox Ridge. She'd been told to let Crane in and opened the door for him. He crossed the hall to a room where men in sterile clothing bent over the body. Ted Benson stood to one side, talking to a man who was adjusting a camera on a tripod.

'Hello, Frank,' he said. 'Terry says you were working for her.'

Crane wondered if he detected the faintest note of contempt in Benson's voice. 'Yes, Tracey was a client of mine,' he said flatly.

Benson said, 'Ronnie, could you all stand back and let Frank take a gander for ID.'

The three men straightened up. The body was being arranged to go into a body-bag and at present lay on its back. It was Tracey. Crane gazed down bleakly, feeling as if he'd been kicked in the guts. He couldn't have felt a death more intensely, it was as if his mother or father had been killed or the kid sister he'd never had. She'd been wearing her elegant working gear, a little white jacket and a leaf pattern skirt. The clothes were relatively unmarked, but the carpet beneath was soaked in blood.

'You don't want to see the back of her head,' Benson told him. 'Just about half her skull's gone. It's definitely Tracey Sharp?'

'Yes, it's Tracey.' He was having difficulty with his voice again. 'I … suppose the car details gave you an address? Flat in Walbank Villas.'

'And she was a Tom?'

'She was a *call girl*.'

'OK, call girl, Tom, hooker, whatever. If she'd not been a whore she'd not be dead. Christ, we've got enough on back at the nick without having to see to dead whores.'

'Ted, for God's sake, this is a woman in her *twenties*! Look at her clothes and her hair. She was a nice kid; she only put out for respectable blokes and, what's more, she was on the point of coming off the game.'

'That's what they all say, they're coming off the game next week and the crack and the booze and getting a nice job at Tesco's.'

'She was in a different league. I'd fixed her up with an interview for a job as a receptionist in Harrogate. She should have been in Harrogate this morning.'

He caught Benson's sidelong glance. 'And no,' he rasped, 'I wasn't bloody well giving her one. She was just a good-hearted youngster who deserved a chance to get her life back on track, not having her head stove in.'

Benson glanced at the Scene of Crime officers, who were clearly taken aback by Crane's emotional tirade. He gave an embarrassed shrug. 'I'm sorry, Frank, I didn't mean to upset you, you'd obviously got to know her pretty well.'

'That's ... all right, Ted, you weren't to know.' Crane took a deep breath then said, more calmly, 'You know Ken Glover was probably involved in selling this house?'

'I'll be checking that out. And if he is we'll have the bugger in before his feet touch the ground.'

Crane had guessed what Jones was thinking but not saying when they'd been speaking on the phone earlier. It was the same thing Benson was thinking but not saying now: if they couldn't charge Glover for involvement in one death there was now a good chance they could charge him for involvement in another, the death of a call girl or, as Benson had put it, call girl, Tom, hooker, whatever. To be scrupulously fair, Crane accepted that when he'd been in the force and part of the canteen culture, and not known Tracey personally, he'd have seen it the way Jones and Benson saw it. He, too, would have taken the line that had she not been a whore she'd not have been dead, and that she could be regarded as an unfortunate but useful pawn in a longer strategy.

He turned away from the inert flesh and bones that had one day ago been Tracey, whose nose wrinkled a little when she grinned and made her look half her age. Tracey with her clear green eyes and her velvety voice, which sounded so full of hope when she'd talked of living a normal life. 'I'll be getting along now, Ted.'

Benson gave him a faintly sheepish smile, as if in memory of the old close friendship that hadn't held when tested. 'Thanks for the ID, Frank, and passing on the tip about Glover liking a bit of dick in empty houses. It'll give us leverage.'

Crane knew he wasn't finding it easy to say these things. When they'd worked together as colleagues, Crane had usually out-performed Benson, simply because of his single-minded concentration and having the kind of brain that never seemed to know when to stop. But because of the friendship and Benson's own dependable qualities, Crane had always ensured that the credit was shared. In the end Benson had tended to believe he was the equal of Crane and had only become aware how plodding his own skills really were when Crane had had to leave the force.

He went out to his car. The land fell away beyond the far side of the road to give views over the Aire Valley. The single line of houses built on this side of the road had an appearance of privacy and seclusion. Uniformed police would be asking the occupants of other houses if they'd seen anyone apart from the owners entering or leaving this house, or if a car, apart from Tracey's, had been seen moving into the drive. But Crane guessed no one would have seen anything, that was why this house had been chosen.

That poor, bright, pretty young kid. He drove off dismally.

Polly eased the cork from a bottle of Sancerre, poured into two glasses and handed one to Jane. 'Here's to Ranelagh House when it's been transformed. Your magnificent garden makes the old place look a shambles at present. It's like an old wizened hag wearing a stunning dress.'

Jane beamed with pleasure. 'But the house is going to look marvellous. You've worked so hard on your designs.'

'It'll be rather like being back at The Hall.'

That was what it had been called, the old Manning place, just The Hall. Over in Heaton, half as big again as Ranelagh House, with extensive gardens, lots of trees and a high wall. Jane had once walked to Heaton just to see where Polly lived. She'd been able to see the house through the iron-work of the tall double gates. The distant front door had had a pillared portico with a turning area in front on which she was sure a Rolls Royce would once have stood. But Mr Manning had to sell off the great mill at what was rumoured to be a knockdown price and let go his hundreds of workers, and had then had to live on a much more modest basis, and the car standing there was now a Volvo. But enough money had been found to send Polly to Bradford Girls' and provide nice birthday parties to which she could invite her friends. Jane had sometimes heard the favoured few talking about those parties, the delicious buffet food and the single glass of champagne they were allowed (though Polly had secretly topped up the champagne flutes a number of times!) and the big room they could dance in to the latest discs.

'When did your family leave The Hall, Poll?'

'Not long after I left the grammar, so at least I didn't have to face that indignity. Too shame-making. Once I was at the art college it didn't matter too much.'

Beethoven's *Fifth* had recently drawn to its triumphant conclusion and the player now began to play Dvorak's *New World*. Polly waved her arm in appreciation as if conducting an orchestra. She was never still. 'Papa was living on capital and there wasn't much of *that* left. We had to let the housekeeper go and the gardener and the woman who came in to cook dinner. Poor Papa. And Mama. Papa kept the mill going for too long, then had to sell it for buttons to the discount people. And all the workers to pay off. I'd have cut a lot of corners, but Papa had these old-fashioned ideas of honour. I made a study of the textile industry for a thesis I once wrote and I can pin down exactly where he went wrong, but it was too late then for rational thinking.'

Jane sipped her wine and nodded. Polly wasn't bragging. She'd just had the sort of effortless brilliance that meant she'd always been top of the class, apart from her near-professional prowess on the tennis court, or in the swimming pool. All that plus her incredible physical attraction.

'There was nothing in the fighting fund for me when Papa was gathered in,' Polly went on. 'He and Mama were living in a small detached in Nab Wood by then. I ask you, *Nab Wood*! Mama never lived it down. Neighbours wanting to invite her in for cups of tea and slices of cake, all that middle-class nonsense, and not a soul able to play bridge to a reasonable standard, if at all. There was some kind of annuity to keep *her* going until she's gathered in, which won't be for decades yet, the women on Mama's side live for ever. So I can't even count on the proceeds of the Nab Wood dog kennel to help out and in any case the proceeds will have to be shared with Tristram. Not that it makes a scrap of difference now, it would be loose change in our scheme of things.'

'The problems will all be behind us when the will's sorted out.'

'You know, Janey, when we had to leave The Hall I swore I'd never make do with living in a dog kennel. Of course I had to live in a dog kennel when I married Brain-dead, but I accepted that as a temporary measure till I'd got him on his feet. So then he was transferred to London and it had to be another dog kennel, but I thought give it a couple of years and we'd be moving into a proper house with a decent spread of land in Bagshot or Windsor. But Brain-dead simply wasn't up to it. He was in an *investment* bank, for heaven's sake, but he was only making about eighty thousand a year and the pathetic bonuses he was getting wouldn't buy dusters.

'"Where are the *proper* bonuses?" I kept asking. "The million-pound ones so I can launch my own business." He then began to whinge about the pressure he was under. He worked long hours and was considered to be doing well, but said he would need intensive training over several years to tackle the complex deals that brought in the big returns. And my attitude wasn't helping, he told me. And then he went on to Prozac and that was the day I knew I'd married a wimp. The family put me in touch with a good legal man. I flashed my cleavage at him and Brain-dead didn't know what had hit him. There was a settlement that gave me the money to buy this place and I kept intact the money I'd made myself in Town, working *my* long hours. The last I heard he was living in a one-bed flat in Stoke Newington.'

Jane couldn't help feeling a flicker of sympathy for the man Polly always referred to as Brain-dead. However hard Polly worked she never seemed to feel tired and it must have been very difficult for her ex-husband trying to keep up with her. He must have been terribly upset when someone as glamorous as Polly walked out on him. But that was Polly. If you didn't come up to her expectations you were through the door. It gave Jane a warm glow to know that she herself could provide things Polly wanted. Otherwise she too would be through the door. Much as she liked and admired Polly, and despite the friendship that had developed, she had no illusions. But Polly remained the most exciting person she'd ever known.

It really did look as if they'd be in business in about a month. She sipped a little of the crisp chilled wine. Polly would be transforming the interiors of houses, Jane would be working on the gardens, bringing neglected lawns back to life, planting out the beds to provide displays of subtly blending colours, installing ponds and stocking fish, pruning and planting trees, constructing the ornamental features.

That hadn't been the extent of Jane's contribution. But the rest, that had been out of her hands really, as Polly had simply pushed it through in that positive, single-minded way of hers and Jane had just gone along with it. It defined the relationship, she supposed.

Polly did things without a second thought and Jane acquiesced and did as Polly wanted.

Polly suddenly gave a wide smile. 'It's so strange, Jane, you and I now. And yet we were in the same class at Bradford Girls' but never seemed to have much in common then. Why was that, do you suppose?'

'Oh, I daresay we had our own circles of friends.'

But Polly was being disingenuous. Jane's school years had been overshadowed by the unhappiness of not being invited into Polly's group. She'd longed to be one of that band that went everywhere together and had such jolly times, but she'd been a bit of a mouse really who simply wasn't noticed in those days. She was quiet and rather docile. She'd not been able to think of funny things to say that would make her classmates hoot with laughter, or things to do that would enthuse them. And in class she'd been steady and a plodder, rarely having those flashes of insight or perception that seemed to come so easily to Polly and her friends.

But those days were long gone. And now she and Polly shared Ranelagh House and would be sharing it indefinitely.

'Thank you for coming in, Mr Glover,' Inspector Jones said coolly.

'Had I any choice?'

'We'd like to think it would be helpful to you if you could help us.'

They sat facing him in the same small room as before, across the metal table with the green surface.

'I take it you've checked me out for the night my wife died?'

'Yes, we have and we've satisfied ourselves about your movements.'

'So why am I here now?'

'This other matter.'

'The dead woman at Fox Ridge?'

'The dead woman at Fox Ridge.'

'Your colleague went to Grant, Spooner's yesterday. I thought the partners had given you all the information there was.'

'You weren't in the office, Mr Glover.'

'I was trying to sell houses when people haven't much money and mortgages are like gold.'

'That's why we asked you to come in today.'

'Why not come back to the office? Why do I have to do all the legwork?'

'We thought it best to see you away from the office.'

'What's that supposed to mean?'

Jones let the silence ride. Silence in a police interview room could have an unnerving effect on certain people. Glover's eyes passed uneasily from Jones' face to Benson's. He was well turned-out as usual, in a lightweight fawn suit, white shirt and striped tie. His blond hair was neatly combed and he was carefully shaved, but his features had the slightly haggard appearance that suggested he'd missed out on sleep. It was a look Jones and Benson knew very well, they'd seen it many times in the faces of men they were certain had something to hide.

Jones said, 'I believe you handle most of the house sales in North Bradford for your firm.'

Glover nodded. 'I know the area and I know the prices houses should bring. Why that woman should end up dead in a house on my list is something I find absolutely appalling.'

Benson said, 'Whoever killed Tracey Sharp locked the front door behind them when they legged it. How would that person come by a key to that house?'

'How would I know?' Glover said pettishly. 'People leave house keys all over the place.'

'But Mr Fisher, the owner, is a very careful man. He has an intruder alarm, a state-of-the-art door-lock and just two sets of keys: one for him and one for his wife. When they gave your people the selling of the house they deposited the wife's set of keys with Grant, Spooner so you could show people round if they were away.'

Glover paled. 'I hope you're not trying to imply that this murder had anything to do with *me*.'

'Someone got in the house by unlocking the door and neutralized the intruder alarm with another key on the ring. How could that happen, Mr Glover?'

'How do *I* know?' The words were almost a yelp. 'Someone must have got hold of the keys and had them *copied*.'

'Not by that bloke who has a kiosk in Arndale Mall. They'd need to go back to the security firm which issued them. And they'll not copy anything until they're quite certain who they're making copies *for*.'

'Look, I don't know *how* this bloke got in—'

'Where were the keys the day Tracey Sharp was bludgeoned to death?'

'In the office. In a lockable cupboard.'

'Do you sign for them if you take them out?'

'Do me a favour. Someone wants to see a house you grab the keys and run before they change their mind. Especially in today's market.'

'So were the keys in the cupboard, or were they with you?'

'They were in the *cupboard*,' he said irritably. 'No one had asked to see the place. Anyway, look, the Fishers have family. Surely one of them will have a set of keys.'

'You're right. There's an emergency set which the daughter holds,' Benson told him. 'I called on the lady and she could produce her set, which she keeps in a house safe. A very careful family, the Fishers. I wish there were more like them.'

'I can't tell you anything else about how that woman got in or … or how the guy who killed her got in.'

'You've not told us anything at all….'

The policemen let the silence ride again. Glover was beginning to get agitated, which was always a good sign. He couldn't control his mouth from twitching at the corner. Jones didn't speak for a good ten seconds. 'Well, Mr Glover, we have this very odd situation where Mr Fisher has *his* keys and his daughter has *her* keys and the only other set is the one that you alone seem to have access to.'

'And your reputation around empty houses for sale is a bit on the dubious side to say the least,' Benson added.

'How do you mean?' Glover's voice rose. 'All I do is show people round the bloody things. What's dubious about *that*?'

'There's nothing at all dubious about *selling* the houses,' Jones said, 'the dubious bit comes in when you take girlfriends to empty houses for sex.'

Glover's ability to keep his features under reasonable control couldn't help him stop the rush of blood to his cheeks. His mouth fell open briefly. 'What … what are you talking about? I don't take anyone to these houses for sex. Who told you that? It's a lie, it's a *lie*! It's as much as my job's worth to mess about with women in clients' houses. Who told you that?'

'These things get around.'

'How well did you know Tracey Sharp?' Benson said.

The impact of the question and the blunt way Benson shot it out jerked back Glover's head like a physical blow. 'I didn't know her at *all*!' he cried. 'Come on, come on, you can't put that poor bitch's death at my door. I don't know who she is or how she got in the house and, what's more—'

'Just where were you the evening before yesterday?'

'I … I was out with David Grant, one of the partners. All evening, from six o'clock on.'

'David Grant will confirm that?'

'Look … look, don't go giving him any shit about me having sex in empty houses—'

'That's the truth though, yes? You'd better admit it now because if you don't we'll pursue the matter.'

Glover's face had now changed from just being red to having an odd mottled sheen. 'All right, all right, maybe I did take a woman to an empty house once or twice. My wife and I, we lived separate lives.'

'We know all about the separate lives you and your wife lived.'

'Would you be agreeable to us taking a sample of your DNA, Mr Glover?' Jones asked.

Glover's face now had a look of alarm. 'What … what point would there be in that? There'll probably be traces of my DNA all over that house, I've shown several people round it.'

'It might help to eliminate you from any connection to Tracey Sharp. There are certain to be traces near the body that might tie the killing to *someone*.'

'Are you charging me with anything?' Glover burst out.

'Right now we're just talking—'

'Then I'm not giving any DNA. Not for it to go in a police data bank and stay there forever.'

'We certainly can't insist, not at this stage. What we shall be doing is keeping you under observation because we're not happy about the things that seem to go on around you. Lydia dying in strange circumstances and now Tracey Sharp being killed in one of your houses when you have form for taking women in houses for sex.'

'A *coincidence*! All this … this questioning because of a coincidence.'

'In the CID we hear of an awful lot of coincidences, ninety per cent of which prove not to be coincidences at all.'

'Can I go now? I'm trying to sell houses. My salary isn't guaranteed like you people in the public sector. It goes up and down depending on the houses I sell.'

When Benson had seen him out and returned, Jones was standing by his office window which gave a view over the city. 'Well, Ted?'

'We handed him a shock or two, but I'm pretty damn sure he'll prove to have been with this Grant character when Tracey was having her head smashed in.'

'I'm sure you're right and it's all too pat. A rock-solid alibi for when his wife died, a rock-solid alibi for when Tracey got killed. He may not have been involved in either death but I'm certain he knows a man who was.'

'But if the deaths are linked what was the point of Tracey's? He stands to benefit from his wife's death, but what could be the motivation for a call girl's?'

'Frank Crane.'

'Can you speak, Frank? It's Terry.'

'Go ahead, Terry.'

'Tracey Sharp and the Fox Ridge place. I'll not go into our saga of the house keys, but Ted's made a thorough check on them and there were definitely only three sets. And it could only have been the Grant, Spooner set that unlocked the door for Tracey to get in and the killer to lock up behind him.'

'Meanwhile, Glover was having a nice quiet game of blackjack at Napoleon's.'

'He's upped the ante on that one. He was at a restaurant called The Cottage with a David Grant, one of the partners. Ted didn't approach Grant directly for two reasons. The first was that there might be a slight chance Grant himself was involved, and the second was that he didn't want to dirty Glover's ticket with his bosses if he really isn't in the frame. I suppose we have to be fair to the lying scrote.'

'So how did Ted check his story?'

'He went direct to the restaurant and questioned the *maître-d*. The man could show him the dinner reservation in his book. Apart from that he actually knows Glover and Grant very well, they'd been to the restaurant a number of times. They were in his place that evening from about six. They ate at seven-fifteen then sat in the bar till going on ten.'

'I can't get it together, Terry.'

'It's just too neat, old son.'

'Those house keys. You can't prove he had them on the day?'

'No. All the keys Grant, Spooner hold are supposed to be in a locked cupboard and the key to that is kept in the office junior's desk with his boiled sweets and his lad mags. He admits that anyone could get hold of it as the staff are forever wanting to show folk houses. I suppose that's how estate agents do go on. The last house the wife and I bought there was no one available to show us round at all and they just bunged us the key and told us to show ourselves round.'

'Could something similar have happened in this case?'

'The junior swears not, but then he would, wouldn't he?'

'Glover's got to be in there somewhere.'

'That goes for the three of us. Ted got in a good shot across his bows. Asked him how long he'd known Tracey. The bugger's face went all colours. He obviously had known her, but he denied it naturally.'

'Why kill a call girl? Him or anyone?'

'We'll have to check out her clients.'

'I'd not waste your time, Terry. She was a bright kid. She'll not have kept any records, but she'd not go near anyone she couldn't trust. I'd concentrate on Glover, though God knows how he fits in.'

'You were working for her. Remind me of the details.'

'She had a close friend who worked Lumb Lane. The friend went missing. Tracey wanted me to find her.'

'Any connection, do you think?'

'Not that I can see. What I did find out was that on the night she took off she was seen going with someone the Toms called the tract woman.'

He gave Jones a brief rundown of Libby's lapsed Catholicism and his feeling the tract woman had taken her under her wing, maybe to help put behind her her life as a common prostitute and make a new start, even if it meant not contacting Tracey for a while.

'Doesn't *look* to have any bearing,' Jones said. 'I suppose you'll be knocking the case on the head anyway, seeing as it looks as if you're going to have to whistle for your fees.'

'I'll not be putting in any claims on the poor kid's estate,' Crane said. 'It could be quite sizeable, oddly enough. She was careful with her money. Told me she was in a position to buy a house of her own.'

'I wonder who might gain financially from her death,' Jones said thoughtfully.

'That's a good point, Terry.'

*

Crane drove on. He wondered if Glover had any idea yet that Lydia had changed her will. It seemed possible that the change of will might now rule out the idea of Glover's involvement in his wife's death. Maybe the death *had* been suicide after all, or the sort of accident that amounted to the same thing. What if Glover's taking up with Pam Draper had been just too much for Lydia to accept, in that the affair with Pam had appeared a great deal more serious than any of his other liaisons and could possibly mean the end of their marriage. Perhaps the unhappiness Glover had brought her had driven her to the point of ending it all, but not before she'd ensured the bulk of her estate went to Polly Manning. Crane shook his head. It still left the problem of why she'd taken out all that insurance in the first place and where Polly Manning fitted in. He wondered if anyone would ever know.

He was still in a low state of mind about Tracey. He couldn't get her out of his thoughts for very long. He'd loved that kid, it was as simple as that, it was an emotion as inexplicable as it was intense. He compulsively replayed the last time they'd been together, when she'd asked so many questions about how she should present herself for the interview in Harrogate.

'You know, Frank,' she'd said at one point, 'I do wish I'd been able to complete my education. I've begun to dream about being back at school. It's so strange, the classroom is full of thirteen year olds, just as I remember it, but I'm myself as I am now but dressed in the sort of clothes they're wearing.'

'There was a play once on the telly, by Dennis Potter, I think, where grown-ups are dressed as children.'

'Was there, was there really? You know, one day *I* want to be able to make those sort of connections. Anyway, in my dream, the children are all fooling about and talking in whispers, just as I used to do, with poor Miss Rawson trying to keep discipline and *teach* us something. But now I was irritated by the bad behaviour. I was keen on being taught, on learning things, I *wanted* to learn. I woke up so disappointed not to really be back at school but just the usual Tracey who rented by the hour.'

Crane sighed. No, she wasn't a woman it was easy to get off your mind.

He pulled in to the car-park of a hotel at Burley-in-Wharfedale.

The couple in the car he'd been tailing were now entering the hotel, the man carrying two small suitcases. Crane strolled into the reception area. It was busy at this time of early evening and he didn't stand out. The man completed a registration form at the reception desk. The smiling receptionist gave him a folder which would have an inner pocket containing key cards. The couple made for a lift and Crane returned to his car.

It was a sad modern morality tale. A woman called Victoria had engaged him to keep an eye on her partner who she suspected of having an affair. This man had persuaded Victoria to leave her husband and join him. But he was now having an affair with another woman. 'I wish I'd never left Oliver,' Victoria had told Crane bitterly. 'He was a tad on the dull side but he was good-hearted and kind, and generous with money. I'm sure the bastard's seeing someone else.'

How right she'd been. Crane drove off back to Bradford. Not long ago it had been fifty per cent of marriages that broke up, now it was going on for two-thirds.

His mind was made up. Whatever it cost him in time, money or frustration, he wasn't going to stop searching till he found Tracey's killer.

Pam sat in her little study feeling depressed. Another fine sunny day and she still dare not sit out on the patio with a drink in case Glover caught her there again. In fact, she hardly dared go out at all in case he was waiting here when she got back. She realized with a start she never now thought of him as Ken Glover, just Glover. He'd frightened her so badly, her wrists had throbbed for two days. She was sure he'd have broken something had she not pretended it had been her who had confessed to the police he'd not been with her that night. But she was glad she'd kept Frank's name out of it. She wasn't sure why, she'd just had a strong feeling it would be for the best, even though Frank was a man very capable of looking after himself.

She shuddered, as she often did when thinking of Glover. How could a man who'd seemed so warm and friendly have such a dark side? Frank had been very even-handed, pointing out that Glover might have nothing to do with Lydia's death, but it had been clear he strongly suspected it. And then the gambling addiction that meant he was on his uppers. She felt she'd been very badly used.

The sex had been great, she had to admit, and she still missed it, but she also knew that she too gave good value under the duvet. She must have seemed an excellent proposition to a man like Glover: good in bed, her own house, an allowance from wealthy Matt, who at least had had a conscience if nothing else.

She dreaded to think how her life might have gone if she'd let Glover live with her or, God forbid, marry her. How soon before there'd have been other women? And if he had got Lydia's insurance money how long would it have taken him to fritter it all away? He'd simply have used her as a makeweight. Someone to feed him and pay the bills and sleep with him when he was between girlfriends. And what if he really was involved in Lydia's death? Even if nothing was proved one way or the other, she'd never be able to put the possibility out of her mind.

There was a sudden tapping on the study window. It startled her and her hand jumped, making some of the liquid in her glass spill over her jeans. She glanced through the window and felt her heart lurch. Ken Glover stood outside on the patio. He had that little peevish look about his mouth and was making movements with an arm that indicated he wanted her to open a door and let him in.

Trembling, she got up and moved slowly to the window. 'What do you want?' she said in a loud voice, but he screwed up his face, making it clear he couldn't hear very well through the double-glazed panes.

'Come on, darling, let me in,' he shouted, but even those words came in only faintly. 'You seem to have all the doors shut and locked.'

She watched him in silence, feeling shivery in spite of the warm weather. With great reluctance, she reached out and opened a small upper panel of the window. 'What do you want?' she said again.

'Oh, come *on*, Pam, let me in, we can't speak through a window.'

'You are *not* coming into my house ever again,' she said coldly. 'Not after last time, when you nearly broke my wrists. Go away *now*, I don't ever want to see you again.'

He gave her the warm smile then that had been such a turn-on for her when he'd been showing her round this same house that she now owned. It still did things for her, but the flicker it gave her inside was now due to fear. 'Oh, come on, darling, it was just a lover's tiff. I said I was sorry and I *am* sorry. Let me come in for a drink. We can go for a meal if you like, there's that little place round the corner in Highgate.'

She watched him sadly. He looked so maturely handsome in his chinos and sports shirt: slim, strongly built, well-groomed, fine gold hairs gleaming on his bare brown arms. And such a way with him: the smile, the ready words, the easy manner. If only he could have been what he'd seemed. 'Go away, Ken, I've had time to think about it. I've done nothing *but* think about it. I've made up my mind: you and me, it's over.'

'Oh, come on, honey, let me in. Let's talk it through over a drink. I'll do anything you ask to prove how sorry I am for hurting you.'

She watched him again in silence. Now that she knew that virtually everything he did was part of a clever act it had begun to *seem* like an act. She should have spotted the flaws earlier, but earlier she'd been without a man in her life for many months and she'd been more than ready to see the best in a man who looked and sounded the way he did. He was like the skilled illusionist whose patter drew the attention away from what he was really about.

She said, 'I suppose you're going to say you'll never hurt me again like you did last time.'

'That's exactly what I'm going to say. And mean it. Like you, it's been on my mind ever since. I can't think what possessed me. Now please let me in, darling. You can't believe how much I want to put my arms round you.'

Or how much she wanted it, to have the old Ken with her, his hands stroking her naked body, his fingers feathering her inner thighs. To hear him murmuring endearments, to know again the lovemaking that had seemed to be an endless series of ecstatic sensations.

'Go away, Ken, there's no place in my life for a man like you,' she said, but the desire he still aroused in her had given her voice a slight edge of hoarseness. It was a tone he instantly responded to.

'Oh, come on, love, I only lost it because of what you told the police. They began to hassle me then and it caused such a lot of trouble. All right, I over-reacted.' He couldn't control that slight petulance from infecting his smile.

'Is that what it was, an over-reaction? When you almost broke my wrists. I will never, ever, have anything to do with you again.'

'Pam—'

'Why are the police hassling you? They must think it very, very odd Lydia driving round drunk and drugged while you were throwing money away in a casino but saying you spent the night with me.'

His mouth suddenly hardened in that frightening way it had once before and she felt almost weak with relief that she was inside a house with locked doors and he was outside. 'All right, you stupid bitch,' he snarled, 'I'll tell you why I'm really here. You've been blabbing to the bogies again, right? Telling them you met up with me for nookie in empty houses I'm flogging. Well, that's given me *another* shedload of hassle.'

Her mouth fell open with the shock. She'd said nothing of that to the police. Why should she? It had nothing to do with anything. And then she remembered: Frank had been shadowing Glover and seen her meet up with him at the house on Haworth Road. It must have been Frank who'd told the police, though she couldn't think why. She said, 'I never told the police anything about seeing you in any houses.'

She spoke so quietly he had to screw up his face again to show he could barely hear her, despite the open window. 'It could only have been you,' he bawled. 'Who else could possibly have known?'

Once again, even though she was flustered, the instinct was to keep Frank's name out of it. 'It must have been someone in your office. Or a neighbour who thought we were spending too much time in the same house.'

'Rubbish! It was *you!*'

'I didn't, I *didn't!* What difference would it make anyway?'

'A hell of a bleeding lot, as it happens.' His entire face had become hard now, not just his mouth. She remembered the look so clearly and began to shake as if he could somehow hurt her again. 'Listen to me, silly bitch, listen very carefully,' he said, in a low, raw tone. 'If you say one more word to the police about me, one single solitary word, you'd better look out because it won't just be your wrists you'll be worried about me breaking. Have you got that quite clear in your head?'

She stared at him. The menace in his voice was like a physical blow. His stony gaze never left her face for several long seconds. And then he turned and stalked off, anger showing in the tense way he held his body.

EIGHT

Crane had begun to check out Polly Manning's movements in the evening. She lived with another woman in the big old place called Ranelagh House. Around half past eight, the two women set off to walk through the walled estate of modern houses and along the main road the short distance to the Mayfield. The Mayfield was a small hotel with a pleasant lounge bar which attracted a lot of local custom. The residents tended to be business people who needed to be in the area for one reason or another and seemed to prefer the location of the Mayfield and its ambience to the hotels in central Bradford.

This was the second evening Crane had spent in the bar lounge. The softly lit, comfortably furnished room was about half-full at this time of the evening but would get busier towards eleven, at which point it closed to non-residents. People sat or stood in pairs or groups, with a handful of men on their own, such as Crane, who stood at the bar. By taking a corner position at the L-shaped counter he'd been able to study the women carefully. They had stood on both evenings towards the centre of the room and on each occasion had been rapidly joined by cheerful chatty men who in turn included the women in the drinks they bought. The women seemed only to buy themselves a single drink, and that on arriving. As they'd sipped these, their friends had steadily gathered and from then on they were free-wheeling all the way.

So far, he'd not been able to work out the relationship between the women. His first thought had been that they might be lesbians but he'd dismissed the idea when he'd seen how very popular they were with the men in the bar and how much they enjoyed male company. They were both attractive though in very different ways. The taller one was Polly, the other was called Jane; he'd heard their names spoken by the men. Polly had lustrous brown hair in a loose flowing style. She had well-defined features and a wide mouth. She had rather broad shoulders for a woman, well-shaped breasts and a slender figure. Tonight she was wearing striped trousers in muted shades of brown, fawn and white, a pale-blue top and a short fawn jacket, all in cotton. She gave off a riveting sexiness. Crane could think of few women he'd known, if any, who'd possessed such an incredible allure. Had she been a film actress she had the sort of magnetism, it seemed, that would have volleyed through the screen just as Marilyn Monroe's had done. It wasn't surprising she didn't have to be in the room very long before the regulars began to home in, with men who stood alone shooting her glances that Crane could only define as wistful lust. He recalled Jeremy Green's words about her: she'd been a wild one who ran around with a fast crowd. A young football-player had been badly injured climbing a trellis to her room. When he could walk only with a limp and his football ambitions ended, he'd been dumped. Crane could now see the powerful attraction that had made him take the risk.

The woman called Jane was more rounded and softer-seeming and gave an impression of having a very agreeable disposition. With short, dark, curly hair and wearing glasses, she was smiley and seemed eager and looked to be a good listener, which very much appealed to the sort of men who liked an audience. Polly was the talker. She spoke intelligently and with a cheery conviction on any topic that came up and had a keen sense of humour that provoked frequent bursts of laughter. She made her friend, also dressed in trousers and summer jacket, appear a little colourless by comparison, though popular all the same with her unassuming manner.

On the previous night, when the women had set off home from the hotel, at about ten o'clock, Crane had followed at a distance, on the opposite side of the road, leaving his car temporarily in the hotel car-park. He'd watched them go into the big house and seen lights go on in a downstairs room. Then he'd seen two cars drive up along the road that ran centrally through the small estate and ended at Ranelagh House, where the cars had then moved on to the drive. Six men got out of the cars. It was clear they were expected as the front door was opened instantly and the men welcomed in. Crane, watching through miniature binoculars from just inside the semi-circle of wall that enclosed the front of the estate, could make out that two of the men carried packs of what looked to be beer or lager and the other men had plastic carriers which he guessed also contained drinks.

A party. First the pub and then a bit of a do at Polly and Jane's. He'd smiled. Polly had form when it came to night life. Well, maybe the people she mixed with these days weren't the sort of fast crowd she'd once run around with and perhaps she'd crossed over from the wild side in what would she be, her early thirties? But it looked as if she still liked to party. And also that she still seemed to have a very strong personality.

Crane had returned to the hotel to pick up his motor and had gone home for the night. He wondered how the men at the wheels of the cars could risk drinking and driving. He doubted they'd be spending the night on orange juice. Perhaps, like the footballer, it was something about a party at sexy Polly's that made it seem a risk worth the taking, though surely they could be in the same position that Crane himself was in: no car might mean no job.

Crane had come back to the Mayfield this evening, to see once again Polly and Jane buy themselves a single drink before the men had begun to gather round them like moths to a candle. Then the jokes and the chat and the laughter had begun and the free drinks pressed upon them. He wondered if he'd ever be able to figure out why Lydia Glover had left this vital and attractive woman all that money. In any case, it seemed that Polly could have had her pick of wealthy men to take up with, even if they happened to be already married. He'd decided that the only way he could find out anything at all about why Polly should be in line for all this largesse was to try to get in with the women. It didn't look as if it would be too difficult going by the way their bar friends appeared to be freely invited to parties at Ranelagh House. Just so long as they could be counted on to roll up there festooned with plenty of clinking carriers.

His mobile was muted but it began to vibrate. 'Frank Crane.'

'It's me, Frank, Pam.'

'Hello, Pam.'

'Am I calling at a difficult time?'

'I'm in a bar, that's the noise you can hear. It's in the line of duty, as it happens. I'll move somewhere quieter ...' He left the bar for the small reception area. 'Go ahead, Pam.'

'I'm sorry to trouble you at this time of night. Ken Glover's been round and scared me again. I didn't let him in. I opened a window. He still scared me though. Badly.'

'Shall I come round?'

'Would you? But it's so late.'

'I'll be there in half an hour. I'll ring the bell three times so you'll know it's me.'

'Thank you. Thank you so much.'

He put away his mobile. At that moment Polly and Jane came out into the reception area, looking to be on their way home. He wondered if they'd arranged for another knees-up. He caught Polly's eye as she passed and gave her a friendly smile. He knew she'd clocked him earlier, looking hopefully at the two popular women holding court with their little circle of admirers. He felt certain that Polly was a woman whose antenna could be safely counted on to pick up the vibes on any man in the vicinity who could be relied on to amuse her or buy her drinks. Polly returned his smile with an equally friendly one of her own and said, 'Goodnight.' He was pretty sure it was the sort of smile that meant, 'Join the gang, big boy.' Just as long as he'd grasped the basic rules, that he'd need to put his hand in his pocket on a regular basis.

'A drink, Frank?'

'I'm afraid I'm on the limit with alcohol, with the driving, but if you've got any sparkling water ...'

'Of course.' She poured some at the drinks table and mixed herself a gin and tonic. 'Thank you so much for agreeing to come so late.'

'That's all right. I don't really do leisure time. When did Glover show?'

'About ... seven. I was just thinking of making a meal. When he'd gone I couldn't face food at all.'

'How did he scare you?'

'First he wanted to oil his way into the house, but I didn't fall for it, not after what he did last time.'

She told him how the meeting had gone, how Glover had turned when she'd refused to let him in. 'What he'd really come for had been to accuse me of telling the police he used houses on his list for sex with his girlfriends. He said it could only have come from me. I denied it, but he wouldn't believe me. I'm sure that's why he'd really come. You can't believe the change in him from the nice smiles and the charm to this man who looked so *vicious*. And the things he came out with. Jekyll and Hyde.'

'He threatened you?'

'Said he really would hurt me if I went to the police again. But I hadn't *been* to the police, not after the first time when they asked me to confirm that Glover had been here that night.'

'I suppose you guessed it was me.'

She nodded. 'I knew it could only have been you.'

'You should have told Glover it was me, Pam. It would have saved you the pain he gave you the other night.'

'I didn't want to do that. It was just an instinct, to keep you out of it. I was sure it would bring you a lot of trouble.'

'Well, I'm very grateful for that. If my name had come into it it could have caused endless complications.'

If not an attempt on his life, if Glover really was in the frame and anxious to make sure no one was looking into his activities too closely, especially a PI, who didn't have to work to a police rule book.

She said, 'I can't understand why he was so angry anyway about the police knowing he took women to sale houses.'

She'd sat down with him on the sofa, as if needing him close by after the shock Glover had given her. The hand holding her drink trembled slightly.

'This is something that has nothing to do with Lydia's death,' he told her. 'They had him in again in connection with the Fox Ridge murder.'

She gave him a startled glance. 'The … Fox Ridge murder?'

'It was in the evening paper.'

'I don't take one. I make do with *The Times*. And I only skim through that.'

'A young woman called Tracey Sharp was killed in a house on Fox Ridge. It was a house on Glover's list. The only key that could have let in Tracey and the killer was the one Grant, Spooner's were holding.'

'Dear *God!*' Her voice was almost a whisper and she'd gone very pale. Her hand now trembled so badly she had to put down her glass. 'Does this mean…?'

'We simply don't know. The police have had Glover in, knowing from me he used his sale houses for sex, but he had an unshakeable alibi for the woman's time of death, as roughly fixed by the forensics team. But both me and the police think the alibis, both for the murder and Lydia's car crash, have been too carefully organized. When I was in the CID one of our biggest problems was in trying to establish exactly where a suspect was on the day some offence had been committed. Few people can remember what they were doing on a certain date two or three months past, not unless they keep a diary. But if these things Glover might be involved with had happened a *year* ago he'd still be able to say exactly what he'd been doing and able to prove it too convincingly. That's why he's under suspicion.'

Pam was shuddering uncontrollably. 'This is terrible, *terrible*. Thank God I didn't let him in. But who ... who *was* this woman?'

Crane sighed. 'Tracey Sharp was a call girl. By coincidence I got to know her pretty well. I was working on a little job for her. She was trying to trace a friend who'd gone missing.'

'Oh, Frank, that's frightful, you knowing her.'

'I got to like her an awful lot. She never made any secret of what she did for a living. By the time I knew her she'd stopped wanting to do it, but it had paid her well and she'd saved most of what she'd made. She took good care of herself and paced herself sensibly. Her clients were all reliable middle-class types, young chaps getting experience in a district sales office and feeling lonely, that kind of bloke. She was ... she was a bright girl and just wouldn't go to anyone's place unless she was certain he could be trusted. That's ... that's why I can't get my mind round her being beaten to death in a house on Glover's list.'

He knew the tone his voice had taken, knew the hesitancy was beginning to show how difficult he was finding it to talk about her, that pretty and affectionate kid he'd begun to feel so protective about. He could sense the picture Pam was being given. He gave a crooked grin. 'It wasn't about getting freebies, Pam. That's the way my old police colleagues were thinking, but nothing could have been further from the truth.'

'She ... it looks as if she made a big impression on you.'

'She ... she really was bright. Desperate to get back into the straight world. The sort of world people like you live in. But she'd had little education and I gathered she came from a broken home. She was so keen to make a new start – like someone in a desert searching for an oasis.'

'We tend to take it for granted, don't we, people like me?' she said in a low voice. 'A mummy and a daddy and a good education. University. My people weren't well off, but they were so supportive. I can see the temptation, in Tracey's shoes, if you're pretty and have a good figure, to take the path she took.'

He nodded. 'I was in a position to help her. I arranged an interview for reception work in Harrogate where her background wouldn't be known. She had an excellent speaking voice, due very much to her own efforts, and the looks, of course. The job was nailed on for her. With training and study it would have given her a chance to make a new career for herself. The day before the interview she was killed.'

'Oh, Frank ... I'm so very sorry.' She put a hand on his arm.

She had no difficulty in believing sex hadn't been involved in that friendship. Not with this man. The way he'd talked about her had given her the impression he'd begun to see himself as a sort of guardian to Tracey Sharp.

'It makes no *sense*, Pam,' he said bitterly. 'I'm sure she had no enemies or that anyone was stalking her. If she had had she'd have told me, because that's how things were between us. It makes no sense Glover coming into it either, though I'm sure in some way he does.'

Pam finished her drink and put down her glass with a hand that still shook. 'Oh *God*, Frank, all these things you've told me, I'm terrified. I'm beginning to think I could believe anything of that dreadful man.'

'Let me get you a top-up, it'll calm your nerves.'

'Alcohol's not really doing me much good. And it's certainly not helping being penned up in the house like this. I daren't leave the house now in case ... in case, *he's* lurking about, ready to accuse me of talking to the police yet again.' She sighed. 'And I love to get out in summer: sit on the patio, go for a walk, pop into town now and then.'

'I could speak to Inspector Jones if you like. He'd be sympathetic. He could arrange for Glover to be given a warning to keep right away from you. They could possibly install a panic button.'

She considered this but looked dubious.

'Or,' he said, after a few seconds thought, 'you could stay at my place.'

'You ... you can't mean that. You have your own life to live. You must have a partner ... a wife ...'

'Neither. Not living in, anyway. I have a girlfriend. She lives in her own place out at Gargrave. We both work long days and meet up maybe once a week if we can get our diaries in synch. It sounds an odd relationship and it has a complicated history, but it goes back a long way and it works.'

'I still don't feel I could impose....'

'You wouldn't be. You'd hardly see me. I leave the house early and usually get back late. A lot of the people I deal with are only available in the evenings.'

She looked rueful. 'It sounds great, but I need to be here for my work. The jobs come through on the Internet.'

'Leave a message to say you're taking a few days' holiday. It is summer, after all.'

'Are you quite sure it wouldn't be inconvenient?'

He put a hand over hers. 'I really wouldn't like to think of your being here if Glover came prowling round again.'

'You must let me pay you.'

'No, Pam. Regard my place as a refuge. About a year ago I was in a position not too different from yours. My house wasn't a good place to be at the time and I was given a room by a woman involved in the case. I was in a low state and I've not forgotten her kindness. Well, now I'm in a position to do the same for you.'

'Do you ... do you mean I should leave my house now?'

'I do. Pack a bag and follow my car in yours. My place isn't too far off.'

'How long do you think I'd need to stay?'

'I couldn't begin to guess. But the police have Glover in the crosshairs and so have I. Let's give it a week and see how things go.'

'I'll pack a bag then.'

She did so rapidly, locked up her house, then followed Crane's Renault in her Fiat. He let her put her car in the garage and left his own in the drive to give the impression he was home alone as usual. In the kitchen he said, 'Would you like a night cap? Or tea perhaps?'

'I'd just like to crash, Frank. I feel all in with the stress of that frightful man.'

He carried up her case to the second bedroom where the bed was always kept made up for the infrequent visits of his girlfriend Colette, not that she actually used it much when she did stay over.

'I'm an early riser,' he told her, 'and clear of the house by eight. You feel free to get up when it suits you. I don't do breakfast, but if there's anything you'd like in the way of cereals and marmalade and so on I'll stop off at Morrison's on my way home tomorrow evening and stock up.'

'Please don't go to any trouble. Tea and toast will be fine. It's all I usually have.'

'We can run to that. Sleep well.'

'I think I shall, you know, now I'm in your refuge. And thanks, Frank, thank you so much.'

'Could I get you ladies a drink?' Crane said, with his practised friendly smile.

'How kind,' Polly said. 'Yes, thank you, that would be most welcome. Mine's a gin and Dubonnet and my friend a dry Martini.'

Crane moved to the bar and ordered the drinks. He'd got to the Mayfield early, aiming to approach the women before their circle of friends had had a chance to form. The plan had worked, the women had walked in about fifteen minutes after him and Crane's timely offer of drinks meant they'd not even had to buy the first round. They had rather expensive tastes too, the gin and Dubonnet came at twice the price of a single short drink. No question of them making do with soft drinks or shandies, whoever was buying.

'There you are, ladies,' he said, passing the glasses to them. 'I'm Jim, by the way. Jim Parry.'

'How do you do, Jim,' Polly said cheerfully. 'I'm Polly and this is Jane. You're rather new here, aren't you?'

'I live in Heaton. I was in the area working with a client and thought I'd call in for a drink. It seemed such a pleasant place and drew me back.'

'Oh, yes, great boozer. Good food too, we often come for Sunday lunch. What would your line be?'

The voice went with the sexiness: full, slightly throaty and with a cultured drawl. The drawl wasn't a way of speaking you could successfully adopt, outside the acting profession, it had to have been in place from childhood but, according to Jeremy Green, Polly's had been a privileged childhood.

'I'm a financial adviser, for my sins.'

'Good God, can you find any financial advising to do with the recession, which the pundits can't decide if it's going to be U-shaped or W-shaped?'

'I get by,' Crane said. 'You learn to take the rough with the smooth.'

'An FA indeed. I may need to pick your brains before very long. We're expecting an improvement in our finances.'

She spoke with assured confidence. It didn't come across as if she was asking a favour, more that she was issuing an instruction.

'Anything I can help with, just let me know.'

'Good man.'

'I daresay you and Jane live locally?'

'The Ranelagh estate. Know it? We're not in one of the dog kennels, we have the big old ruin at the end. It gave the estate its name. The builders wanted to ball it and use the site, but the old gel who owned it wouldn't sell, so there it stayed. Lucky for me. I bought it from the daughter when the mother died; she was glad to get shot at any price. The money came out of my divorce settlement. When our finances improve we're going to make it over, eh, Jane?'

'Polly's got some great ideas for doing it up,' Jane said quietly, gazing at Polly with what looked to be a mixture of affection and admiration.

'Polly, Jane, hello there! Can I get you girls a drink?'

'Our friend Jim here has just got them in, Ralph.'

'Well done, Jim. How do you do.'

Other men began steadily joining the group, until there were eight or nine of them. They were all types who looked to be well-heeled and who were possibly funding their drinking with expense accounts, as several of them were staying at the Mayfield. Crane gathered that the hotel had a homely atmosphere, a good chef and comfortable rooms. It was also cheaper than the central hotels.

Crane was quickly accepted as a member of that band of men who stood around Polly and Jane on what appeared to be an almost nightly event. Drinks for 'the girls' were bought on a regular basis, but the convention seemed to be that rounds weren't bought for the entire group. Each man bought only for himself, or possibly a colleague, and included Polly and Jane if their glasses were empty. This was convenient for Crane as he could quietly buy himself a tonic and lemon and give the impression to the others he was really drinking gin and tonic.

For the next hour he stood with the group, giving his ready smile, listening to the gossip and banter and occasionally throwing in the odd one-liner of his own. He responded agreeably if he was button-holed, gave his pretend occupation if asked and courteously enquired in his turn what others did for a living. As he'd guessed, they tended to be all either businessmen or professionals, working from Bradford as a good base to cover the West Riding area. During all this he kept a watchful eye on the women, who stood always to the centre of the group. Polly seemed effortlessly to dominate the main strands of any group conversation. She was almost as tall as most of the men.

'Ralph,' she said, in her imperious drawl, 'do you know of a first-class joiner? He must be able to interpret my ideas and not believe his own to be superior.'

'I think I can lay my hands on such a man. One of the modern school and not cheap.'

'He'd be no good to me if he *was* cheap. However, I'd know how to cost the work involved and so his prices would have to be realistic.'

She gave Crane an impression of being a demanding woman to work for but also possibly had the knack of getting from the people who did the best results they were capable of. She was wearing similar clothes to the previous night: trousers, a blouse and jacket, all of good quality. But she had such incredible sensuality, enhanced by the delicate scent she wore. Women with her kind of attraction tended to use it as an instrument of manipulation, and that alone, in someone like Polly, would have been formidable enough, but Crane suspected there was a lot more to her than sexual pulling power, in the way of brains and knowledge and drive.

Polly was the star of the bar, a woman who gave clear signals to her compelling personality, and this seemed to leave the smaller quieter woman something of an enigma. She seemed very much in thrall to Polly, but why? Her gaze went to the other woman's face so often, with an almost dog-like devotion, but which didn't, in a way Crane couldn't exactly pin down, relate to anything remotely sexual. Perhaps she was like a schoolgirl who developed an inno-cent crush on the games mistress. The contrast between the women couldn't have been sharper, apart from Jane having curly hair and rather heavy glasses and a softer more rounded body. She looked to get a great deal of pleasure from the non-stop jokes and chatter that went on around her from the cheery group. Polly hoovered up most of the attention, but Jane had her own admirers from the handful of men who perhaps fancied a break now and then from the one who took the attention as an automatic right. Jane was the one who was delighted to *give* attention, with her endless agreeable smiles as if programmed to please. And she gave it in an appealing almost wondering way, as if she somehow found it difficult to quite believe she was having such an enjoyable time with such nice people. Crane suspected the good times were only coming to her because of being Polly's friend. It was a symbiosis that went back, of the woman who dazzled and the companion of lower wattage who shone with a dimmer light.

Crane edged a little closer to Jane and said casually, 'When are you hoping to make a start on your home improvements, Jane?'

She gave him one of her eager smiles but hesitated, sipping a little of her drink and glancing towards her friend, as if the question had been one that required careful consideration. 'I ... we ... well, Polly is in line for a legacy from a relative who died recently. When the money comes through she'll sort out the house and I'll work on the garden. Gardening's always been my hobby. We'll work as a team then, doing the same thing for other people, preferably people who buy houses that need a lot of renovation. The money will come in handy to get the agency off the ground.'

'Sounds a good idea. You've got experience of that type of work?'

Again there was what seemed to be a thinking time delay: a sip of Martini, a glance towards Polly. 'I ... haven't, but Polly has. She did a lot of interior designing in London, but always wanted to have her own business. She has a wide circle of friends and acquaintances in Yorkshire. County types. Polly's a Manning. Does that mean anything?'

'The mill-owners?'

'That was a long time ago. There should have been money for Polly to realize her ambitions before now, but, well, the family went through a crisis.'

'The textile industry had a rough old time in the 1960s, I believe.'

'The Mannings suffered badly.'

'Do you and Polly go back a long way?'

This produced the longest hesitation yet. She coloured slightly and gazed down into her glass. After a delay of a good many seconds, she said, 'I've ... I've known her since ... since she was at school.' She seemed somehow to be searching for exactly the right words, but looked uneasy with the words she'd selected. 'You must excuse me, Jim, it's about our home time. Polly, should we be making tracks?'

Polly, who'd been deep in conversation with a man called Angus, looked briefly distracted, but nodded. 'Any of you chaps want to come back to the ruin?' she said. Most of the men looked very pleased with the idea of going back to the ruin. Several others had to decline, with much reluctance, saying that calls had to be made, or that reports needed finishing touches. 'Some other time,' she told them graciously. 'How about you, Jim? We sometimes have a nightcap back at our place.'

'There's a half of gin in the car,' he said, 'if that would help with the drinks.'

'Well done!' she said approvingly. Crane felt he'd earned his membership of the Polly and Jane fan club. He picked up the gin from his glove compartment and rejoined the group. The men had decided not to take any cars this time and they all walked either with or behind the women the short distance to the Ranelagh estate on a warm summer night, the carrier bags some of the men carried clinking gently with bottles or cans.

Crane, while making idle conversation, thought over those last awkward words Jane had said to him: '*I've known her since she was at school*'. Not, 'I've known her since *we* were at school'. And yet they must both have been at school at about the same time, if not the same school, as they both looked to be around the same age. But she had hesitated for so long before putting this odd choice of words together and seemed herself to have been aware of the oddness. He wondered if there was something about her relationship with Polly she felt she had to be guarded about. And, if so, did that mean she knew the real provenance of Polly's legacy, that it would be coming from the will of a woman who'd heavily insured herself then driven herself to destruction? And who'd changed her will some time before her death so that Polly benefited instead of her husband?

The group of people walked through the small estate and along the garden path of Ranelagh House. Jane unlocked the front door and Polly said, 'Well, chaps, welcome to the 1930s again....'

Glover let himself into his house. He'd not been back since breakfast time and there were a couple of letters on the door-mat. He picked them up and walked through to the kitchen where he poured himself a large Scotch. He'd had a poor night at the casino. He knew in a part of his mind, a part he tried to keep suppressed, that in the long run he was always going to end up the loser at Napoleon's. But it was like telling an alcoholic that if he didn't forgo alcohol he would damage his liver and probably die young.

It was the *look* of the roulette table he couldn't resist: the little columns of coloured chips beneath the lights, the spinning of the wheel and the rattle of the little ball as it hopped along the numbered grooves, sometimes settling into a black groove, then being dislodged into a red one. But the *kick* when his elaborate spread of chips paid off! And those occasions when he'd had a 'straight up' and the little glass dolly had been placed on his square and a mound of chips slid over to him by a smiling croupier girl. It had happened three times to Glover and in each case he'd not been able to sleep because of the frisson.

But he knew, in that part of his brain he tried to keep the lid on, that all the money he'd made with each of those three wins had gone back to the casino the following night. And he was now broke. Cleaned out. He had barely enough to live on till his next pay cheque and that pay cheque wouldn't begin to cover his outstanding bills for Council Tax, the mortgage and a Barclaycard account on which he could barely meet the obligatory five per cent. But he was quite relaxed. Before too long Lydia's will would kick in and he'd be able to settle all the outstandings, including on a house that was on the verge of being threatened with a repo.

He'd go back to Pam, cap in hand. He was quite confident he'd be able to talk her round. There'd not been a woman in his life he'd not been able to talk round in the end, and there'd been a *lot* of women. He smiled faintly. He wished he'd not needed to get tough with her. If she'd just gone along with the original plan and confirmed he'd been with her that night. And kept her mouth buttoned about meeting him for sex in his sale houses. That was the trouble with middle-class women, the minute they saw a bogey they panicked, couldn't keep schtum.

Not that it mattered too much; he'd been able to prove exactly where he was both nights. But it had just meant too much attention from the police. Anyway, he'd give her a few days to get over it and then go back and get the old charm going. He was certain she'd be as keen to get under the duvet as he was. He'd work on it. There was just too much to lose. Apart from being good in bed she was so nicely placed. You didn't let a woman like Pam slip out of your grasp, even if your own boat was shortly to come steaming in.

He picked up the letters from the kitchen work surface. He'd not looked at them closely, certain they'd be more bills or threatening reminders, but one of them was from Green, Newbold and Turner, the solicitors. It had to be about the will and when he was going to touch the dibs. He quickly tore open the envelope and unfolded the letter:

Dear Mr Glover

I am the partner responsible for the probating of your late wife's will and I should be glad if you would regard the details to follow as a preliminary outline of the way it affects yourself.

Your late wife wished you to have, as tenants in common, her share of the equity in your property at Comstock Crescent, together with all her possessions contained in the house. She also wished you to have any monies payable from the pension scheme to which she contributed at the firm that provided her employment. Further, she wished you to have any balances remaining in her bank accounts: current and investment. I am hoping to conclude the probate within a month and will provide a comprehensive statement of your position at that time.

With my sincere condolences for the sad circumstances of Mrs Glover's passing, I remain,
    Jeremy Green.

Glover could feel the blood rising to his cheeks and his hands began to tremble. What about the insurance money? He read the letter again. Two million pounds-worth of insurance money and not a bloody word about it. Did Green *know* about it? Surely solicitors had their systems for tracking down every last pound of a client's estate. Thoroughly agitated, he paced distractedly about the ground-floor rooms. Christ, he'd been expecting news of the big pay-out and when the cheque would be in the post. If Green didn't know about the insurance money he'd better be put in the picture PDQ. But there was nothing he could do at this time of night. He poured himself another large whisky. But it wouldn't help him to sleep. He knew he'd not sleep properly till this was sorted.

The rooms of the house were lofty and spacious with plaster moulding in the ceilings and large marble fireplaces and heavy fabric shades on the overhead lights. Polly had been spot on in welcoming them to the 1930s. The house must have been sold furnished as the sofas and armchairs were all very old and faded, the solid tables marked and discoloured and in need of french polishing, the patterned Axminster carpets worn in places almost to the floorboards.

'And how about this radio?' Polly said. 'Though I suppose the old lady, who lived to be ninety, called it a wireless.' She indicated a vast machine in dark-brown wood with an ornate fretted façade. 'It still goes, would you believe, so long as you give the valves a couple of minutes to warm up. She didn't have a television. I daresay she and her companion would settle down in the evening to a nice game of bezique once they'd listened to *The Archers*.'

The men chuckled, standing about one of the scarred tables on which stood the array of bottles and cans they'd imported from the Mayfield. Music was provided from a modern music-centre which stood incongruously against the ancient decor of peeling and unfashionable wallpaper. There were shelves holding dozens of thick books that gave an impression of not having been taken down in half a century and glass-fronted cabinets in which could dimly be made out port and sherry glasses of ancient design.

'What do you think of these, Ralph?' Polly said briskly, opening a framed canvas bag of the type that would keep art-work flat. She propped up several drawings in stiff white card against the rear wall. The drawings had been completed in fine felt-tip and in great detail with considerable skill.

'This will be the new kitchen,' she said, pointing at one of the drawings, 'only it now becomes the dining kitchen as I'd knock through to the old dining room, extend the kitchen space and have an arched opening to a much smaller dining area, to separate one from the other. A far better use of space.'

'Then we'll be able to have a central fixture in the kitchen area and a place for every possible machine,' Jane broke in in her eager way. 'Look, an American-style freezer, a double oven, washer, dryer, micro. A small table by the window when it's just the two of us, a modern dining table in the part of the room beyond the archway when we have guests.'

'And here's my take on this drawing-room,' Polly went on, pointing to other drawings. 'A modern fireplace that will have very delicate Adam styling and on this wall a feature. It will take books and ornaments but be broken up by spaces for paintings, and below this sideboard effect that will conceal a superior music-centre and speakers. The television will go in a separate reproduction cabinet. Mama can't abide televisions and musical equipment to be on show when not in use and nor can I. And then two chandeliers with tear drop ornamentation. The carpets, woollen and plain of course, and the rug Chinese, very large and very intricately patterned. I intend to design the furniture myself, the sofas and armchairs, and they'll blend comfort with styling. There'll be two or three good antiques and the wallpaper must really lift the room, paper that is light and delicate and with a hint here and there of gold. I've decided to contact the firm who designed papers for the Speaker's chambers in the Commons. There'll not be any of this minimalist rubbish, it won't wash with the sort of people I'm aiming to work for. It will be sort of neo-trad. What do you think, Ralph? The dining-kitchen, will it work? I've taken a lot of very precise measurements.'

Ralph studied the drawing for some time in silence. Crane gathered he was an architect by profession, whose brains Polly was vigorously picking. 'It looks good to me,' he said eventually. 'I tell you what, when you're in a position to go ahead I'll drop by and draw up a plan your builders can work to. I can also put you in touch with a reliable team.'

'Oh, would you? That would be a tremendous help. You see, what Jane and I are aiming to do is to show clients what we've done with our old property and what we could do with theirs. And you know what women are like about kitchens and bathrooms; we want ours to be so eye-catching they'll not be able to rest till theirs look the same.'

She pointed to another drawing. 'This would be the bathroom, knocked through to a small bedroom. That would give space for a shower cubicle, a separate claw-foot bath, two hand-basins, loo and bidet. It'll be very warm in winter and air-conditioned in summer and there'll be piped music if they want it. And some first-class lighting to make them think their bums really aren't too big. Would you mind having a look at the bathroom, Ralph, to see if you think that'll work too?'

'Delighted! Lead the way.'

With Polly out of the room the atmosphere seemed to flatten slightly as if the lights had dimmed. Polly appeared to have boundless energy to go with the awesome sexiness. She seemed totally unaffected by the many drinks she'd put away and gave an impression that sleep was something she could take or leave. Crane had noted surreptitious grins and winks going on among the other men standing at the drinks table when Polly had borne Ralph away and he wondered if the inference to be drawn was the obvious one.

This was confirmed when the pair returned. Ralph's tie had been removed, his shirt collar was open and his pink face was a shade pinker, but he seemed very relaxed and contented. It looked as if he'd been repaid for his expertise with a session under the duvet and he gave every indication it had been a good deal. There wasn't the remotest change in Polly herself, she seemed almost to vibrate with her usual crackling energy and was now asking around if anyone knew of a decorator who could be relied on for really superlative work. 'Someone young,' she said firmly. 'People who work for me must be young. I can mould young ones and they'll not have developed fixed ideas. When Jane and I get going with the agency we'll need to provide the complete package: builders skilled in adapting, decorators *au fait* with the latest methods, a really top-hole sparks....'

Crane looked again at the drawings that stood against the back wall, showing the various rooms that were to be given priority, from different angles. The design work was excellent, at some stage she must have had formal training in art. Everything showed flair: the lines of the new fireplace, the detail of the woodwork on what she called the feature, with its elegant bookshelves and the irregular squares that would contain the paintings, the paintings themselves skilfully mocked up, the storage unit below on the surface of which would stand a silver tray with several decanters in simple clean lines, not cut glass. Neo-trad in Polly's phrase.

Crane found himself admiring the woman though this fell short of actually liking her. Her ambitions had had to be put on hold but she'd not let them go and wouldn't settle for working for anyone else. She wanted her own show with a single partner who had complementary skills. She had energy, presence and drive and knew how to make the most of her sensual body. All she'd needed was capital and now, almost magically, the capital would be provided, from Lydia Glover's estate.

He knew she was going to make it. He'd worked for a number of business people and they'd all had the intense focus of purpose Polly had. But why *had* Lydia left her all that money? She must have known Polly, known her well. Had she too been a Polly admirer? Changed her will to benefit Polly as she herself could no longer live with the bouts of depression? Well, strange things happened in life, but Crane couldn't quite sell himself a scenario as strange as that.

It always came back to the original problem: why had Lydia taken out all that insurance in the first place? What if she'd had an incurable disease? Something she'd kept to herself but which might have explained the depression and the decision to kill herself in her own way and her own time? Maybe she'd met Polly in some way, been impressed, then decided Polly was more deserving of the insurance pay-out than her womanizing husband. He dismissed the idea. If she *had* had an incurable disease it would have come out in the post mortem. Her doctor would have been consulted, the hospital people.

As usual, none of it made sense and in the end he knew that all he could do was to keep seeing the two women and hope that at some point one of them would let something slip that would give him some kind of a ball to run with. He moved to where Polly was locked in earnest discussion with two of the men about the detailed plumbing that would be required to make her new bathroom an airhead's dream, as she put it.

'I must go now, Polly. I've really enjoyed the evening.'

'Goodnight, Jim. We'll see you tomorrow night, yes?'

'I'll look forward to it.'

He couldn't take leave of Jane as she was no longer in the room. When Polly had returned to the drawing-room with Ralph he'd seen Jane discreetly go off with one of the other men, who was also perhaps to be paid in the sort of kind the women tended to work in. What was the man to be rewarded for? Advice on how to clear up an outbreak of Japanese knotweed? The best way to trim a topiary bush into the shape of a peacock? It was as if Jane had to live exactly as her idol.

And just exactly where did Jane fit into the Lydia Glover affair?

N I N E

'Hi, Frank. You're late. Can I get you a nightcap?'

'Please. I hope you didn't stay up on purpose. My days are open-ended, as you're probably beginning to gather.'

'I got hooked on *Sliding Doors*. And I don't usually go to bed before eleven.'

She went off to the kitchen and came back with gins and tonic. 'What sort of work was it kept you out so late?'

'I'm in the process of keeping an eye on a woman who looks to have been involved with Lydia Glover when she was alive. I'll spare you the details, but the woman looks as if she might benefit in a big way by Lydia's death. You weren't educated at Bradford Girls' by any chance?'

'Too expensive for my old dad, I'm afraid. Why do you ask?'

He drank a little from his glass, stretched out in his armchair. 'My researches tell me the woman I'm watching went there, Polly Manning.'

'*The* Polly Manning?'

'You know her?'

'*Of* her. I think we all do who were part of the young scene when she was on the go. Those who went to pubs and clubs inside a twenty-mile radius anyway.'

'I had heard she ran around with a pretty fast crowd.'

'An awful lot of us wanted to be part of that crowd. A girl I knew tried to get in with her but had to retire hurt. Polly was just too demanding. You had to do things for her. You had to amuse her, or buy her drinks, or be able to get her into the best clubs when the heavies were turning you away.'

'No big change there then, from what I've seen recently.'

'She really was a hard case, though good fun by all accounts and a tremendous draw for the blokes. There was some ghastly incident when a boyfriend fell trying to climb to her bedroom. He was walking with a stick from then on.'

'And Polly didn't do cripples. I'd heard that too.'

They sat for a short time in silence, then Pam said, 'You say Polly might benefit from Lydia's death. Does that mean she knows Ken?'

'I really couldn't say. It's a very odd business. Something to do with Lydia changing her will in Polly's favour. That detail is confidential, Pam, but you've been involved in all this and I know you'll keep it to yourself.'

She nodded pensively as he told her how he'd mulled over ideas so much of the evening, at the Mayfield and later at Polly's, but hadn't got any answers he could hold up to the light. He said, 'I'm getting nowhere. All I can do is bear in mind the old police mantra, ABC: assume nothing, believe nobody, check everything.'

'Have you ... any more news about your friend who was killed at Fox Ridge?'

He sighed. 'Not a thing so far. My contacts in the force will keep me informed. I work on it when I can, not that there's much to go on, apart from her being killed in a house Glover was selling. When, and if, I can get this Glover business out of the way I'll give it my full attention. I owe it to the kid.'

'Do you still think Glover might have anything to do with *that*?'

'He's completely in the clear. But the key to that house, which Grant, Spooner were holding, somehow got into the hands of the man who killed her, and that's what we'll have to work on, me and the police.'

'You're a driven man, Frank. Why don't you let it go for a while and put your feet up?'

He nodded. 'You're right. I try to let go but my brain seems to have its own agenda. By the way, you mentioned a friend who was keen to be a member of Polly's gang. Well, the Polly effect looks to be working on a woman she lives with called Jane. She gives the impression that the best thing that's ever happened to her is to be able to share Polly's life. They aim to set up in business together: Polly designing house interiors and Jane working on gardens. I'm pretty sure there are no lesbian overtones.'

'My old friend, who wasn't called Jane and now lives in Australia, she said Polly made things happen they could all enjoy, apart from being funny and a bloke puller, but there was an element of danger about her too that was part of the turn-on for her chums.'

Crane thought about this. 'It might have been the element of danger that made the boyfriend climb the trellis, but this Jane woman seems the type who'd run a mile at the slightest hint of danger. She's rather quiet and reticent: the opposite of Polly. I suppose Polly's calmed down a lot by now. People do. I wish you could see this Jane. There's something about her that defies analysis. My analysis anyway. Maybe your woman's instinct might help.'

'I'll help in any way I can. And now shall we have one more drink and talk about anything except the Glover affair? You've got to switch off sometime.'

'You're right. Same again?'

He picked up her glass and went to the kitchen. It had made a pleasant change to get home and see rooms lit up and then to have a drink and a chat with a woman like Pam.

'I like your house,' she told him when he was back in the living-room.

He gave a wry smile. 'You surprise me. The decor isn't quite as old as that at Ranelagh House, Polly's place, but not much has been done with it since the seventies. I bought it from my father when he retired and he and Mum went to live on the coast.' He glanced round at the chocolate-boxy pictures and the elderly suite and the big square television that operated with a cathode-ray tube. 'I've had a few big disappointments in my adult life and this house, and the way it looks, takes me back to my youth, when I was happy and seemed to have everything to play for.'

'Tell me about it,' she said, with a wry smile of her own. 'Don't I know the scene? When Matt and I were together, my ex, it seemed life couldn't possibly be better. Big detached at Wilsden, lots of holidays and weekend breaks, enough money to be very comfortable, planning to start a family ...'

'And then he legged it.'

'Oh, *God*, does any marriage work in this bloody country unless you were born seventy years ago? My grandparents' generation seemed to be able to make do with just the one partner.'

'I'm sure you know the L.P. Hartley quotation: "The past is a foreign country ..."'

'Yes, I know it,' she said, nodding sadly, '"... they do things differently there". Oh, Frank, I'd never have got mixed up with Glover if Matt hadn't cleared off with one of my so-called friends.'

'You had bad luck. You'll meet a worthwhile bloke one day, Pam. You're attractive, clever, outgoing.'

'From where I'm sitting they all seem to have been snapped up.'

'You're still young. Plenty of time to meet someone, start a family.'

'Have you ever taken an antibiotic called amoxicillin?'

He gave her a puzzled glance. 'Can't say I have.'

'In powder form and water it's the most repellent stuff I've ever forced myself to swallow. You need to drink something else to get rid of the taste of it. Ugh! Well, that's how I feel about Glover. I need an antidote to clear him out of my mind.'

'What do you think might do that?'

'Would you sleep with me? Oh dear, that *does* make me sound a right old slapper, doesn't it?'

He smiled. 'The first answer is yes and the second is no.'

'I'd be no threat to your girlfriend,' she said, speaking quickly. 'I need time to assess my life, think the future through. But it would be so nice to go to bed with a decent bloke like you, to get that vicious piece of garbage off my mind. Perhaps I should lay my cards on the table and admit that I do *like* sex. In fact I miss it.' She shook her head. 'I can't believe I'm saying all this, it must be the gin. I was carefully brought up. I didn't let anyone touch as much as a leg till I was eighteen. Look, Frank, if you don't fancy me I'll go and sit on the naughty step.'

'Just cut yourself some slack, Pam. You've made me an offer I don't want to refuse.'

'What if the semi-det girlfriend were to find out?'

'Colette and me, there are no rules. We live completely separate lives, but it's a very strong relationship. When I met her she was going through a bad time and I was able to help her. She had a partner who died on her and he was the sort of bloke who took a lot of getting over.'

'Dying, legging it, it comes to the same thing, you know. Except that if they die on you you aren't forever asking yourself did he go because of my inadequacies?'

'Men go because some woman gives them a come-on smile. And, when the glamour wears off in six months to a year, they very often wish they were back with the partner they had so much in common with. Oddly enough, one of the things they miss most is no longer being able to reminisce about a shared past. But it's usually too late then, the original partner has finally dealt with the pain of him clearing off and moved on. Believe me, I know the territory, a fair amount of my work comes from women who want to know if what they suspect is true. It always is, but they are hoping and praying I'll prove them wrong.'

'How sad so much of modern life is.'

They arranged that she'd come to his room as it had the larger bed. She came in ten minutes later in a frilly nightdress. She turned off the bedside lamp and he heard the whisper of the fabric as she removed the nightdress. Then she slid into bed with him.

He was being a stand-in for Matthew just as Glover had been. It was a role he was accustomed to. Several women in the past, in the throes of divorce, had wanted him to spend the night with them. They were vulnerable and it wasn't so much the sex as simply wanting a man in their bed who'd not turn his back on them. They knew there'd be no complications. To Crane it was a kind of pleasant bonus that sometimes went with the job and, like Pam, he too liked sex. And it came as a decided relief tonight to share his bed with her. He'd had a long day and his brain had given him little or no respite from its endless revolutions around those same names: Lydia Glover, Ken Glover, Polly, Jane and Tracey.

And he'd had enough, though left to himself he'd have slept badly. But this fragrant women had come to his rescue and they'd both been able to escape from their dark thoughts in the pleasure and release they could give each other. Later, she said, 'God, I needed that. You've *almost* cleared him out of my system, that bastard Glover, but I'm pretty sure I'll need a repeat session before very long to make sure he's gone for good. I'll not forget you, Frank, for all the right reasons.'

'Your Matthew, he needs his head looking at, to walk away from someone like you.'

'Bless you. I feel I ought to send Colette some flowers and a thank you note....'

'Mr Green, please. The name's Glover, Ken Glover.'

'Putting you through, sir,' she said, shortly afterwards.

'Mr Glover, Green speaking, how can I help you?'

'It's about the letter I received yesterday.'

'Yes, about Mrs Glover's will. What seems to be the problem?'

'My wife's life was insured. You make no reference to it in your letter. Do you want the details?'

There was a short silence. 'I … know about the insurance, Mr Glover.'

'Why leave it out of your letter then?'

'Mr Glover, there's been a development that you may not know about.'

'What sort of development?'

'I think it would be best if we could talk it over in my office. I could find time at eleven if that would be convenient.'

'I'll be there.'

At ten, Glover was to show a young couple around a semi in the Bolton district. He drove up there with his insides churning, his mind going obsessively over Green's words. Development. What could the man mean? How could there be a development? Did it mean the insurers were making difficulties? How could that be? There'd been a death and the insurers paid out on death. Did they think there was something about the death that meant they could suspend payment? He couldn't understand, the coroner's verdict on the death had been an open one. Were the police causing problems? All right, they'd had him in for questioning, but that was quite normal when a spouse died in unusual circumstances, it was always the partner the police went to first. But he could show proof he'd been at the casino that night, the police had checked it out.

He showed the young couple round the semi in a preoccupied mood, unable even to put on a pretence of the charming bloke he'd turned himself into over the years, who had such mastery of the tricks of the trade: the vendor *might* be persuaded to take an offer from a serious buyer; yes, there's been a *lot* of interest in the house; no, no need to worry about a mortgage, I can fix that. He couldn't get his mind on to any of it, but showed the couple around almost in silence. It was left to them to prise out of him the answers to questions he would normally have provided full information about: the council tax band, when did the vendor want to complete and so on. Disappointed with an agent who answered their questions almost tersely, they drove off without a further word and didn't look as if they'd be back. Glover was indifferent and jumped into his own car and drove, careless of his speed, down to the city centre, where Green, Newbold and Turner's offices were sited in Hustlergate.

His appointment with the young couple had taken so little time he was early for his meeting with Green. He paced about the reception area, so preoccupied he never heard the receptionist ask if he'd like a cup of coffee, and she had to repeat the question. He gave a vague shake of his head, which she took, correctly, as a no. At a few minutes after eleven he was finally shown into Green's office, with its shelves of legal reference-books and its view of the imposing entrance to what had once been the Wool Exchange. It had been built in the style of Venetian Gothic and Green felt it had a calming effect on clients in a nervy state. This wasn't the case with Glover, who began speaking the moment he sat down.

'A development, what does that mean? Are the insurers dragging their feet?'

'Insurers always drag their feet, Mr Glover, but that's not the situation here. The position is that you are not named in your wife's will as the beneficiary of the insurance to be paid out on her death.'

Glover paled and his mouth fell open as he stared at the solicitor. 'What … what are you saying, what can you possibly be *saying*?'

'There's no mistake. The insurance money is willed elsewhere.'

'But there *is* a mistake,' Glover said in a raised voice. 'A bloody big mistake. My wife and I made the arrangement together; she'd insure herself in my favour and I'd insure myself in hers. That was to ensure we'd be in a comfortable position if either of us died while we were still working. We made a decent living as a couple, but our income would be virtually cut in two if one of us were to die.'

Green tried to look as if he believed any of this. 'And you insured yourself for a similar amount?'

Glover began to redden. 'I … I couldn't run to it right then. Things were bad in the estate agency business. But that's got nothing to do with it. If the money doesn't come to me who does it go to?'

'I'm not sure I can tell you that if your wife didn't give you the information.'

'It's Polly Manning, isn't it? It can only be her. Those two were as thick as thieves before my wife died. It's that bitch, Polly Manning.'

Green was silent for a short time. Then he nodded uneasily. 'Very well, it is Miss Manning.'

'Why did you let my wife *do* that? Why didn't you tell me what was going on? I was her husband, for God's sake!'

'Mr Glover,' Green said coolly, 'I'm a solicitor and I was acting on instructions. It was *her* will, *her* estate and it was insurance she'd organized and paid for herself. She was quite free to apportion her estate as she saw fit.'

Glover leapt to his feet. 'I'll see her, that Manning bitch, I'll see her. Today. She had my wife mesmerized. If you think I'm going to take this lying down—'

'Mr Glover, you must *calm* yourself,' Green said firmly. 'You mustn't attempt to harass Miss Manning about this. Your wife offered no explanation why she was changing her will and there was no reason why she needed to. I'm just sorry that you should be the last to know.'

'I've got it together now,' Glover said, in a low, raw tone. 'If she thinks I'm going to let it rest this way she's out of her tree.'

He'd begun pacing the room in his agitation and now suddenly yanked open the office door. 'Mr Glover,' Green shouted, 'close the door and listen to me!'

Glover paused, shaking with rage, but a few seconds later let the door swing shut.

'You must *not* cause any trouble for Miss Manning,' Green went on. 'If you feel you must dispute the will I can advise you how to go about it, but quite frankly if you believe you'll get any redress through the law, when there's no question of genuine hardship if you *don't* get the money, I can assure you you'll have to whistle for it.'

Glover stared down at him balefully, mouth twitching as if there was a great deal more he wanted to say, but Green had a strong impression he'd realized he'd already said too much, though Green couldn't begin to guess what that might be. Turning on his heel, Glover pulled open the door again and strode out.

His mobile rang. 'Frank Crane.'

'It's Jeremy, Frank. Could you ring me back on a landline? It's confidential but there's no rush.'

'I'll be in my office at five, Jeremy. I'll ring you then, OK?'

'That'll be fine.'

When he rang the solicitor later from his little office, Green said, 'Didn't want any of this to go off into the ether from your mobile, Frank. It's about Ken Glover.'

'Let me make an inspired guess. You've told him the insurance money will go to Polly Manning and not him.'

'I lit the blue touchpaper and stood well back. He was *incandescent.*'

'He had a hell of a lot riding on Lydia's very convenient death. That's why I'm keeping tabs on the beggar on a daily basis and so are the police.'

'He was certainly a sight more broken up about the money than the death itself, that's for sure. He couldn't even pretend to be the grieving widower.'

'My friends in the force say he's not shown any real distress about the death since day one. And he's in a desperate state money-wise. I ran a check on him and he's so broke I reckon the men in the big boots will be knocking on his door any day now. Gambling losses. I don't think he could begin to clear off his debts without the money he thought he had coming.'

'I had to admit that Lydia had changed her will in favour of Polly. His attitude worries me. I think he might go round to her place and cause a lot of trouble.'

'I'm keeping an eye on Polly too. As you know, I'm still trying to find out *why* Lydia took out all that insurance cover. We all know there was something dodgy about her death. We don't know how, we just know there is. Polly lives with a woman called Jane. I haven't got a surname yet. Would you know anything about her?'

'Afraid not. Polly always had a lot of friends.'

'And hangers-on, I believe. People who wanted to join the magic circle.'

'Wherever Polly was, it was party time.'

Crane told Green about the party times at Ranelagh House and the women's plans for a design agency. 'They'll be a good team and I'm certain Polly's drive will make them very successful. But they do need capital. I'm rather torn. On the one hand I'd like to find evidence of wrongdoing in connection with the insurance, but on the other I'd like these women to get the funding they need and have the success I'm certain they've got the potential for.'

'Knowing you, Frank, I'm sure you'll not let it stop you trying to ferret out the truth. And yet Lydia's death might be exactly what it seems, after all: depression, pills and booze.'

'You could be right. These things happen. Blame it on my CID training. You learn inside the first half-hour that the only view you can take is the cynical one.'

*

Polly drew the cork on the bottle of chilled Chablis and poured into two glasses. 'That blessed hour, six o'clock,' she said brightly, 'when we can pop our beaks into the first drink of the day.'

Jane giggled. She, too, really did love this time of day, when she could come in from the big back garden, where she was working on an elaborate rockery and Polly could put away her design ideas for when they were in business, and they could have their showers and dress for the Mayfield. She couldn't imagine a day now without what Polly called the sundowners.

'Well, Janey, about three weeks, that's what Jeremy says.'

'Probates always take time.'

'The longer it takes the more they can charge. Not that it'll make much impact on *my* inheritance.'

They both giggled this time.

'I'm counting the days, Janey. Once the agency's up and running it'll lead to other things, you'll see. Success in one field will lead to success in others. We'll build up so many contacts, have so many ways of building on a sound base. I'll want the firm to grow, take on staff, make Manning a name again. The family had such prestige when Papa was on the council. He did such a lot for the city, quite apart from giving so many people a livelihood at the mill.'

'You'll get what you want, Poll. You always do.'

And always did. Jane could remember so vividly Polly leading her side to victory on the hockey pitch, swimming in the pool two yards ahead of the nearest competitor, striding across the stage, word and character perfect, as Portia in *The Merchant of Venice*.

Jane, small and retiring, had always been there in the background to see her idol excel, as if by divine right, in everything she did, her long brown hair always perfectly cut and styled, her clothes so fashionable. She'd always drifted around in Polly's wake like an insignificant sail-boat in the wake of a gleaming cruise-ship.

And then, when they were older, and she had a boyfriend, Jane would get him to take her to a club or a pub that she knew Polly favoured, just so that she could be there when Polly erupted into the room like a film star with her dozen-strong retinue of the chosen ones, all laughing and joking and having such a marvellous time. The landlords all loved Polly: she gave the takings such a boost, could make their pub seem *the* fun place to be.

Jane sipped some of the steely wine. It was a wonderful feeling to know she'd be sharing Polly's guaranteed success, to be a partner as the new opportunities were detected and developed. One day she would have the satisfaction of leasing superior office accommodation and be involved in the hiring of additional staff when they could no longer cope with all the work that came through the door as the firm expanded.

The phone rang at a distance. It was a free-standing handset and tended to move around a lot. 'I left it in the kitchen,' Polly said. 'It'll be Ralph. He knows some people who've just bought a great house near Ripon with an acreage. It's in a worse condition than this. On his recommendation they want me to look it over and draw up a renovation plan. They know Mama, of course, everyone who is anyone knows Mama. Good old Ralph. I'd say that was well worth *two* sessions with my legs in the air and describing figures of eight with my pearly buttocks, wouldn't you?' She went off, chuckling.

Jane poured herself a little more of the Chablis, smiled. She was having her own sessions with her legs in the air with Paul, who'd given her such a lot of help with the heavy lifting of the rockery stones. It was all such fun being with Polly, just as she'd always known it would be in the days when you had to be able to bring something to Polly's table to be allowed to sit at it: make her laugh or have access to a decent motor, or be in a position to spend a lot of money.

Well, now Jane had been able to bring things to Polly's table at last and what a great life it was proving to be. Take the sex. She really enjoyed it, but didn't want to be involved with men any more, not after her own marriage had been so awful and she now had Polly for companionship. And, like Polly, she could use sex as an incentive scheme. Polly had taught her how to go about it, of course; she'd never have mastered the art without her expert tuition and encouragement. And then party time almost every night. The future seemed to unwind before them like the yellow brick road which would lead them to certain glittering success.

Jane loved the swimmy sensation she got from the white wine on an empty stomach. She'd learnt how to pace herself and drank sparingly at the Mayfield, not having Polly's ability to drink as if she had hollow legs and feel no ill effects. She supposed she'd come to rely on the sundowners. After a long day in the garden she would feel just a little jaded and depressed. She still couldn't quite keep the shadowy side of this enjoyable existence out of her mind. Polly had told her again and again that if you wanted something you just went for it and if people sometimes got hurt, well, it showed they weren't up to the job of life anyway. That's why Polly had had to split with her husband, he'd not been fit for purpose, as she put it. And the young man who'd fallen from the trellis all those years ago, Polly had dismissed that as a man having had bad luck and she'd insisted she couldn't be around people who had bad luck in case it rubbed off on her. 'Bonaparte thought the same way, Janey, he always asked of an officer being put up for promotion, did he have the luck?'

There were other things Polly had been dismissive about, but, 'All that matters is that you and I have this chance and with this money that's coming our way we shall have. Never look back, never apologize and never explain. Just take what you want from life, work hard, have a little fun and always live for the future.'

She was right. Jane knew she was right, but she always needed the reassurance of Polly's presence and attitude. It was just that sometimes Jane couldn't stop herself remembering the quiet studious girl she'd once been. She felt that that girl would never really have been able quite to understand how she could become the woman she'd turned into by seizing the chance she'd always forlornly dreamed of, of being a Polly person.

'Great stuff!' Polly cried, bursting into the drawing-room. 'Top me up, Janey, before I get too much blood in my alcohol stream. Ralph is taking us to meet the Hartneys. Me to say what can be done and take photos and measurements and you to cast an eye over the grounds. The legal work has only just begun and will take a few weeks yet, so by the time they complete, our money should be in the bank and we'll be in a position to fund the renovations. The rich, as I know, do *pay*, but they always pay very late. As for Ralph, I really do believe he's in line for a three-bonk special. He's not bad on the duvet, you know, it's with him being on short commons at home, it puts a very keen edge on his appetite. And he knows there'll not be any comebacks. I don't think he'd be particularly bothered if his wife *did* do a bolt, though he'd be pig-sick if she tried to take the dog....'

Crane had kept tabs on Glover on a daily basis. He'd checked that he went to the office then did his rounds with the houses for sale. Having ensured that he still seemed to be working normally Crane would then go off to cover routine work, only returning to his main task to check that Glover was to spend his usual evening at the casino. God only knew what he was using for money these days, perhaps he just couldn't keep away from the place and went to watch the play even if he couldn't find a tenner to join in.

But today Glover had been given the bad news that the insurance money would be going to Polly and Crane felt certain this would make a change to his routine. It did. Glover hadn't left his house that evening until eight o'clock. He'd then driven not to the casino but on a route through the outskirts to Harrogate Road, where he'd left his car in the car-park of the Mayfield and gone in the hotel.

'No prizes,' Crane muttered to himself, 'a man on a mission.'

He waited five minutes then strolled into the Mayfield bar. The usual group of men was there, clustering around Polly and Jane, with Glover, slightly flushed, standing apart at the bar.

'Hi there, girls,' Crane said. 'Ready for another drink?'

'Hello, Jim,' Polly said warmly. 'A top-up would be very welcome.'

He got the drinks, passed the women theirs, then, with his own, joined in the general chatter, ready as usual with the quips and the easy laughter and an opinion about Federer's chances at Wimbledon. At the same time he kept a practised eye on both the women and Glover, who still glowered alone at the bar. Jane, who wasn't as good a dissembler as Polly, looked decidedly uneasy behind her agreeable smiles and ready laughter, but Polly looked to be exactly her usual self, full of a house that Ralph had lined up for them as their first major commission. But it took one to know one and Crane could tell that Polly, behind what was really a class act, was watching Glover as attentively as he was. At one point, when the men were locked in an excitable discussion about the differing merits of manual and automatic cars, which briefly excluded the women, Crane saw Glover take a step nearer to Polly and say quietly something that sounded like, 'I can't stand here all night.'

Polly gave him an imperious stare and also spoke quietly but in a voice that had an edge, 'We'll be leaving at ten, no sooner.'

Glover's flush had deepened slightly. He had the look of a man who'd had a very bad day.

The chatter flowed on for another half-hour and at five past ten Polly said, 'Look, chaps, we can't invite you back tonight, Jane and I have things to sort out. See you tomorrow night as usual. Got to go now. *A tout à l'heure.*'

The women moved off to a cheery chorus of 'Good night, girls', and a little proprietary kiss on Polly's cheek from the man called Ralph. 'Jolly good sports, those girls,' Ralph told Crane with a knowing wink. Agreeing that as good sports went the girls were in the first division, Crane joined in the appreciative comments about them for a few more minutes, then said that he too would have to go, early start in the morning.

He passed through the reception area and was about to leave the hotel when he saw that the two women and Glover were standing in the forecourt in lamplight. The entrance had double doors, one of which had been closed, the other left open. He stepped behind the closed section and could just hear what was being said. Polly was speaking decisively in her cultured drawl, 'You can drive if you want to but we're walking back. We *always* walk back.'

'I need this sorting *fast*.'

'It'll just have to wait till we're back at the house.'

'I've waited two bloody hours in that bar.'

'Then another ten minutes will make no difference.'

'You've got a nerve.'

'Good job one of us has.'

The women walked off with Glover trailing behind them. At a distance Crane began to follow. When he reached the Ranelagh estate he stood for a while in the darkness of the perimeter wall, waiting for the front door of Ranelagh House to open and lights to go on as the three entered, but that didn't happen.

He wondered if the women had led Glover to the back door. He moved then quickly through the modern part of the estate. At Ranelagh House there were flagged paths that led to the rear on both sides of the house. He took the right-hand one that skirted the garage. The back garden was immense and ended in what looked to be a copse of trees. It was as carefully tended as the front garden, with an oblong pool in the foreground and an elaborate rockery, close-cut lawns and many flower-beds in differing elegant shapes and full of seasonal blooms, miniature hedges, well-shaped bushes. Crane looked warily around the corner of the house. The two women and Glover stood on the patio just beyond a conservatory built out from the rear entrance to the house. They stood in the light of a security lamp that operated when anything moved within its range. Polly looked as calmly controlled as ever, but Jane stood apart from the others, looking very troubled. Her right hand fluttered near her mouth in an odd gesture, as if a child was having to listen unwillingly to a parental row.

'We are *not* going inside, Ken,' Polly was saying firmly. 'Neither of us would trust you across the doorstep. We know all about your violent streak when you don't get your own way. Not that you'd not get as good as you gave from me, but I can do without a black eye or a broken tooth.'

'And you think you're safe out here, do you?' Glover sneered.

'Safer than inside. Jane is a dab hand with rockery stones. I'm sure she could inflict considerable damage on you with one of those.'

A neat pile of rockery stones stood at the edge of the patio, but Crane doubted Jane really would be of much help in a crisis. She looked very small and frightened in the glare of the security lamp, the hand that had feathered now held over her mouth. Glover watched them both in a baleful silence. Then he said, 'What the fuck's going on, Polly? The deal was a million each, with the entire estate willed direct to me.'

'Maybe it was decided you couldn't be trusted with all that money.'

'So you got her to change her will and not a word to me. Stupid bitch, can't you see how it'll look to the police when they find it's going to you? I'm having trouble with the police as it is. When am I supposed to get my end?'

'Three or four weeks, but it won't be a million.'

'What's that supposed to mean?'

'Exactly as it sounds. You'll be getting a hundred grand and think yourself lucky.'

'Run that past me again,' he said, in a low menacing growl, his face darkening, 'if you dare.'

'Of course I dare,' she said in her drawl, not showing the slightest flicker of fear. 'You'll be getting a hundred grand and that's all your input is worth.'

'Nothing could have *worked* without my input!' he shouted.

'The detailed planning was all mine. I planned while you were playing roulette.'

'You'll pay me a million, you bitch, as agreed, or—'

'A hundred grand, Ken, to throw away at the casino, which is what you'd do if we *gave* you a million.'

Red-faced, quivering with rage, blond hair dishevelled because of the hand he'd kept passing through it, he suddenly lurched towards Polly and seized her by the upper arms.

'Forward with the rockery stone, Jane,' Polly said calmly. 'This was why I'd not let the bastard inside.'

All at once, Jane had stopped looking frightened. Her face twisted into such a feral mask that Crane was taken aback. It was as if she was determined to show herself as fearless as her idol. She darted to the mound of stones and hefted a sizeable one. Glover froze, hands still grasping Polly by the shoulders. He was a strong-looking man but Polly also gave an impression of strength. She had height and the erect carriage and had probably never really lost the wild streak that had once given her the aura of danger. The three people stood as motionless as figures in a tableau. Glover had to be aware that the women as a combination could cause him serious injury. By keeping him outside the house they could tell the police, if it came to it, that they'd been attacked by a marauder and had had to defend themselves. Polly was a good strategist.

Glover released his grip, let his hands fall to his side, but brought his face close to Polly's. 'Look,' he said in a low harsh tone, 'if I don't get the million you'll be in one heap of trouble. You won't know the direction it's coming from, but believe me, it'll come.'

'We're shaking in our shoes. I'm sure we'll not get a *wink* of sleep tonight. What makes you think I'm remotely concerned about anything a man like you can do? It won't be anything much going by what you've done so far.'

'Maybe it won't be me doing it. Maybe it'll be the police. Acting on a statement I'll send them which will give all the dates, all the details, all the planning. You try, bitch, just try to rob me of my share and before you know it you'll be having your collar felt and the next thing after that you'll be finding out what it sounds like to be banged up.'

'Nonsense! It cuts both ways: what you know about me and what I know about *you.*'

'But I'll have done a runner,' he rasped. 'I'll have gone where I'll never be found. You'll find out when it's too late that I can make plans as well.'

He turned away abruptly and walked off quickly, taking the path that ran along the far side of the house, fortunately for Crane.

'Safe to go inside now,' Polly said, her drawl still unwaveringly intact. 'I could do with a drink.'

TEN

'Frank, how're you doing? Sit yourself down.'

'Thanks, Terry. I thought I'd better see you as soon as possible. This Lydia Glover business. I need to tell you what I've found out. But the first thing you *should* know, and this is confidential at this stage, is that Jeremy Green told me that Lydia changed her will so that all the insurance money goes to a woman called Polly Manning.'

Jones's eyebrows went up. 'You don't say. Is this Polly Manning connected by any chance to the late Wilfred Manning who owned the mill and was a JP, councillor, all that stuff?'

'She's the daughter. The family came out of it badly when the mill had to close. Look, Terry, she's involved in what has to be a conspiracy between her and Glover to get the insurance money. But there's been a falling out among thieves.'

He told Jones what he'd overheard the previous night at the rear of Ranelagh House. Jones listened closely, eyes widening from time to time. 'This *is* a turn-up,' he said, when Crane had finished speaking. 'But it poses more questions than it answers. What do you make of it?'

'I've kicked it around ever since. All I can come up with is that Polly got to know Lydia and somehow persuaded her to take out the insurance and leave it to her, knowing she was in a state of near-chronic depression.'

'I'd say that that seems just a little bit far-fetched.'

'I couldn't agree more. The thing is I've given myself a false name and got to know this Polly quite well. She's very clever, very ambitious and very manipulative. She can get people to do things for her and she can inspire great devotion in the people she takes up with. She's also the sexiest woman I've ever known and she has nothing to learn about using her favours.'

Jones thought about this for a short time. 'Are you *really* saying that this Polly woman manipulated Lydia to the point where she insured herself, committed suicide and left Polly with a pot of money?'

'Polly needs capital for a business she's aiming to set up. She's certain to be successful. She's focused and talented and can call on a lot of expertise. Maybe, just maybe, Lydia couldn't shake off the depression, didn't want to live, but thought that at least she could do Polly a good turn.'

Jones slowly shook his head. 'I've heard of some bizarre motivations in my time, but *this* ... and anyway where does Glover fit in?'

'He was probably giving Polly one at some stage. Maybe he puts her in the picture about Lydia and her depressed state and this gets Polly's mind going. Perhaps they both worked on Lydia together, Polly telling her how frustrated she was about not being able to get her business going and Glover telling her he couldn't bear to see her go on having to live such a desperately unhappy existence. They are both good with words. Maybe Polly says *she'll* pay the insurance premiums.'

'But Polly persuaded Lydia to change her will....'

'Maybe it was agreed that the entire estate would go to Glover, and he'd give Polly the insurance money to start her business. Only Polly, having the measure of Glover by now, tells Lydia it might be safer to will the insurance money to her before Glover can start throwing it at roulette wheels.'

Jones sat in another sceptical silence. 'Working on your scenario, no one's really guilty of anything, not that's against the law anyway. Lydia insures her life then tops herself, and if the insurance has been in place for more than a year the insurers pay out. Maybe we ought to come back into the real world, Frank.'

Crane gave a crooked grin. 'In the real world Glover would have organized Lydia's car crash.'

Jones nodded gloomily. 'The forensics have DNA from the vehicle, but even if it matched Glover's, which we can't obtain without charging him, what would that prove? It was his wife's car and blokes often use their wives' cars. Anyway, none of the samples match anything on the data base.'

He got up with a sigh, came round his desk and clasped Crane by the shoulder. 'Thanks for finding the time to come in, old son, you've put a lot of effort into this thing, but we're not really any nearer, are we? We'll just have to wait and see if anything turns up.'

Crane said, 'I'll give it a few more days. I can't think Gillis, the broker's man, will want to retain me much longer.'

He got up and Jones opened the door for him. 'Keep me up to speed, Frank, and if you can give me anything to act on I'll act. By the way, we're getting nowhere with the Tracey Sharp killing. Any line on that?'

Crane shook his head. 'I've given that a lot of thought too. I daresay you've spoken to any of her clients you can pin down?'

'Ted has. A fingers-of-one-hand job. There were no punter details in her flat.'

'It just makes no kind of sense.'

'But that bugger Glover is in the background *again*. Macavity the sodding cat. The forensics have plenty of DNA but no luck. God, Frank, if people really want zero crime they could have it next year. Put the DNA of the entire population on the data base by law. From then on we'd be able to pin down anyone who'd been involved in a murder, a rape, a stabbing or a robbery. The villains would be running shitless. But the civil bleeding liberties people want it *destroying* after a few years, the DNA we're allowed to collect now. So when some hard case has done his porridge he can go and smash someone else's head in and we have to start all over again with nothing on the base. This bloody *country*!'

Jones was on his hobby horse like probably every other policeman in the land. 'I know, Terry, I know,' Crane said with a faint smile. 'The trouble is, the civil liberties people all make sure they live well away from where all the trouble is.'

'Can I get you girls a drink?'

'Thank you, kind sir, we do seem to be running on empty.'

Crane went to the bar for the usual round. He wondered how Polly could put away such quantities of drink without ever slurring a word, or giving the slightest sign she was any other than totally sober. Jane wasn't in the same league. At the Mayfield she tended to have only one drink to Polly's two and was noticeably affected by the drinks she did have: lisping a little, looking slightly spaced, gazing at her friend with an affection she made no attempt to conceal.

'Jim, have you been able to give any thought to how I should invest my inheritance for the best return?' Polly asked. 'Bearing in mind I'll need to keep a good slice of it fairly liquid for bills I'll need to settle up front.'

'If you could give me a rough idea of the sort of money you'll be looking at I could work on a plan for you.'

'I'll give you exact figures when we're at the house. You'll be coming back? Good man. But think big.'

Crane knew how big. 'What with the credit crunch, Polly, cash is still king so I suggest you keep say a hundred K in a decent interest-bearing current account, with the rest of the money in maybe a spread of short-term bonds, not junk, and not the very cautious building-society ones, but those issued by reliable mid-range companies. And then perhaps we could tiptoe into the stock market. Morrison's are looking good and so are Halford's and Glaxo Smith Klein. I reckon we could get you a pretty safe five per cent on a careful spread. Going for a higher return is too risky at present.'

'That sounds good to me, Jim.' She put a hand on his arm. "You won't be wanting to charge me any of those fancy fees FAs tend to be keen on?'

'You're a friend. I don't charge friends.'

'If you can look after my finances as well as that,' she said, her voice dropping seductively, 'I'll be able to find other ways of rewarding you.'

It was clear the reward was to be the freedom of her lithe, vibrant and naked body in a softly lit bedroom. He smiled. 'You can't say fairer than that, Polly.'

'I get the impression you're a bit of a financial whiz so I'd want to look after you *very* well.'

He gave a modest shrug. He'd simply done his homework on the financial pages. She'd moved so close to him their bodies were almost touching. He'd never known a woman of such powerful attraction. He wondered how many men in the past had been ready to ditch wives, partners, girlfriends for the chance to help Polly out of her clothes and run their hands over her delicately scented flesh. He was tempted himself; she was like the embodiment of the sirens whose beguiling voices drifting across the sea had given Odysseus such a bad time. And like Odysseus, he knew that to give in to temptation with a woman like Polly could only be a seriously bad move. He didn't know how or why, he just knew instinctively to keep her at arm's length.

With a final squeeze of his arm, Polly began to join in the general conversation of her faithful band of admirers. She was totally her usual self despite the ugly scene Crane had witnessed the night before. Jane though seemed marginally subdued despite the smiles and laughter.

Crane simply couldn't get Jane together and it bugged him. Polly had once run around with a fast crowd and to become one of her friends you had to be able to give her something she wanted. You had to be as fun-loving as she was. But Jane was the opposite of confident and gregarious. Had it not been for Polly Crane couldn't see her being here at all in the middle of this group of cheerful, chatty professional men. She was a skilled gardener but so were many other women, women who had a great deal more charisma and assurance. Why hadn't Polly teamed up with someone who could have given the partnership her own brand of dynamism? What special benefit had Jane been able to provide to this demanding woman? As with everything else in this case he wondered if he'd ever know.

As usual, around ten, the women and the half-dozen or so men began the short walk to Ranelagh House. 'Listen up, chaps,' Polly said, when they were in the drawing-room and the drinks being poured, 'we've decided to have a proper party here on Saturday. Eight o'clock kick-off. We'll do the buffet and the wine if you boys will help with the cocktails. We'll be having a few people in from the estate. Maybe I can talk one or two of them into a Polly-designed kitchen or bathroom. Jane can advise on gardens. If word gets about it could provide decent bread and butter work for when we get going. Bring any wives or girlfriends by all means, there'll not be a peep out of us about what naughty boys you can be at our place while they're doing the ironing.'

Crane joined in the laughter. He knew that whatever Polly had been up to with the insurance money he'd always feel an admiration for the sort of person she was. She simply never stopped working, even when it was fun time and the gins and Dubonnet were on the go. She was one driven woman, though she kept it carefully hidden behind the laughter and the clink of glasses and the alluring glances she gave out that always seemed to be offering someone or other even more fun upstairs.

Pam was sitting in the living-room reading a novel when he got home. It really was very pleasant to have a woman about the house, ready with a night-cap and keen to chat. 'How did your day go?' she asked, handing him a gin and tonic, the first genuine one of the evening.

'Frustrating. How about you?'

'A lazy day. But I managed to make a trip to the supermarket. I saw you were out of a few things so I stocked up.'

'That was very good of you. How much do I owe you?'

'Frank, for heaven's *sake*. I should be asking how much I owe *you*. And I owe you a lot. I feel so much more relaxed now. I sat in the sun in your back garden most of the afternoon. It's been the break I needed, to get away from my translating deadlines for a while, not just … from him. And to be able to feel I can come and go without having to glance over my shoulder.'

She was beginning to look very well. Lightly tanned, her mid-length auburn hair freshly washed and glossy, she was wearing a silky shell top in green, and white linen trousers.

'Sorry I couldn't make it home for dinner. It was just a quick meal on the hoof. I've got several kettles all boiling at the same time at the moment.'

'I had one of your ready meals. I've just about got my mind round the incredible hours you put in.'

'At present, a lot of them still go on the Lydia Glover case. I saw Terry Jones and put him in the picture about Polly having a head to head with Glover on the patio.'

He'd talked over the details with Pam when he'd got home last night and now told her about the discussion with Jones. 'Terry's name for Glover is Macavity. He's somehow involved in everything but never seems to be there when anything actually happens.'

She watched him for a short time in silence. 'You don't really think Lydia deliberately took out insurance and then killed herself?'

'No. It was all I could think of that seemed to fit. Well, truth is stranger than fiction but neither I nor Terry think it can be so strange.' He sighed, drank some of his gin. 'I can't really see how any of us are going to be able to pin down the real truth. It could be the perfect crime. And if anyone can think out a perfect crime it's got to be Polly. She's got the kind of brain that's never in neutral.'

'Rather like yours,' she said, smiling.

'I have the dismal feeling that Polly's has the edge on mine. She must have had one bunch of good fairies dancing round her cradle.'

'Not all good if she's involved in something fraudulent.'

'They're having a party at the big house on Saturday, Polly and Jane. Would you mind going with me as my pretend partner?'

'I'd be delighted. You want me to see what I can make of the one called Jane?'

'Ah, you remember. Yes, it would be a help. She really is an enigma. I don't know who she is, or how she came to team up with Polly. I've checked the electoral register but it just lists Polly as being at the address. I've tried quizzing Jane in the most casual way, but there's always a five-second gap while she thinks out a guarded reply. Your reactions would be welcome and it would help my cover to have you by my side.'

'It'll be a pleasure, Frank. By the way, just when do you think it would be safe for me to go home?'

'I reckon Glover has so much on his mind right now that his relationship with you will be the least of his problems. But I'd give it a few more days.'

'Fine by me. Being here is like a lovely peaceful holiday.'

She was the ideal guest. She made no demands and after the long discouraging days he was going through it was a great relief to have her to talk things through with over a couple of drinks, to have her in his bed and know she'd be able to provide the relaxation that would ensure sleep.

Later, as they lay silent and drowsy and within minutes of sleep overcoming them, he reflected that when she was gone the fragrance of her scent would linger on, even after a change of linen, and he would remember the rustle of her nightdress as she slipped it off. He would also remember the way she looked in the morning glow of summer sunlight through the curtains with her hair spread on the pillow and her face in sleep almost as smooth as a child's. But he felt it had been a welcome interlude for both of them.

She began to speak quietly. 'If I'd known you earlier I'd never have got involved with the creep. You see, you'd never have given the impression you wanted to make the relationship permanent. With Ken it was very tempting to try and replace Matt with him. It was something you said the other night about moving on. I've been thinking about it a lot. I've begun to realize that I can't move on until I've stopped being in love with Matt, and if I can't stop being in love with Matt I'll just have to live my life the way you live yours. And I have a feeling that something happened a long time ago between you and a woman that you never quite got over.'

'What makes you think that?'

'When it's happened to you you're alert to the signs.'

He was silent for a short time. 'For some people, Pam, there seems to be only one person who really fits the bill. I was in love with the lady, but she wasn't in love with me. She *liked* me a lot, but it wasn't the same thing. I hope one day you *will* be able to move on, but it could take a while. Or, if you're like me, maybe never.'

They sat on in the drawing-room when the men had left, Polly over a drink and Jane, dry-mouthed from the earlier alcohol, sipping a cup of Earl Grey tea. Jane would never understand how Polly could drink so much and be so little affected, could sleep so little and still stay so incredibly animated. Jane would have to go to bed soon but Polly could quite easily take out a piece of white card and begin yet another of the designs her brain seemed to teem with.

Polly said, 'I can't quite get the hang of our new friend, Jim.'

'In what way? He seems a nice chap.'

'He's not like the others. The others are always trying to find things to do for us so they can take off our knickers, but Jim, he just doesn't have that randy gleam in his eye that I know so well. I couldn't have made it clearer tonight that if he looked after the investments he'd have a free pass to my fanny, but his reaction simply wasn't the bodice-ripping one I know to expect.'

'He must be gay,' Jane said, as it seemed there could be no other reason why Jim should be the only man they'd ever known who couldn't wait to get Polly into bed.

'No, he's not a shirt-lifter,' Polly said pensively, 'I can spot those in milliseconds. He's definitely hetero and he definitely finds me fanciable, but I can tell he's holding back and I can't think why, the chaps know we're totally discreet.' She began to speak in a declamatory voice, 'Let me have men about me who I can sense are having an erection. Sleek-headed men and such as sleep o' nights. Yond Jim, he looks as if he thinks too much, such men can be dangerous.'

Jane could remember as if it were yesterday Polly as usual playing a lead in another of the Shakespearian plays put on during their school years. She was paraphrasing one of the speeches and it made her smile; yet Polly did have a remarkable knack for picking up vibes that didn't quite hit the right spot. It made Jane feel vaguely uneasy.

'He asked me one or two questions the other night,' she volunteered, 'about how long we'd known each other and your back-ground.'

'Did he now?'

'It could have been idle curiosity, the other chaps often ask things like that. And as for holding back on you perhaps he's got a gorgeous partner back at home he's quite happy with.'

'Ducky, for pity's *sake*. Have you ever known a man who was happy with what he's actually got? Especially when I'm around giving them the false eyelashes?'

Jane nodded. It was a given in their relationship that Polly always had first pick of the men, invariably those she could sense would provide the more useful services. Jane was quite happy to sleep with the men who were handy with clippers and edging tools. She could tell that Polly, despite her usual cool drawl, was rattled about Jim failing to rise to the obligatory erection on being given an unmistakable hint of the delights that could be in store.

Polly finished her drink. 'Yes, he's a tiny bit of a puzzle is our Jim. Now then, Janey,' she went on more briskly, 'this other matter. We can't just let it hang. He's like one of those IEDs they bury under the ground in Afghanistan, we could step on it not knowing it was there. Something must be done.'

Jane hadn't wanted to think about it. It was one of the things she didn't want to dwell on in her life with Polly. Most of the time she succeeded, such being the pace of that life. There wasn't much time for dark thoughts to cast a shadow over things. She said, 'Perhaps when he's mulled it over he'll take the hundred thousand. As you said, it really is good value for his contribution.'

'That may be but he'll not take a hundred.'

'Perhaps if we upped it to two hundred?'

'He'll want what he considers to be his full share, and we don't know what he'll really do if we don't agree.'

'Maybe we *should* give him half then.'

'That would leave us under-capitalized. It sounds quite a lot, but the early days of the venture will be very expensive as I know from my London days. Our money going out fast to pay tradesmen, the client's money coming in very slow to pay us. We need that cushion, Janey, and this is the best chance we'll ever have to get airborne. And once we're flying, once we can show what we can do, the money men will advance us *more* capital to take on bigger and bigger projects, as soon as the credit crunch is over.'

Polly's gaze was unfocused in the way it was when she talked about that wonderful future she was determined they were going to have. 'My big ambition, Janey, is to design an entire *house*. It would have Georgian overtones, especially the windows, you know, tall ones on the ground floor, then reducing in size on the upper floors to give that perfect visual balance. And to have a free hand in laying out the rooms, the last word in comfort and style. I've talked to Ralph about it and he'd be keen to work on the architectural detail. Might even invest to get it built. He has a friend who owns several small parcels of building land in good country.'

'Polly, it sounds *marvellous*! Just imagine, people putting down their names to own a Polly Manning-designed house.'

'That's right. That really would get the name going, wouldn't it? Just single houses in an acre or two, all different but having the Manning style.'

Jane knew Polly would never rest until the Manning name became once more as well known as when her father had owned the mill. She'd been born to excel. Jane's heart beat a little faster. All she'd ever be able to do would be to lay out the gardens and she knew that when all these exciting things began to happen she'd really be hanging on to Polly's coat-tails. But she'd always be able to remind herself that she'd been crucial to helping Polly into a position where she was able to have these awe-inspiring dreams in the first place.

'Frank Crane.'

'John Gillis, Frank. Any news?'

'Look, John, you were right about Lydia Glover's insurance pay-out *not* going to Glover. In confidence, Jeremy told me Lydia changed her will so that the money went to a Polly Manning, daughter of the late Wilfred.'

'Go on. What can it *mean*?'

'It means that Ken and Polly were involved in some sort of a scam, but it's impossible to prove at present.' He gave Gillis a brief rundown of what he'd heard on the patio at Ranelagh House. 'It's definitely crooked, but they look to have covered their tracks incredibly well. I'm afraid my account's getting a bit hefty, John. If you want me to quit I couldn't blame you.'

'No, stick with it, Frank. I'm offsetting your charges against a possible colossal pay-out. I reckon that having got so far you'll get there in the end.'

Crane wished he had the same confidence.

'My name's Jim Parry as far as Polly and her coterie are concerned, Pam.'

'I'll not forget. I'll be interested to see Polly again. Not that I ever knew her. It was just that you couldn't miss her, whichever pub or club you were in, sooner or later you'd see Polly and her tribe, all screaming with laughter and having a marvellous time. Polly the Ubiquitous we used to call her.'

'She's a phenomenon. Incredible energy, full of ideas, brilliant networker, sexiest woman in town. If she does get her hands on that insurance money success is guaranteed.'

Crane was driving on the familiar route that would take them to the big house off the Harrogate Road. He was dressed in a sports shirt and jacket, Pam in navy straight-leg trousers and a short mauve jacket in slub silk over a dark top. Her hair was well-brushed and her make-up skilfully applied, and it occurred to Crane that perhaps it hadn't been one of his best ideas to take such a good-looking woman to the party. He knew he should be giving Polly the impression he could barely sit still until that red-letter day when he took charge of her finances and was to be welcomed into her bed with open legs. And yet he did want the reactions of an intelligent and perceptive woman like Pam to the Polly Jane set-up.

It had been a mixed day of sun, cloud and the occasional shower but the evening was more settled and Ranelagh House looked good in declining sunlight despite the neglect it had suffered over the years. The flowering trees and the manicured lawns were perfect, of course, and there were stone tubs at each side of the porticoed front door, filled with geraniums.

'Ah, Jim, do come in.' Polly stood in the hall wearing a floral shirt dress that enhanced her femininity without reducing that impression of driving energy that went with her frame and shapeliness.

'This is Pam, my partner,' Crane told her. 'And this is Polly, Pam.'

'How do you do, Pam.' For all her self-assurance and relaxed drawl, Crane didn't miss the swift appraising glance Polly gave the other woman, a glance that produced a near-subliminal impression that she didn't much care for what she saw. 'Ah, gin *and* Dubonnet, that really is very thoughtful, Jim. I'm asking the Mayfield contingent to help themselves to drinks from the kitchen. Jane's looking after the estate people.'

She gave the words 'estate people' a subtly disdainful note that seemed to imply they were very much 'not one of us'. She led them into the drawing-room which, for all its dated style, had been carefully hoovered and polished, almost certainly by Jane. It wasn't possible for Crane to visualize Polly in a head-band, overall and Marigolds, a duster in one hand and a spray-can of Mr Muscle in the other. Some of her designs were on display for the benefit of the estate people and she began to explain all the changes she would be making in the renovation of the house. While doing this she inserted carefully spaced plugs for the partnership she and Jane were on the point of forming, and that they were already prepared to offer advice on interior design and landscaping. The wives and girlfriends of the men, who were beginning to make the usual admiring circle around Polly, looked both impressed by, and decidedly envious of, her hypnotic charm, drawling self-composed manner and obvious expertise. Crane went off to the kitchen to get drinks for Pam and himself. On his return he heard one of the estate wives asking Polly, rather shyly, if she was one of the mill-owning Mannings.

'Wilfred Manning was my father,' Polly told her. 'He had to close the mill in the seventies at a considerable loss. Many years later, when I'd been able to research the situation in the industry, I was able to show Papa where he'd gone wrong. The mill was a vertical operation; all the processes done under one roof: fleece wool in at one end, finished products out the other. "Papa", I told him, "the industry was being undercut by the countries that could draw on cheap labour. The spinning and weaving and cloth manufacture were moving away. You should have closed down all those processes and kept only the combing and topmaking."'

'Topmaking?' one of the men asked.

'When the fleece wool's been cleaned and combed it's drawn into a sliver and wound into a sort of ball. That's a top. All the other processes follow: the spinning, weaving, dyeing, finishing and so forth. Now Papa's business was losing out on those processes, but at the time there was still an intensive demand for tops, which the home industry was still leader in. Papa should have switched to producing tops only, extended the combing facilities and closed down all the other procedures. But he didn't and in the end, by the time he'd paid off all the workers and sold the mill at a thumping loss, there wasn't much left in the Manning kitty. He'd used too much of his own money to keep an unprofitable business going, you see.'

'Perhaps he was thinking of the workforce, Polly, and not wanting to put so many people on the dole,' one of the men said mildly.

'It was the only way to make the business viable,' Polly said crisply, 'convert the mill to a combing operation and just keep a tenth of the staff. I told Papa he wasn't supposed to be a welfare department. But that was Papa's Achilles heel. "I regarded my work people as part of the family", he told me, "I knew every one of them by their first name." Well,' Polly went on, 'how can one make the correct business decisions unless one is completely objective about staff, hiring and firing as conditions demand?'

'That's our Polly,' Crane said to Pam in a low voice, where they stood by the window. 'I'm sure she had the economics exactly right and wouldn't herself have thought twice about putting all the workers on the dole in a declining industry. It would be old Wilfred who'd have the sleepless nights having to let go all the people he knew by their first names.'

'She really is one tough lady,' Pam said softly. 'And she's changed so little in the past ten years. It's not fair, she's not put on an ounce, and a perfect bust and a narrow waist. Plus a bum that's never going to look too big in *anything*. Such a glamour-girl.'

'And master class at making full use of her charms.'

Crane glanced round the room. Jane was dutifully serving drinks from a tray to the estate people while Polly talked on to a receptive audience. She answered question after question, patiently and with a pleasant smile, about kitchens and bathrooms and furnishings and decorative schemes. The estate people were clearly beginning to regard her as very much an upper-class person to whose house they'd been very privileged to be invited.

'Hello, Jim,' Jane said, as she edged past them with her loaded tray. 'You don't mind looking after yourselves with the drinks? Jolly good. I'm Jane, by the way,' she told Pam.

'Hi there. I'm Pam.'

'Nice to have you here. We see Jim now and then at the Mayfield. There'll be a buffet supper in the dining-room at nine.'

She moved off and Crane said, 'I'll get you a refill. We needn't stay too long. Polly doesn't do anything for nothing and she may want to talk to me about her investment options for when her ship comes in. But we'll get away as soon as we reasonably can.'

'And have a proper drink at home when you'll not have to worry about driving.' She gave him the little special smile, so familiar to him now, which meant she'd also love to share his bed again if he wanted her to. He returned a similar smile, but was careful to make sure he had his back to the room. He knew that Polly, for all the women clustered around her, was keeping a speculative eye on him from time to time.

He walked again into the kitchen, with its elderly machines and plain wooden surfaces on which were spread the many bottles the Mayfield men had donated. He rinsed out Pam's glass at a stainless-steel sink, dried it, and put the old slice of lemon into a bin he located in the cupboard below. There was a crumpled piece of writing paper in the bin. He took it out, hoping it might supply some slight clue to anything that went on in this house of secrets.

But it just appeared to be a list of figures Polly had jotted down to do with the repairs of the exterior of the house. That the figures looked to be guesses was shown by the question marks that followed the figures. Repairs to roof tiling: £10,000? Replacement windows: £40,000? Painting of exterior: £5,000? Replacement of front door: £2,000? The list went on and told Crane nothing worth knowing. He turned over the sheet of paper expecting more of the same, but read this: *'Joy shall be in heaven over one sinner that repenteth, more than over ninety and nine just persons, which need no repentance.'* The writing went on, *'These words from the New Testament are just as meaningful today as they always were and I invite you to join with me in prayer that repentance may be yours and mine.'*

There were further quotations from the Bible and Crane stood baffled. The writing seemed to be in Polly's hand as it was the same as the writing of the repair figures. It made no sense. From what he'd seen and knew of Polly she had to be just about the last woman in the Western world who'd feel the need to repent about anything. He wanted to keep the sheet of paper as it was so odd, the sentiments so absurdly out of character with Polly. Yet he had a feeling they just might mean something if he could give time to them. But he memorized the quotations as well as he could and then replaced the paper in the waste container just in case Polly might by any chance want to retrieve it.

At that point the kitchen door burst open and Polly herself walked in, closely followed by a small red-haired woman and a man who was one of the Mayfield group called Trevor. Polly turned on the woman and said in her usual calm drawl, 'Look, Penelope, I really don't know what you're getting so very agitated about but my only contact with Trevor has been to have a chat with him now and then at the Mayfield. And if you've got something to accuse me of don't attempt to do it in a roomful of guests.'

'You've slept with him, haven't you?'

'No, Trevor is simply an acquaintance.'

'He's made a full survey of this house but he's not charged you fifty pence. I know, you see, because I do the invoices.'

'Let it rest, Penny, let it rest,' Trevor put in sheepishly. 'I'll sort out the invoice—'

'But she'll not pay it, not in hard cash anyway. She'll have paid you already, on her back.'

'I can't imagine what leads you to believe I've had an affair with your husband.'

Penelope leant towards Polly and began to sniff noisily. It was obvious she'd not been able to cope with the drinks she'd had, possibly because of the low tolerance for alcohol redheads were said to have. 'It is the scent!' she cried. 'The one he came home *reeking* of.'

'Perhaps he likes to indulge himself in a dab behind the ears. Some men do, I'm told,' Polly said, rising almost indifferently above the other woman's excited state.

'You *slept* with him. Payment in kind. That doesn't put food on my children's table. But it's the only kind of payment women like you understand. You're no better than a common harlot.'

Polly gave the woman a rapid, accurate blow to the side of her face with a clenched fist. It sent her reeling across the room and sprawling over a table. Penelope slowly levered herself up, looking dazed, and made no attempt at retaliation. Trevor rushed to her side and helped to support her. 'Come along, Penny, I'll get you home. I did tell you not to have that last drink. Come along. We'll go the back way, Polly. I wish you hadn't done that.'

'And I wish your wife could learn to hold her drink.'

Trevor almost carried his wife from the room. Crane guessed that that would be that. The man was a middle-class professional, he'd want no trouble, least said, soonest mended. He was also in a delicate position, having provided Polly with several hundred pounds' worth of expert information for the bounty of her silky inner thighs.

Polly mixed herself one of her gins and Dubonnet, gave Crane a wry smile. 'Sorry about that, Jim. Don't let it spoil your evening. I don't at all mind being called a harlot but I object very strongly to being considered common.'

'What did you make of Jane?'

'I have a vague feeling I know her from somewhere, but I can't for the life of me think where. The hair's a wig, by the way.'

'Really? You surprise me. I can usually tell.'

'It's a very good one and would have been expensive. I had a feeling too she might have had something done to her face, but if so very skilfully. And the glasses puzzled me. They're rather heavy and unfashionable and I couldn't see why she didn't use contacts or a pair of those light modern ones.'

'She takes off the bins when we all go back to the house from the Mayfield. She seems perfectly able to see without them.'

'I'll keep on trying to think where I might have seen her.'

'It could be a help.'

They were sitting in Crane's living-room over a final drink. They'd left the party not long after ten, Crane making the excuse they'd need to be up early for a trip to the coast to see his parents. Polly had clearly thought it decidedly odd as the party was then in full swing and looked as if it would go on until midnight at the earliest.

Crane took out a note-pad from a sideboard drawer and began to write on it. 'Just give me a couple of minutes, Pam.' When he'd finished writing he told her about the piece of paper he'd found in the waste bin of Polly's kitchen. 'These are some of the things that were written on the back in what looked to be Polly's writing.'

He handed her the note-pad and she began to read, rapidly beginning to look as mystified as he'd done. 'What *can* it mean? Prayer and repentance are the very last sorts of words I'd ever associate with Polly Manning.'

'That makes two of us.'

'Do you ... think it might have been some kind of a rough draft of something she was going to type up and print off through a computer?'

'Could be, but why?'

She frowned and began to study the words again. 'It's ... it's like a sort of tract. The sort of thing batty old ladies stick in you hand when you're walking round Lister Park lake. But Polly's not batty and it's unlikely she's ever walked round Lister Park lake in her life.'

Crane was suddenly given the sort of frisson he had maybe once a year if he was lucky. 'Well done!' he said. 'Bloody well done, Pam.'

She gazed at him wide-eyed. 'But what *have* I done?'

She slept quietly at his side. For once the lovemaking hadn't brought him his own almost guaranteed drift into sleep. His mind wouldn't let go tonight. It was that word: tract. It was Tracey of fond sad memory who'd told him about the woman who'd handed out tracts to the prostitutes. The prostitute he'd spoken to in Lumb Lane had confirmed Tracey's description of a woman with brown hair taken back into a bun, who one night had gone off with Tracey's friend Libby. And Tracey had also talked of the tract woman visiting Libby earlier in her flat.

Crane had been elated to hear the word on Pam's lips. Perhaps it was some kind of a breakthrough. But mulling it over had brought back only too keenly and painfully the times he'd spent in her own flat with that pretty young kid and found growing between them such a powerful and caring relationship. He'd forced the images out of his head by the many jobs he'd taken on and the long days he'd worked, but tonight they were back: one day Tracey, eyes gleaming with the anticipation of starting a new life, the next day Tracey lying crumpled in a pool of her own blood.

He tried hard to concentrate on the idea of the tracts but couldn't really begin to see where it was taking him. It had been tempting to think Polly might have been the tract woman, handing out Bible extracts on neat little fliers, but how could that possibly be? Polly was one of the most focused women he'd ever met. She had a career carefully mapped out and seemed able to find a use for every minute of her time. How could she remotely have anything to do with the handing out of tracts like someone not entirely right in the head? As usual in this case, none of it seemed to make any sense.

And then there were the things he'd learnt about Jane. A woman in an expensive wig who wore glasses away from the house and might have had some expensive surgery to her face that had subtly altered it. Why did she want to look different from the woman she'd been?

Pam's steady breathing seemed almost to taunt him. It would be two hours at least before he could get off himself. He knew him.

'Thank God they've all gone back to their dog kennels,' Polly said, sipping a last drink. 'All those bloody *women* wanting their kitchens and bathrooms to look the way ours will. My designs wouldn't be any bloody *good* in a dog kennel, I kept wanting to tell them. But I jolly them along, we shall need the little people and their budget-price mentalities in the early days to help with the cash flow.'

'It's been much the same with me,' Jane said wearily. 'How do they get their lawns to look like ours, where can they buy gera-niums in that particular shade, would the back garden be big enough for a small pool?'

Jane was very tired. Much as she loved being with Polly, much as she admired and revered her, she did wish that occasionally, just very occasionally, she'd lend a hand in the kitchen, help with the clearing up and the debris after a party, take round a drinks tray now and then. Jane had barely had time for a glass of wine with all the work that had needed to be done looking after so many people. Fatigue brought on depression, the sort of depression she some-times had after a long day in the garden and before the first sundowner had begun to stimulate her to see things in a more posi-tive light and replace gloomy thoughts with those of the days to come. Days that would be so crammed with exciting things to do they'd be like suitcases you had to sit on to be able to fasten the catches.

Polly said, 'What did you think of the Pam female?'

'She seems nice. I feel I've seen her before somewhere. Can't think where though.'

Polly finished her drink and said in a musing tone, 'I do wish I could get a fix on Jim. It's rather tiresome. Just why *did* he latch on to our little group? Our chaps all understand the situation: if they look after us we look after them. That's why they hang out with us. And looking at some of the dismal creatures they dragged along tonight I'm not at all surprised. But the Pam woman isn't like them. She's no older than us and she's attractive. She's fond of Jim and he's fond of her. So why does *he* feel the need to get out of the house of an evening? And why is he so willing to give me the benefit of a shrewd financial brain and not want the soft lights and the flying fanny?'

'Perhaps he just likes the bar lounge atmosphere.' Jane was bone weary and anxious for her bed. If she couldn't keep that shadowy depression at bay through lack of alcohol, sleep would have to be the answer.

'I don't think he's the pub *type*,' Polly said. 'Not like the other chaps. He suddenly pops up from nowhere and takes us up overnight.'

Jane yawned. 'I'm whacked, Poll, I'll have to turn in.'

'You can't go till we've sorted out that other matter, Janey. We can't let it drift, it'll bring endless problems. We've got to get a straight edge on it.'

Jane felt near to tears, she was so tired and low. 'Oh, Polly, can't we just let it go and sort something out with the money? We can't go on and on and on like this.'

'We,' Polly said coolly, '*we*? Just where have you yourself come in to it up to now?'

'Oh, Polly, how *could* you, you know perfectly well none of it could have worked without me.'

'The planning was all mine, Jane, every bit of it. And I'm going to need your help this time, no two ways about it.'

E L E V E N

'What's your name, dear?'

'Myrtle.'

'Would you like to get in the car, Myrtle?'

Myrtle made a discreet hand signal to a woman a little further on the road. It could have meant, 'See you later', but Crane guessed its message would be interpreted as, 'I'm getting in the car of a punter who's not a regular', and that the other woman would commit to memory the make and colour of the car and its number. He'd read that street prostitutes developed good memories for these kinds of details. They had to.

'Look, Myrtle,' he said when she was sitting next to him, 'I talked to you a fortnight ago about a woman called Libby who went off one night with the woman you called the tract woman. Well, I'll pay you your usual rate plus twenty sovs on top if we can go somewhere where we can talk again. Nothing else.'

'You a bogey?'

'We've had this discussion before and the answer's still no. I'm a private investigator and I'm trying to find Libby. Where do you normally go with your ... clients?'

'Either my pad or the road above Lister Park. That's where I generally go with the blokes if it's just a hand job.'

'We'll make it the road above the park,' he said, smiling, 'but I'll not be needing a hand job. I'm Frank, by the way.'

He drove to North Park Road. It wasn't far away and was deserted at this time of the evening, when it was near dusk. 'Never no fuzz along here,' she told him. 'Christ, these days there's never no fuzz *anywhere* except when the city boozers are throwing out.'

'Sometimes you do need them and sometimes you don't. I know.'

Crane took two small photos from an inner pocket. He'd gone to the Mayfield last night and contrived to get snaps of both Jane and Polly on his mobile while pretending to make a call and their attention had been diverted chatting with their friends. The mobile was a superior model designed to take good clear photos in existing light without flash. He handed the photos to Myrtle. 'Do these women look at *all* like the tract woman and Libby?'

She studied the photos, forehead lined in concentration. She'd once had reasonable looks, her features and bone structure must have made her passably attractive and she had a well-kept figure, though that was possibly due to the cocktail of drugs and alcohol that would help to kill her appetite. She wore the short skirt and simple top she'd worn before, both very clean if well-used, but her long mousy hair was lank and her face had the slight unhealthy sheen that went with substance abuse. Crane pitied her. He'd always felt pity for these women, who'd been a regular feature of his duties when he'd been a uniform in his early days in the force. Could the life they'd turned away from to go on the streets possibly have been worse than a life *on* the streets?

'This *does* have a look of the tract woman,' she said eventually, 'but she had her hair in a bun and wore old clothes. She was a bit broken-down looking. This woman looks a bit, well, sort of ... you know ... posh.'

'How about the other woman?'

'Can't make my mind up. She has a bit of a look of Libby ... them glasses don't make it easy. Trouble is, I never knew Libby all that well, never saw her too close. Kept herself to herself a bit. They say she was pally with that woman who had her head bashed in up Fox Ridge way.' She gave a sudden shudder. 'Couldn't get that together, mister. She wasn't working the pavements like us. You had to ring her up before she'd take her knickers off, know what I'm saying, and she had to know who was doing the ringing.'

Crane sighed, nodded. 'She was a call girl, Myrtle, as you say. Her name was Tracey Sharp and it was Tracey herself who hired me to try and find Libby.'

She watched him, dull-eyed. He wondered if her eyes ever showed any spark of animation these days except briefly perhaps, when she was shooting a line or throwing down a straight vodka. 'Why bother going on looking if Tracey's dead? She can't pay you if she's dead.'

He nodded again. Payment for services rendered would be the top priority for women like Myrtle. 'You're right,' he said, 'but I got to know Tracey quite well and she was a nice kid. I want to know who killed her and why, and maybe if I could find Libby I might get some answers. Nobody's paying me to keep looking, I'm just doing it in my spare time. I feel I owe it to Tracey to find out who ended her life before it had really got going.'

Myrtle looked vaguely alarmed, as if she found it barely possible to believe that anyone would do anything for nothing. But there was also an element of wistfulness there that seemed to suggest that she knew quite certainly that if anything frightful were to happen to her it would, overnight, be as if she'd never existed.

'I'll take you back to your patch in a couple of minutes, Myrtle, this has helped me a lot. Now this woman you think has a look of the tract woman, do you think if her hair was taken back and she wasn't wearing make-up she really would look like her?'

'I … think so,' she said slowly, 'but I really only saw her close to the once when she pushed the leaflet into my hand about the Bible.'

'Can you remember anything that was written on the leaflet? Anything at all?'

She shook her head. 'Sorry, mister, I just slung it. I can do without the holy stuff.'

'OK, not to worry. And this other woman *might* have a look of Libby?'

'A bit of a look. That's the best I can do.'

'One last question. You girls, you probably talk among yourselves. Have any of you got any idea at all why a call girl like Tracey should be murdered at Fox Ridge? I don't want to frighten you, but do you think any of the men you all see could be a nutter on the loose?'

Her pale face went paler. 'There's always a chance, mister, we get really scared when we hear about some bloke cutting up a street girl or throttling her or whatever. But … well … the geezers that pick us up, they're mostly guys we see regular. But if they aren't and if they come across as a bit weird, well, there's no way we'll take them on. And if there *was* a nutter on the loose I reckon we'd have him sussed by now.'

'Many thanks, Myrtle.' He took out his wallet and began counting notes. 'I'll not take up any more of your time.'

'No problem, mister,' she said in a low voice, briefly touching his hand. 'It's been a great break for me, just being able to sit in a bloke's car and not have to do nothing except just have a chat.'

On these sad words, Crane started his car.

*

Polly drove steadily in third gear. Bradford was encircled by hills, virtually every road out of the city went upwards. Queensbury was the highest district of all. In fact you drove through an area called Mountain to reach it, but Queensbury wasn't their destination. They passed on to the Halifax Road with a deep valley to the right and to their left land, mainly open, that went on rising. Several isolated houses were dotted about on this terrain. Polly, naturally, had perfect vision and was the first to spot the house they were seeking. 'That's the one,' she said, 'I can just make out the sale board.'

She drove on to a narrow road that angled left from the main road and began a climb so steep she needed to engage second gear. The house had been built on land that briefly plateaued before continuing to rise again. It was a tall rather narrow building with white-painted stucco walls, a mansard roof and wide windows. It stood in lengthy gardens. 'Spectacular view,' Polly said, 'and when you've said that you've said everything. It must have cost a few bob to build and they'll be lucky to turn a profit when they sell, especially in today's market. Who'd want to live up here? The people we'll be dealing with will want houses near water and close to some decent shooting, like people right in the head. What *is* the matter, Janey?'

Jane couldn't stop the tears running down her cheeks. She was having a bad time. She felt she was reverting to being that shy timid girl she'd once been who'd never been able to stop longing to be in Polly's circle and yet had kept wondering if she'd be able to cope with the sort of life they led if by some miracle Polly had allowed her in. The frenetic rushing about, the clubs, the drinking, the sleeping around. She'd had to accept that even if you did get into Polly's circle you were still very much on trial, had to meet Polly's inflexible demands or were rapidly discarded.

She took out a tissue and dried her face. 'I'm sorry,' she said, in a thin mewing tone. 'I want to go home. I can't take any more. I want to go home and go in the garden. Please let's go home. Let's agree to give him half and go home. Please.'

'No, Janey, you're really not thinking this through. Whatever we gave him he'd throw it away on the tables and its money we really do need. It's only just enough to get this kind of business off the ground. Even a couple of mill doesn't go far in this day and age.'

'I can't go in there, I *can't* ...'

Polly pulled in to the side of the narrow road and glanced at her watch.

'Look, old girl, I'll tell you what we're going to do. On the way back we'll buy some decent champagne for our sundowners and get it nice and chilled while you're in the garden and I'm in my office and then we'll have something really special for dinner. And I'll ring Jeremy and get a fix on when the probate should be completed so we'll have something to focus on. And then we'll be *away*! The old house exactly as we want it, our first wealthy client raring to go. And Ralph says the man knows everyone in Yorkshire worth knowing, just like Mama. We'll be going from one client to another, you watch. And nothing really lost ... with you know who....'

Jane finished dabbing her eyes. It was always the same. Polly was such an incredible force, her confident drawl always driving you along. Champagne, a nice meal, a jolly time at the Mayfield. She just needed to get through the next hour.

'Look, Jane,' Polly said, in a gentle tone Jane had heard only rarely, 'I can't do this on my own. Not with him. You know I would if it were possible. This is the last loose end. Just fix your mind on our future. And what a future! We'll make the house perfect and we'll be together as long as ever you want to stay with me. I shall never remarry. I've tried it and found it a ghastly bore apart from the bonking. Well, I can just have the bonking now and it suits me fine. And *you* don't want to marry again, do you? We'll have the perfect set-up, working partners and the best of friends. So let's get this thing sorted, eh?'

Jane was silent for some time but eventually nodded. She opened the car door. 'You've got it all straight in your mind?' Polly asked.

Jane nodded again. She said, 'Do my eyes look swollen?'

'No. Slightly bloodshot, nothing more. You've got the flask?'

Jane went into the garden of the white house through a side gate. Then she walked up to the house along a drive that led to a garage. From there a path of crazy paving ran along the front of the house. The BMW was parked in front of the garage. Nervous, feeling nauseous, she rang the front door bell; the door was opened almost instantly. 'You're definitely alone?' he said.

Polly's car was screened off by the garden wall and if he'd gone to the gate to ensure Jane was alone Polly would have ducked out of sight. But he took her word. Glover held open the door for her and closed it without locking it, she was glad to see. He took her into a room whose windows overlooked the steeply falling land to the main road and the valley beyond. The room had a minimalist look. There was no fireplace or radiators. There were several modern armless chairs and a plasma screen television was fastened to one of the pale-blue painted walls, together with several abstract prints. A white-wood bookcase held books that looked as if never read and in front of the window was a narrow drop-leaf table with a single leaf opened out towards the room and a spindly upright chair on each side of this section.

'We'll sit here and talk this thing through,' Glover said, pointing at the table. 'We'll not be disturbed, the vendors are long gone. Bridging loan. They'll be lucky if they can sell this place before Christmas. The people who have looked at it are put off by the underfloor heating and say it looks as if it'll be cold in winter. Know what, they're dead right.'

Jane forced a sympathetic smile and sat down, Glover wore one of his expensive-looking lightweight suits, his blond hair was carefully cut and he smelt faintly of good after-shave, but both she and Polly knew he was near broke, the BMW of course being a company car. Jane knew little more about him. It was a very strange situation but most things had been strange since she'd met up with Polly after those long years in an unhappy marriage.

'I told that bitch I'd not deal with her direct under any circumstances, not after the other night. She's just not playing the game, we both know it. I told her I'd only deal with you and if we couldn't agree a deal I'd set things going that would put you both inside. I mean it.'

'I'm ... I'm sure we can sort something out, Ken,' she said quickly. 'Shall we talk about it over a drink?' She took out a small leather-covered flask from the pocket of her linen jacket. 'It's a single malt. You're fond of that, aren't you?'

'All right, just the one,' he said, giving an impression he was relieved the meeting might be going his way. 'I'll see if I can locate a couple of glasses.' He went off and returned with tumbler-type glasses that matched everything else in the house for modernity. She poured a good measure for Glover, a smaller one for herself.

'If we doubled the figure Polly offered to two hundred K?'

'We might as well go home now. That doesn't begin to—'

'Five hundred K?'

'If this is supposed to be a Dutch auction you start with the top bid first. And the top bid is a million and that's all I'll consider.' He swallowed a good half of the whisky with an irritable gesture.

'Look,' she said, 'Polly insisted I tried to negotiate on the off-chance you'd agree a lower figure. I knew you wouldn't. I told her so. I think both Polly and I want to see an end to it, even though she thinks she's done the bulk of the work. We've talked it all through. I know she's ready to accept we share it equally.'

'Good. You've used your head. I really could have done without all this hassle. Well done. When do you think that legal scrote is going to cough up the dibs?'

'Polly's going to give him a bell this afternoon to try and pin him down. We're anxious to get our business going.'

'Fine.' He finished the rest of his drink. 'A good drop of the hard stuff this. I'd have another if I wasn't showing folk round houses this afternoon.'

Jane, still feeling nauseous, her own drink untouched, didn't push him to risk another. One drink would be quite enough.

Crane normally ate lunch out but with Pam staying at his house he'd taken to coming home these past two or three days. She would prepare tuna or ham salads with crusty rolls and they'd eat them with a single glass of white wine. It made a pleasant break for Crane in his long day and he was enjoying her company for the short time they'd be together.

'Could I use you as a sounding board?' he said today, after they'd eaten and she was pouring the coffee.

She smiled. 'For what good it would do.'

'It could do a lot of good. You know the background, you were involved with Glover, and it was you talking about tracts and batty old women that gave me the lead.'

When he'd got home last night it had been so late that Pam had gone to bed. But it had been his bed she'd gone to and though a little drowsy she'd been keen to provide her usual affectionate embraces. So he began to tell her now about the photos of Polly and Jane he'd shown to Myrtle.

She looked puzzled. 'But why do you think Polly and Jane might have been the tract woman and Libby?'

'Just a hunch. We can connect Polly to the writing of tracts and this mysterious woman called Jane lives with Polly.'

'I really don't understand. Jane's a skilled gardener and she's going into business with Polly. How could a prostitute become Jane?'

'Libby was Tracey Sharp's friend. They were both keen to get off the game, not just Tracey. Maybe Libby had once been a good gardener, maybe she'd had some crisis in her life that had made her take to the streets. She was a bit aloof from the other girls according to Myrtle, and Tracey once told me Libby hadn't quite the looks or the confidence to be a call girl. She had a Catholic upbringing and that's why the tract woman stroke Polly could get her to leave the streets.'

'And ... become Jane?'

'It's the only construction I can put on it. These seem to be the facts: let's say Polly *is* the tract woman. She goes off with Libby and Libby seems to vanish but then we have Jane, who has a *look* of Libby, living with Polly at Ranelagh House.'

Pam drank some of her coffee, drew her mouth down at the corners. 'I really can't get any of that together, Frank. *Why* does Polly pose as a tract woman, why bring Libby back to Ranelagh House to become Jane? I just can't equate Jane with Libby. Jane is middle class. She speaks well and dresses well and she really is a good gardener. And where's any pay-off for Polly? Polly being Polly there has to be one.'

'She gets a gardener and can then offer the full package to her clients.'

'There must be half-a-dozen women with good gardening skills, and maybe even capital, who'd be keen to work with her.'

Crane sighed. 'I'm up to my old tricks, Pam, trying to make things fit the few facts I've got. You're right, why *would* Polly be doing these weird things and why is Jane altering her appearance and, most important of all, how does Polly gain?'

'I still think I've seen Jane somewhere,' Pam said musingly. 'And if she *was* Libby why not go on looking like Libby?'

'Maybe she wants to distance herself from Lumb Lane Libby. Who knows? I certainly don't. It still boils down to having been an insurance scam but though we all know it's a scam none of us knows *how* it's been a scam. I hate being unable to solve a case but I suspect Polly's expertise is going to make it insoluble.'

Pam was silent for a time, then said slowly, 'You've given a lot of time to keeping an eye on Polly and Jane, but it was Lydia who put you on to Polly by changing her will in Polly's favour. Perhaps if you did a little research into her background....'

'You could be right. It does after all all go back to Lydia.'

Glover got to his feet as if it was an effort and opened one of the windows. 'I need some air. I've come over very drowsy for some reason.'

The tension was making Jane feel ill. She had to clench her teeth to stop her lips trembling. 'It is ... it is pretty hot today,' she said. 'Perhaps it's getting to you.'

He almost staggered back to his chair. 'Can't understand it, I almost feel I could nod off. I'll be better in the car, it's got air-con.'

'That's ... right. You'll be fine in a cool atmosphere.'

'I might just have forty winks in the car, can't understand it.'

He yawned. He was so sleepy he didn't register the room door opening and hardly felt the first blow as the baseball bat struck his skull. After that he didn't feel any of the other blows.

Jane leapt from her chair and scurried off to find a place where she could be violently sick.

TWELVE

It was a big old house in Airedale that had been converted to offices. The firm was called Airedale Books Ltd. It fronted on the main road but backed on to open country with views over the River Aire itself. Crane parked his car in a small rear car-park.

A sign on the door read, 'Please ring and enter'. He did so and walked into a cramped reception area where a small desk stood unattended. The business was clearly run with minimal staff. A good minute later a girl in her late teens in jeans and T-shirt came out of a door near the desk. She looked flustered and gave an impression there was still a good deal of work to be done on her multi-tasking skills.

'Can I help you?'

'I have an appointment with Mr Robertshaw. The name's Frank Crane.'

'I'll tell him. Please take a seat.'

There was a visitor's chair but a pile of books rested on it. The girl fingered a small modern switchboard uneasily as if she might get an electric shock. She seemed unable to make it work and eventually drifted off again. After another delay a plump, middle-aged man burst into the reception area. He was red-faced and white-haired and looked harassed, as if his own multi-tasking put him under considerable pressure. 'Mr McShane?'

'Crane, sir. Frank Crane.'

'I knew she'd got it wrong. She gets most things wrong. Work experience! Perhaps one day they'll send me someone who can get names right, operate a foolproof switchboard and count. Do come through.'

He led Crane along a corridor off which people sat in small offices speaking on phones and operating VDUs, and into an airy but cluttered room which overlooked the rear view of fields, hills and the river.

'Sit down, Mr Crane. How can I help you? I'd offer you a coffee but by the time work experience has traced the coffee and the milk and mastered the art of boiling water it'll be lunchtime.'

Crane smiled. 'Not to worry, sir. And thanks for agreeing to see me when you're so busy. As I explained on the phone, I'm a private investigator working for the insurers who covered Mrs Glover's life. The amounts involved were considerable. The insurers aren't refusing to pay out, but with it being such a large sum they simply retained me to ensure there's no reason why they should hold up payment. The ... death *was* unusual and it was undecided whether it was an accident or suicide.'

'An odd business that. Lydia always gave me the impression she hardly touched alcohol.'

'Really?'

Mr Robertshaw watched him across a desk where no single inch of its surface wasn't covered with printers' proofs, typescripts and completed books with covers of laminated card. He ran a hand over his hair. 'This big insurance pay-out ... I'm surprised. Oddly enough a solicitor rang the other day who's sorting out Lydia's will. I was able to tell him there was a modest pension involved, payable to the spouse. But there was also a lump sum payable on death during employment of four times her salary, which in her case would be about a hundred thousand. I can't imagine why she thought she needed all the extra cover. There were no children and her husband had a good job.'

'What did Mrs Glover do here, sir?'

'She was a commissioning editor. We publish books with a strong local flavour, fiction and non-fiction. Lydia looked after the fiction side: romance, crime, general, the usual stuff. We have steady sales and a loyal readership. Lydia's instinct was for selecting novels she knew would work for us. She's very much missed. Gifted people like her whose ambitions are satisfied by working for a modest outfit like ours are not easy to find.'

Crane gave a sympathetic nod. 'What sort of person was she?'

'Quiet, unassuming, steady worker. She was always ready with a pleasant word and a smile and was well-liked. She had periods of depression when she could be a little withdrawn, but she always seemed to get over them and be her normal self. That was until she had some kind of a domestic crisis. And that was down to that beggar she was unlucky enough to have married.'

'Ken Glover?'

'Good-looking and did he know it. Our Mrs Peel, she had him sussed. She and her husband dine out a fair amount and she said they'd come across the beggar everywhere, wining and dining different women. But Mrs Peel said Lydia would never hear a word against him. Then there was the bust-up at home and Lydia seemed to retire into her shell. It didn't affect her work but she was never the same. She was off work for the best part of a month before her accident. I believe the sick note mentioned depression and stress.'

'You've no other details about the domestic crisis?'

'Our Mrs Peel may know. She's our office and personnel manager. People tell her things in confidence knowing they'll go no further.'

'Would it be possible to speak to Mrs Peel?'

'She's away at present, back the day after tomorrow. I'll ask her to give you a ring, if you like.'

'I'd appreciate that, Mr Robertshaw.' Crane got up. 'Well, thank you very much, sir, you've been very helpful.'

'I'll get Mrs Peel to contact you, I'll make a note of it now....'

On his drive back to Bradford Crane's car phone rang. It was hands-free so he could take the call. 'Frank, it's Terry here. Ken Glover's been murdered. House up Queensbury way. And before you ask, yes, it was in a house he was trying to sell and where the vendors were away.'

'Gordon *Bennett!*'

'I know you're a busy man, Frank, but could you find the time to call in?'

'Give me half an hour.'

When he was shown into Jones's office Ted Benson was also there. 'Sit yourself down, Frank,' Jones said. 'What in hell is going *on?*'

'This house—'

'Built into the hillside above Halifax Road. The owners have already moved but left it partly furnished. A Nicola Christie, friend of the wife, calls in once a week to check the place is OK. It's very isolated.'

'Like Fox Ridge.'

'The papers will be calling them the death houses,' Jones said gloomily. 'You watch.'

'The woman who found the body, she's clean?'

'We'll check her out,' Benson said, 'but she is. I reckon she's still hyperventilating.'

'Head smashed in like your Tracey Sharp,' Jones added. 'Well, with Glover out of the mowing it opens up a new can of worms, bumper size.'

'Any ideas, Frank?' Benson asked.

'Someone with a definite motive is Polly Manning. Glover warned her that if he didn't get half the insurance loot he'd blow the whistle on her to you lot.'

'Christ, I only wish he had done,' Jones growled, 'so we could have cleared up this sodding lot.'

Benson said, 'Do you think Tracey Sharp's killing and Glover's could be connected, Frank?'

'It's possible but I can't think how.'

'There are similarities. The type of blunt instrument used could have been the same in both cases. The forensics think it might have been our old friend, the baseball bat.'

'Too soon for a DNA reading, I suppose?'

'There'll be sod-all matching it on the database,' Jones said. 'Well, you know my feelings about the sodding database.'

'Will you do anything about Polly Manning?'

'What can we do? Everything we know about her and the scam has come from you and you've gathered the information by methods not allowed to us.'

He sat in a moody silence for a short time, then said, 'Apart from anything else we need to be very, very wary around Polly Manning. Remember Alan Parker? He's been retired some little time, but few people in the force had a better feel for this city and the people who really counted than Alan. I dropped in on him, asked him what he could tell me about the Mannings. Well, Polly's mother was born a toff, *her* father was in the House of Lords by birth and they can trace the line back six hundred years. She was an arrogant bitch. Thought she was making do when she married a wool baron just for the brass. So, you'd got brass and lineage and the old lass had top-drawer contacts and access to powerful legal brains. Polly herself was a handful, as you know, what you probably don't know is that she had several brushes with the law, two of them pretty serious and car-oriented, but somehow the Mannings always managed to get them swept under the carpet. Alan told me that in the end the

Mannings were considered almost to have divine rights, and what I'm saying, Frank, is that Polly isn't someone you tangle with without wearing your body armour.'

Crane nodded. 'I hear you, Terry. But the woman might be involved in Lydia's death or even in Glover's. What do you want me to do?'

'Keep her under obbo. Carry on doing what the insurance people hired you to do. It's us, the police, who'll have to go canny. You'll have to have gold-plated admissible evidence of Polly's wrongdoing before we can even begin to think of feeling her collar. And let's face it, all right she'll be getting the insurance money fraudulently, I fully accept that, but murder, well, I think that's got to be a non-starter. It's not really a woman's thing, except in domestics when they lose it. My gut reaction is that it was the husband or partner of one of the women Glover had had an affair with, who attacked him in a jealous rage.'

'I tend to agree,' Benson said. 'It's happened before and Glover did a lot of womanizing. I reckon there's a good chance that sooner or later some woman will come forward because she suspects her husband or partner has done it and she can't live with it.'

'Hello, Frank. Any news?'

'Prepare yourself for a shock. Ken Glover's been murdered.'

'*No!*' She paled and stood very still, hands shaking on the plates she was laying on the table.

'It was in another of his houses for sale.'

She flopped on to a dining chair as if her legs had given way. He told her what he'd heard from Jones and Benson.

'What ... what can it *mean*, Frank?' Her voice was almost a whisper with shock.

'I don't know. I really don't know. Obviously Polly had everything to gain by the death, but Jones tends to think that's coincidence. He and Benson think it was the husband or partner of a woman he'd had an affair with. If I was back in the force I daresay it would be the line I'd take myself.'

She began to shake her head, then still speaking in a low voice said, 'I really can't buy that. He was always very, very careful about making sure there were no other men in the background. I think he must once have had an ugly scene with the partner of one of his women. He would only tell me which house to meet him in at short notice. He'd make a joke about it. "I don't want any of your old boyfriends or even your ex-husband coming after me with a flick-knife", he'd say. It was only later I realized that behind the jokiness he was almost paranoid about covering his tracks.'

He nodded. 'Men who play the field tend to pay great attention to that kind of detail.'

'Oh, *Frank*! It's only a fortnight since I imagined myself in love with him. I really was thinking in terms of marriage one day. If you'd not come into my life I'd *still* be thinking that way. I'd not have known about his violent streak or his gambling and ... and the other women. This murder, it's been such a frightful shock, but think of the even more frightful shock it would have been had I really known nothing of his true background. And he gave me such an illusion of happiness for a while. He was funny and attentive and seemed so kind. It's so upsetting to think of him dead in one of his empty houses. It's too ghastly and dreadful however bad a type he was.'

Crane put a hand over hers. 'Glib charmers like Glover *can* bring a lot of happiness to vulnerable women,' he said gently, 'for a time.'

'It's good of you to see me, Mrs Peel.'

'I was very fond of Lydia and very much saddened when she died.'

'Mr Robertshaw explained about my working for the insurers?'

'It does seem very odd, I must say, that she took out so much insurance on her life, especially when she seemed more than adequately covered through the firm's scheme.'

They were sitting in the comfortably furnished front room of a spacious terraced house overlooking Bradford Road. Mrs Peel had insisted on him having a cup of tea and she now poured from an elegant silver pot. She was a woman of middle age and spare, dressed in a white blouse and dark skirt. She had plain features and dark wavy hair arranged in a rather rigid style. Her thin lips added to a slightly forbidding impression and Crane could see her being very much in control of the administration at Airedale Books. He guessed she would be respected rather than liked, but probably admired for her efficiency and dedication. He felt sure Mr Robertshaw would now be sitting at a clear desk and that 'work experience' would either be showing genuine promise or be out through the door.

'Lydia was a very hard worker,' Mrs Peel said, handing him the cup of tea. 'It's been a nightmare trying to replace her. There's only one in a hundred who has a genuine flair for being able to spot a viable manuscript. Lydia could get through a tremendous number in a day of the many offerings that bombard our business. I doubt we publish more than one per cent of the unsolicited manuscripts we receive so you can see the size of the task.'

'Mr Robertshaw said she was subject to depression.'

'It wasn't surprising. Did he say why?'

'Her marriage wasn't too happy and he believed there'd been a domestic crisis that changed her in some way.'

'Lydia told me a lot in confidence. She'd talk to me because she knew I thought a lot about her and genuinely cared. Her father died in his sixties and her mother began to develop dementia. They'd been a close family and it upset Lydia very badly. Quite apart from that, as if that weren't enough, she had that dreadful Ken to contend with.'

'He made her unhappy?'

She sipped her tea, watching him in silence for a short time. Bradford Road was a busy highway and the soft hum of traffic noise was endless to Crane's ears. He supposed it was the sort of noise you never consciously heard when you lived with it permanently, like the circulating of refrigerant or the firing of a central heating boiler.

'Lydia adored that man, Mr Crane. I knew perfectly well he cheated on her and I'm certain she knew herself. I got the impression she always forgave him simply because she couldn't live without him. Her depressions always coincided with his affairs. They'd clear up when he'd finished with his latest girlfriend and she'd be quite happy and cheerful for a few weeks.'

She hesitated for a few seconds. 'And then one day she came in the office in a terrible state. A black eye, bleeding gums, swollen face. She'd not let anyone see her but me. She had her own little office and I kept everyone at arm's length including Charles, that's Mr Robertshaw. I was horrified. At first she said she'd had a bad fall in the shower, but then she broke down in tears and it all came out. After his last affair Ken had sworn he'd never have another. He did, of course, within a month. For Lydia it was the last straw. They'd had this dreadful row and he'd ended up knocking her about. I finally calmed her down and got her to stay with me a few days to get over it. She'd only come in the office that day because she couldn't stand being at home. And then she said, "I'd like to kill him, Kath. I wish the swine were dead".'

She watched him for a few seconds in another silence. 'It gave me such a shock. You see, she didn't blurt it out hysterically, which would have been understandable and not have meant too much. She said it when she'd collected herself. She said it very quietly and with intense loathing.

'Well, after that, as Charles said, she changed almost out of recognition. She worked just as hard, but kept everything locked in, if you know what I mean. I really wasn't too surprised when she had her ... accident. I wanted to contact the police and tell them about the frightful beating he'd given her. He deserved to be punished for driving her to do what she did. My husband talked me out of it. He said it wouldn't make any difference to anything, now Lydia was dead. But he should have been punished, Mr Crane, for making that poor woman's life such a wretched affair.'

'You won't know this, Mrs Peel, as it's not got into the evening paper yet, but it seems someone else wanted Ken Glover dead as much as Lydia did. He was found murdered yesterday in one of the houses he was selling.'

'You'll have to buck up, Janey. No one can connect us to it. We weren't seen coming or going. It had to be done. We *must* have the full amount and he was just enough of an idiot to have caused us trouble with the police, even if it meant it would do him no good.'

Jane sipped a little of her wine. Normally it dispersed the shadows or at least pushed them into the background; tonight they seemed immovable. It had been because of having to *be* there. It had been a first for her. Polly was right, he could have made such a lot of trouble for them. He was cunning. It wasn't that she was worried about being connected to the house. Polly had thought it out very carefully. They'd not gone in Polly's car. That had been left conspic-uously on the drive of Ranelagh House and they'd crept out through the back garden and on to a footpath that bypassed the estate houses and connected diagonally to the main road. There, in sun hats and dark glasses they'd taken a bus to Bradford, where Polly had hired a car for the day. It would seem to the people on the estate that the pair of them had been in and around the house all day, as they usually were. They would never be linked to the white house beyond Queensbury, but if somehow either of them ever was they could say they'd been at home. 'We're each other's alibi,' as Polly had said confidently. Polly could think it all out, without a flicker of nerves.

No, she knew they'd not be caught. Jane had been anxious about DNA traces, but Polly had pointed out that the police had to have DNA specimens on the database to compare any traces *with*. And the only details on the database were to do with people who already had some kind of police record. 'And we haven't,' Polly said cheerfully. 'So all we need to do is behave ourselves like about ninety-nine per cent of the population.'

But Jane was in a state. She couldn't shake herself out of it. It would go in the end with Polly always being so relentlessly positive and jollying her along and making her remember how much she'd always longed to be a Polly person. If only it hadn't been so *big*, the offering she'd had to make to be allowed a place at Polly's table. Polly was left completely unaffected by the dark things that had had to be done. She had sorted them out with her usual calm expertise while assuring Jane that they really didn't matter. It had somehow been possible for Jane to put them in a part of her mind that she could then seal off, especially when it was time for sundowners and the loud triumphal music and their animated discussion about the future, and their stroll to the Mayfield to see the chaps. But having to *do* something like that, having to *be* there, having to pour him the doctored Scotch, having to see his head smashed ... oh God, oh God, oh *God* ...

'I really shan't be able to work with a partner who mopes, Janey,' Polly said, pouring more wine. 'We'll be selling a service to *le gratin*, and that's the toughest market there is, so we have to be positive, positive, positive. And if you can't be positive I may have to look for someone who can.'

'Oh, *Polly* ... without me it wouldn't—'

'I *know*. But I've got big ambitions riding on this venture. I need to rescue the family name from the oblivion it's beginning to sink into. It's essential to have a partner who's pulling her weight.'

Jane was seized by an attack of panic that drove off depression. If Polly dropped her! Took on someone else! What would she do then? Where would she live, how could she work, how would it be possible to cope without the sundowners, the evenings at the Mayfield, the parties back here, the sex sessions with the chaps?

How would she get through life without the thought of their golden future? Being without Polly, whom she'd adored from being a teenager, would be like living without sunlight.

'Oh Polly!' she cried. 'Please don't talk like that. I can't bear it.'

'You've had a long face ever since we sorted out the Ken problem, and we both knew how dangerous he could be.'

'I'm sorry, I'm sorry. I've been looking forward so much to making a start on the grounds of the Ripon house. You know I'll do a good job.'

'Yes, but you must be enthusiastic. The man knows we'll be a new outfit and he'll be looking for a hundred per cent dedication. There'll be no challenge we can't rise to, inside or outside the house and we'll have to convince him of that. But one look at your long face—'

'Oh *please*, Polly. It was just that frightful … *business* …'

Polly gave her a faint smile and said in a slightly gentler tone, 'I know, I know. I've kept you away from the sharp end. But Glover wouldn't have dealt with me directly, you know that.'

'I'll be all right,' Jane said hurriedly. 'I'm almost over it.'

'Very well. But when we get to the Mayfield I'll expect you to be back to your usual form.'

'I will be, I will be.' Jane drank off her wine, forced a wide smile and poured herself some more from the near-empty bottle.

'That's more like it,' Polly said briskly. 'Now keep smiling….'

But when Jane was putting the finishing touches to their dinner in the gloomy old kitchen, soon to be transformed, she let her features slide back into the dull-eyed expression that reflected her state of mind. She knew she'd have to snap out of it. She knew Polly only too well. Polly was the most exciting person she'd ever known to be around, but Polly made all the rules and wouldn't hesitate to drop her if she decided she wasn't showing the right spirit, didn't give a constant impression she was brimming with enthusiasm. It wouldn't matter to Polly how unfair it was that none of it would have worked without Jane's input. And Ken's. And where was Ken now?

Jane felt as if her mind was splitting in two. Her future had never seemed brighter, life had never been such fun, and yet the shadows had never gathered so strongly before. When they'd planned it, with plenty of drink always on hand of course, Polly's positive attitude had rapidly rubbed off on to her. The things that would need to be done had somehow been almost airbrushed away, as if there really wasn't much harm involved. 'Better out of it,' Polly would firmly assert, and that would seem to be an end of it. And Polly had insisted that she'd be doing the bulk of what needed to be done and had been as good as her word. Except for that last bit.

Jane tossed the salad in French dressing, checked that the new potatoes were simmering, the pork steaks grilling nicely. Polly tended to regard cooking as a book she was quite happy to keep closed but liked to eat well. 'To give the alcohol a good base,' she would say, and never seemed to put on an ounce of weight. Jane too liked her food but had little appetite for it this evening. Yet she'd have to eat with every appearance of satisfaction. It was going to be a long night and she wished it were over and she could go to bed. Take refuge in a sleeping tablet. Last night she'd dreamt she was back at Bradford Girls', sitting quietly at her desk while Polly addressed Miss Yewdall in flawless French, French that she spoke with considerably more expertise than Miss Yewdall herself, who'd actually graduated in French and German.

It had seemed like a golden age. Idolizing Polly and yearning to be in her exclusive group and yet getting a perverse sense of relief from not being one of the chosen few and having to pay the steep price that went with it. As she was doing now.

'Yes, Ralph, we got on extremely well. He likes the designs, bore copies off to study them with his wife. His cousin's Lord Plover's son, did you know? Mama knew the father very well. He was keen to marry her at one stage. I think she wishes she had done now. She'd be living in a dower house now instead of a detached in Nab Wood.'

Polly's tone indicated that there was little to choose between a detached in Nab Wood and an African mud hut. Ralph said, 'Let me know when the designs are approved. Poll, and I'll get going on the detailed plans.'

'Jolly good. And thank you so much for the intro. I find he's worth a hundred million according to *The Sunday Times* rich list and they doubt he'll have dropped more than five million in the recession. A very valuable contact.'

'By the way, I've completed the detailed work for your Ranelagh House designs.'

'Splendid! I've drawn up a tentative team-list of the people I want to do the work. Perhaps you'd cast an eye over it?'

'Any time to suit you, my dear.'

Ralph was going pink. Crane guessed it was due to the intoxicating scenes that were filling his mind of the rewards he was in line for. He was a man of middle age and putting on weight in the wrong places and Crane wondered if he was being entirely wise in subjecting his heart to the matchless delights of Polly's buttocks. They would be gyrating so gratefully, due to the hours of free work Ralph had put in, as to be almost a blur.

Crane stood once more among the group of men who encircled Polly and Jane. As usual the women were the focus of all eyes. The hotel owner beamed on them for making the bar lounge so popular. The men who stood or sat in other parts of the room looked on with the usual envy of Polly and her people, wondering sadly if they'd ever seen any other woman who looked as stunning as she.

Crane, putting on his usual chatty, smiling act, had to admit that he himself had never known anyone like her. She'd surely been born out of her proper period. She should have been born one of the renowned courtesans, a driven schemer in the palace of a powerful monarch, always ready with her expert sexual favours, her quick tongue, her gem-like mind. She'd have slept with every courtier who could be useful in bringing her to the attention of the king himself. Once in the king's bed she'd never have made the mistake of sleeping with anyone else, especially for the idea of anything as absurd as romantic love. She'd have borne the king bastard children, who she'd have ensured were granted titles, land and modest palaces of their own. She could then forge her own noble dynasty and provide comfortably for her middle and old age. Because one day, of course, the king, with many a nostalgic backward glance, would move on, graciously to bestow bed space to another skilled and wily piece of medieval totty.

Yes, she should have been a courtesan. She was enticing, astute and manipulative. And she'd have been quite up to the task of organizing the efficient demise of any courtier who'd begun to be troublesome. She might have done that without a second's thought then but how about now, in the twenty-first century? Pam had been certain Glover wouldn't have been murdered by the jealous partner of one of the many women he'd had affairs with. So who did it leave?

Not too many by the look of it. And only one who stood to gain a great deal of money if Glover stopped breathing.

But could Polly really be a killer? And if so, where did Jane fit in? Surely Jane couldn't have involved herself in anything like that. She had none of Polly's hard edges. She was a giver not a taker, eager to please. Possibly one of the reasons Polly had taken her in was because Jane could be left to do life's boring jobs: housework, cooking, sending for repair men. He studied her round face again: the glasses, the expensive wig. Could she *possibly* be the prostitute called Libby? And if she wasn't, just who was she? And what had she brought to Polly beyond her housekeeping qualities and gardening skills? Surely Polly must have wanted more than that, she always appeared to have done.

It seemed to him that Jane wasn't quite her usual self tonight. She wore her eager smile and laughed gaily at the jokes and anecdotes that went on almost non-stop, but to his practised eye she gave out a slight impression of strain. While Polly seemed almost to vibrate with the usual high spirits, chattiness and laughter, Jane seemed to be forcing herself to be exactly the same, though he was certain no one else would pick up on that slight but definite difference. There were times too when her face was briefly still that her eyes seemed to give an almost subliminal impression of unhappiness.

Yet what could she be unhappy about? She lived a very pleasant life and was almost certainly assured of a pleasant future. Many other women would stand in line to have the life she led. If Jane really was Libby shouldn't she be giving the impression that she couldn't believe her good fortune?

'Can I get you a drink, Jane, your glass is almost empty?'

'Oh no, Jim, no thanks. I'm fine, really I am.' She put a hand over her glass to emphasize the point, then gave him an oddly endearing little smile that didn't seem to be put on. For a part of a second there looked to be a vulnerability in her expression that appeared to confirm the sadness he felt he'd picked up on earlier. 'We've not seen you since our party,' she said with a brightness that didn't ring quite true. 'Did you have a nice day at the coast?'

'Perfect weather. I'm sorry we had to leave the party early, we were really enjoying it. I daresay it went on a lot longer.'

'Oh, ages. We weren't in bed till the early hours.'

'Did you manage to make it to morning mass?' he said casually with a smile.

'Morning mass?' She gave him a blank look.

'Sorry, Jane, I thought I'd heard one of the chaps say you went to St Mary's. I obviously got it wrong.'

'Not me. I was in bed very late. I'm a girl who needs her sleep. And I'm not a religious type.'

'I got my wires crossed.'

'Your partner's nice, isn't she? Where did you meet her?'

'Oh, she was just wanting some financial advice and someone put us in touch. We just got on,' Crane said carefully.

'Need any help in the garden, Jane? I've got a free afternoon tomorrow,' a man behind her said hopefully. It was the man she'd rewarded in the usual way not long ago for work he'd helped her with earlier.

As she turned away with the bright smile that seemed just a little bit forced, Polly put a hand on his arm. 'Jim, I've managed to prise a date out of the solicitor for when my legacy should be coming through.' She sipped her gin and Dubonnet. 'Now, do you think you could have some sort of investment plan in place for three weeks from today? I'd like it earning interest, dividends and so forth from day one.'

'No problem, Polly. I'll draw something up this weekend and you can cast an eye over it.'

'Good man! Do give me your phone number.'

He gave her his mobile number and made a note of hers. He had to know if it was Polly on the line so that he'd know to call himself Jim Parry and not Frank Crane.

'I'd better have your home and office numbers too. Give me one of your business cards.'

'I'm out of cards, just waiting for a new lot to be printed. I don't work from an office and I'm away from home an awful lot.'

'Where is your house, by the way?'

'Over in Heaton, off Toller Lane.'

'Such a long way to come for a drink. How do you manage with driving?'

'Very, very carefully,' he said, grinning. 'I try not to drink *too* much and, well, take a chance, I suppose.'

She broke into gleeful laughter. 'Tell me about it! The crazy risks I took in my early twenties. A wonder I wasn't locked up.'

Crane joined in the laughter. According to Jones she might have been locked up but for some inspired string-pulling by her family.

'Do you not think your attractive partner feels a little neglected?'

'I like the company here and Pam doesn't mind, she prefers the telly during the week. Can I get you a top-up?'

'Thank you. You'll be coming back to the house later?'

'I'd love to.'

'The pleasure will be all mine, Jim.'

Crane moved to the bar. The slight lowering of eyelids, the moistening of the lips, the forward angle of the upper body, no signal had been neglected to let him know that he could be in line for an advance payment in Polly's softly lit bedroom for the work he'd be doing on her finances. He had to admit to himself that he really wouldn't have minded a glimpse of the ingenious Brazilian she'd have in place to add to the many other excitements guaranteed to increase an exquisite if dangerous fluttering sensation to Ralph's ageing heart. But he was slightly uneasy. He paid for the drinks and stood for a moment thinking about the string of questions she'd asked. She'd spoken as casually as he did when he was trying to obtain information but not arouse suspicion.

He wondered if he was being over-sensitive. There was really no reason why she shouldn't want to be able to contact him easily, and wanting to know where he lived could simply be idle curiosity. Or, being Polly, she might want to know the location and approximate value of his house to be able to decide just how successful he really was. Maybe he was just being too watchful. He was, after all, a PI.

Pam turned off the television. 'A G and T?'

'I really am ready for one after drinking pretend ones all evening.'

Under Pam's regime the gin and mixers were no longer left in the kitchen, which had been Crane's rough and ready way, but now stood on a tray on the sideboard.

'How did things go?' she said, handing him the glass.

He shrugged, gave a crooked grin, stretched out in an armchair.

'Nowhere. I had a chat with Jane, trying to get a fix on her background. I asked her if she'd managed to get to morning mass with the party finishing so late. I knew Libby had been raised a Catholic and I wondered if I could get an instinctive reaction from Jane, assuming she really was Libby.'

'And did you?'

'Not a flicker. I guess you're right, she can't be Libby. So why did Polly go off with Libby, if Polly was the tract woman?'

'I wish you'd call it a day on the case, Frank.'

He looked at her. She'd spoken quietly and very seriously. He said, 'I wasn't aiming to stay with it beyond the weekend. I've made no impact on it whatsoever and I've never come up against anyone as able as Polly. I think we can safely say she's won.'

'I wish you'd let it go right now. Before … before there's another dreadful killing.'

'What makes you think there'll be another?'

'I've had no distractions while I've been in your house. No deadlines to meet and feeling quite safe.' She sipped a little of her drink. 'I've had time to think it all over, the insurance business and all the trouble it seems to have caused: Lydia dying, your friend Tracey at Fox Ridge, then Ken.'

'Everything's circumstantial, Pam,' he said slowly, 'and it's possible none of those deaths is connected.'

'I can't explain it,' she said, 'and maybe I've had too much time to brood. I just keep having these awful feelings of foreboding. Apart from Polly, the only person who's central to all this peculiar frightening business is you. I've only known you for such a short time and yet I now see you as one of my closest friends. I couldn't bear for anything to happen to you, Frank. The shock was bad enough when … when Ken went and by then he meant nothing to me.'

'I'm very touched,' he said, 'I really am. But you know I was trained as a CID officer. I learnt then never to put myself at risk if I could avoid it. And really, I can't believe Polly sees me as any kind of threat,' He gave a thin smile. 'And I'm not standing between her and a colossal pay-out.'

Pam continued to look troubled. 'Just be very careful. I know it sounds silly, as if I'm frightened of shadows, but I simply can't throw off these scary feelings. Can I stay here till you call an end to it, the Lydia case?'

'You know you don't need to ask. Stay here as long as you like. I'll be having withdrawal symptoms anyway when I start getting home in an evening and have to see to my own G and T.'

Later, when they lay relaxed and drowsy in his bed, she murmured, 'Is Polly still coming on to you?'

'I must be the only man in her entire life who's not really wanted to know.'

'Are you not tempted?'

'What heterosexual male wouldn't be? But, call me old-fashioned,

I do need to like a woman before I can sleep with her. I don't like Polly but I can't help admiring her.'

'You will be very careful, Frank, won't you? Humour me.'

'He's evasive. It's the only word that fits.'

'Jim?'

'Impossible to pin down. Couldn't get a business card out of him, says he doesn't have an office. And in the Mayfield every night while the Pam woman is left watching the television. What woman of her age and looks wants to sit watching the box on a summer evening when all the action is at places like the Mayfield? Says he lives in Heaton, refers non-specifically to somewhere off Toller Lane. And still not the remotest interest in feasting his eyes on the minor work of art Jemima's made of my bush.'

Jane wondered if it was that that was really getting to her, that Jim was proving to be immune to her formidable charms. Her drawl had taken on a slightly nettled edge. She said, 'I suppose he can be a little odd. He asked me if I'd missed mass on the morning after the party.'

'He thought you were a Catholic?'

'He did say he had me confused with someone else.'

'Did he now.' Polly became thoughtfully silent for a time, then said, 'The more I think about it the more he seems not to fit in with the rest of the chaps.'

'Oh, I don't know. To me, he seems just the same as them. Buys us drinks, joins in the fun, ready to help with the investments. All right, maybe he doesn't come on to you but he does have an attractive girlfriend.'

'The chaps do things for us, Janey, because we do things for them. They are all pretty wealthy but they do like a spot of trouble-free bonking. Jim seems not to be short of a few bob but is quite willing to work for us for no return at all. Men don't *do* things for nothing, so what is Jim after that doesn't come naked on a duvet, legs akimbo?'

'I'm sure it's just the sort of man he is. He strikes me as a really nice bloke. I think he just likes being with our lot and if Pam is happy enough at home....'

But Polly was again silently lost in thought. 'I get odd vibes about Jim,' she said at last. 'I'm not sure why, I just do.'

The depression Jane had fought so hard to ward off earlier

threatened to take hold of her again. Polly in a pensive mood always made her uneasy. It usually seemed to mean there were complications ahead. She felt she couldn't cope with any more, there'd already been too many hitches to that original simple plan. And yet Polly had such a remarkable instinct for anything even slightly off-key. But what could be off-key about Jim? Jane was beginning to find herself very attracted to him. He was so tall and strong-looking, gave such an impression of being goodhearted and reliable.

'Oh, well, let's forget it,' Polly said, finishing her drink. 'Let's just say he's different.'

Jane gave a sigh of relief. 'Perhaps you're being just a tiny bit paranoid, Poll.'

'You're probably right, old girl. This hasn't been an easy time.'

'I'm sure with Jim what you see is what you get.'

'I must say I was rather looking forward to trying him on for size.'

Polly was back to her usual ebullient form, Jane was glad to see. It was so unusual to see her quite so still with her eyes unfocused, normally she was so animated and chatty whatever time of day it was. Then Jane began to wonder if Polly was now playing down the uneasy thoughts she'd been having about Jim because she knew how difficult Jane found it to cope with any change to the ordered pattern of their days. She knew she was getting to be a bundle of neuroses but she couldn't bear the thought of being marginalized. Not up to helping Polly with some of the things that had to be done. And yet surely everything that had had to be done had now been done. And how could Jim possibly be any kind of a threat? He hardly knew them or they him. Yet she felt she had to stress to Polly her willingness to share everything. She couldn't get out of her mind Polly's threat that if she didn't pull her weight she might have to be replaced.

'Polly, if there's ever anything you want me to help you with I promise I'll always do my bit. I shan't expect to leave everything to you, not any more. It wouldn't be fair.'

Polly said, 'Everything's plain sailing now, Janey, as far as I can see. All the little problems sorted out. There's just one small thing I'd like you to help with....'

'Of course. Anything at all.'

'I'd like a trench in the back garden, up near the trees.'

'A ... a trench?' Jane said, mystified.

'If we do it together it shouldn't take too long. It's to bury certain things it really isn't a good idea to have in the house. Just in case. It would tidy up a lot of the loose ends.'

'Oh, very well. We can do it in the morning if you like.'

'Jolly good.'

Jane didn't ask what was to be buried in the trench, but she had a good idea. She gave a little shudder. Anything that could connect them to anything, if anyone ever became suspicious. Not that they ever would.

'I'll want you to use all your skill when we fill in the trench. The ground will have to look as if it's never been disturbed,' Polly said.

'It'll take a little time and very careful levelling and a covering of moorland turf that'll blend in.'

'You're the expert.'

THIRTEEN

'Anything, Frank?'

'Nothing at all. Anything your side?'

Jones shook his head, drank a little of his Scotch. 'Ted's trying to track down any of the women Glover knocked about with but it's uphill work. The one or two he did pin down were well separated from their exes, like Mrs Draper.'

Crane said, 'Well, I've kept tabs on Polly and her mate, but all I still only know is that they were in an insurance scam with Glover. I'll pack it in at the weekend. I can't keep on invoicing fees for sod-all results.'

'Something might turn up.' Jones's tone lacked conviction.

'If something doesn't turn up soon the loot will be in Polly's bank account.'

Jones shrugged his heavy shoulders. 'If we can prove fraud, at whatever stage, we'll be able to freeze her assets.'

'By the time you get round to doing that, Terry, with someone like her, the money would be long gone.'

'You don't still think Glover's down to her?'

'Glover might have fixed Lydia's death and he might for some inexplicable reason have fixed Tracey's, but I can't see him fixing his own.'

'They *are* calling them the death houses,' Jones said gloomily, 'in the papers, the places where Tracey and Glover were topped. Weren't those my very words? You'd better watch yourself, going to Polly's place for nightcaps, Glover sold that one too.'

'Really? I didn't know that. That's obviously how he came to meet her. Even so, if Polly *was* involved in Glover's death the one thing she'll be very careful about is not having any bodies in her own drawing-room.'

Jones said, 'Even so, it's unthinkable, Frank, you must agree, that the daughter of what used to be one of the most powerful families in town should be involved in a killing. A con artist, all right, I can buy that; I can quite see her being brassed off when the old man ran out of folding, but a *killing* ...'

He finished his whisky and got up. 'I've got to be off. Win some, lose some, eh, Frank? I'll be seeing you.'

For the next two days Crane never had the Lydia Glover case out of his mind. He worked on the easier routine jobs he could select from his always heavy workload so that he had no real distraction from the almost total concentration he gave it. Something that Terry Jones had said had triggered this response. He'd said it was unthinkable that a Manning daughter could have been involved in a murder.

It was that word 'unthinkable'. It reminded him of the words Tony Blair was said to have used when encouraging Frank Field to dream up daring policies for the reform of the welfare system: think the unthinkable. This was what Crane now began to do, as none of the credible thinking had got him anywhere. He drove up to the golf-club car-park, left his motor there and began to walk over the ground beyond the car-park that led to the edge of the gully into which Lydia's car had crashed. He even made his way down the rough footpath that led to the bottom, where the brook ran.

He found that the ground between the car-park and the gully was very uneven. Driving a small saloon car over it wouldn't be easy, not, he'd have thought, by a woman spaced on alcohol and tranquillizers. He got back into his car and sat for a long time, going over yet again every aspect of the case since he'd taken it on: Glover and his alibis, both for Lydia's death and Tracey's. Tracey herself, who'd hired him to find Libby. Libby who'd left her spot on Lumb Lane to go off with the tract woman, and the tract woman who'd almost certainly been Polly. The murders in houses being sold by Glover. And finally, the two women who now lived together at Ranelagh House, with Crane at one time thinking Jane might *be* Libby as there'd been a resemblance. And £2 million very soon to hit Polly's account.

He sat in his car for the best part of an hour, thinking the unthinkable. And if you thought the unthinkable answers did slowly begin to emerge. The more he thought the unthinkable the more the pieces seemed to fall into place. And it seemed to be the only way they *would* fall into place. He took out his mobile, dialled the central police station and asked to speak to DI Jones. 'Terry, just a quick word. When your people examined the wreckage of Lydia Glover's car did they not consider that the uneven terrain between the golf-club car-park and Royds Cliff Gully would have been very difficult to drive a car over in Lydia's condition?'

Jones was silent for a few seconds. 'They probably did but I suppose there was no way of them knowing just how badly she was affected by what she'd taken. As you know, everyone reacts differently to the sort of cocktail she'd had. Motivation counts for a lot; she might have been so hell-bent on doing herself in that that determination would have seen her getting the car into the gully.'

'Let's speculate that what she'd taken had spaced her so badly she'd have had great difficulty keeping her feet on the pedals on that bumpy ground. I'm assuming the car wasn't an automatic.'

'No, it wasn't an auto. What's your point, Frank?'

'Maybe someone *else* was driving the car.'

'There's an easy answer to that. The car would have had to be driven very fast to get it *into* the gully. If there *had* been someone else driving it they'd have gone over with her.'

'What if the driver had been a daredevil type who was very energetic, could drive the car fast and could jump out of it with exact timing when it was a yard or so from the edge?'

'Why does this remind me of a James Dean film from the fifties?'

'Because villains sometimes *get* their ideas from film, as we both know.'

'Well, it couldn't have been Glover and there's been no other bloke across the radar.'

'I wasn't thinking in terms of a bloke.'

'Christ, we're not back to Polly Manning!'

'Polly is like no woman you've ever known, believe it. She's got enough brains and energy to share out among three. She'd consider strict training to pull a stunt like that would be to lay off booze for a couple of hours.'

'But she's a *woman*, Frank. These people who nick cars and tear-arse along the M62 with two pandas on their tail and stingers being laid, it's *never* a woman. Never has been.'

When he handed the drinks he'd bought to Polly and Jane, Polly said, 'I know we talked of discussing the investment plan at the weekend, Jim, but could we bring it forward to tomorrow night? Jane and I want to keep the weekend clear, we'll probably be spending most of it with our Ripon client.'

'Oh, I can quite easily fit in with you. I'll put something together in the morning.'

'Good man. If we could meet here tomorrow night as usual and then just the three of us go back to the house.'

'I'll be here.'

'It really is very good of you, Jim.'

She put a hand on his arm and Crane could almost sense the envy of the others. It was to be Jim's turn, lucky devil, the soft lights, the elegantly sculpted bush, the choice from a sensual menu adapted to suit all tastes, the only stipulation being that it had to be jolly good *fun*.

Later, sitting at home with Pam over the G and Ts, he said, 'Polly wants me to go back to the house tomorrow night to discuss her finances. It'll just be the three of us. Of course the others are all assuming I'll be in for the bonk of a lifetime.'

She smiled uneasily. 'Is that a good idea, Frank?'

'Oh, I know enough to get something down on paper. I reckon I can match the average FA but I'll not be charging three or four per cent.'

'No, no, I'm sure you'll be very convincing, it's just … it's just that I've begun to get very nervy when you're with those two. Well, you know about my hang-ups.'

'Pam, I'm coming off the case this weekend. End of. It just seemed that this is a chance I can't miss out on, the last throw of the dice, if you like. If I could just pick up on anything, anything at all, that would help to bear out a theory I've been kicking around in my head most of today.'

'Do you want to talk about it?'

He gave a crooked grin. 'Not really. I tried it on the dog, that is Terry Jones, and I was blown out of the water inside three minutes.'

'You can rely on me for a kinder reaction.'

'You know me and my theories. This one ticks all the boxes but it does take some swallowing. And even if there was anything in it at all I don't know that I could do anything about it. There's no real line the police could take and they tend to pussyfoot around anyone called Manning anyway.'

'If you're not keen to talk about it I understand. But I'm guessing Polly *is* the leading light in your new theory?'

'Only Polly could have worked it out and had the persuasive powers.'

If she was being honest with herself, Pam knew that she didn't really want to hear any more about the Lydia Glover case. She was just glad, very glad that he'd be out of it at the weekend. She was still trying to get those creepy murders off her mind. She couldn't repress a shudder even now when she thought of Ken lying dead, the man who'd been her lover such a short time ago.

She said, 'Frank, you've mentioned about being in the CID: why did you leave the police?'

He watched her in silence for a time. He'd once found it almost too painful to think about, let alone discuss, but time had helped heal the wounds if not quite clear up the scar tissue. 'I was dismissed,' he told her. 'I fixed some evidence and it was spotted. It was the one and only time I ever did anything like that and there was simply no other way of nailing the man. We're talking Bradford's criminal number one. I acted with a colleague, but I kept his name out of it; he had kids and a sick wife and I was single. No one in the force held it against me even though I had to be got rid of. Terry Jones did everything in his power to help me set up as a private man. I'll always owe him and that's why I help him whenever I can.'

'Oh, Frank, I'm so sorry. It must have been such a blow. I'm sure you'd have gone far.'

'I'll not play the modesty card. I was being fast-tracked. I don't know who was the most disappointed when I got the welly, me or Terry. He'd kept an eye on me from day one.'

'Because of your dedication? I don't know any other PIs, but I can't think there are many who put in the hours you do.'

'I regarded the force as a genuine vocation. The best of us do, men like Terry and Ted Benson. We accept we're doing society's dirty washing, but we really do want law-abiding citizens to be able to live without being mugged, or raped, or burgled, or have their motors stolen. Above all we can't stand for murderers to get away with it. What is your most precious possession? Your life.'

'Is it ... partly because of Tracey you've put in so much to the case?'

'I grew to love that kid, Pam, in the short time I knew her. It wasn't anything to do with sex, on either side. We just got on, liked each other's company. I've never known anything like it and I'm still trying to get over the loss.'

'This … your new theory. Does it take her murder into account too?'

'It would, not that it's going to get me anywhere.'

She leant over and pressed his arm. 'Life's dealt you a pretty poor hand, Frank. It's so unfair.'

He shrugged. 'You and me both. Your husband leaves you and then you get lumbered with a penniless con-man. I suppose most of us walk around with all this baggage, wishing to Christ we could just get shot of it in some kind of a left-luggage office.'

They made love again very fondly in Crane's bed, knowing that these times would soon be over. Pam was returning home on Sunday; she couldn't neglect her translation agency any longer. But she'd enjoyed her days in this house: the peace, the easy mind, the hours in the sun, the late night talks over a drink and of course the shared bed. But she knew she was lotus-eating. Real life waited for her out there, to be made sense of, to be coped with, to provide her perhaps with a new *raison d'être*, possibly even with a man who, if she was really lucky, might have some of the qualities of the man who lay at her side.

She did wish he wasn't going to Ranelagh House tomorrow night. It gave her a nameless and inexplicable feeling of fear. It had to be all the very disturbing things that had happened since he'd first rung her doorbell, had to be. Yet he was a tough, skilled detective. What could possibly go wrong? He was going there simply to talk finance with Polly, in his role as an FA. Polly had no idea who he really was. Pam's nerves eventually settled down and she fell asleep, but it was a sleep filled with troubled dreams, of the type that, when you woke up, give you the impression you've not slept at all.

Crane too was finding that sleep wasn't coming easily, his restless mind still travelling again and again over that scenario which, though it seemed to answer all the questions he'd endlessly put to himself over the past days, he fully accepted was bizarre in the extreme. The problem remained that even if he had hit on some accurate version of the incredibly convoluted chain of events, how would it ever lead to anyone being brought to justice? There really seemed little point in going through the charade tomorrow night of advising Polly on her millions if the case at the weekend was going in the file marked No Result.

But he supposed he should phase himself out in an orderly manner. And you never knew, something of value *might* come out of it. And one day Polly might devote part of her legacy to Oxfam.

'A G and T, Jim?'

He hadn't wanted a drink, but he supposed he'd not be over the limit if he had one more, seeing as the drinks he'd had at the Mayfield had mainly been tonic without the gin. Polly was probably wanting to be hospitable for the many drinks he'd bought her and Jane and he didn't want to appear ungrateful.

'We'll go in the morning-room, Jim, there's a table in there we can spread papers on. I'll just make sure there are some jotters and calculators. Back in a jiff.'

Crane moved about the room with his glass. Polly had stood more of her white-card drawings against the back wall, designs for the renovation of the Ripon house. It had been confirmed that she was to get the work, with Jane to plan a new lay-out for the extensive grounds. There were also enlarged photographs of the house's rooms as they now were to give a sort of before and after effect. It struck him yet again how very talented Polly was.

'Right, Jim, the morning-room awaits.'

Crane had never before in his life heard anyone refer to a room as 'the morning-room'. He supposed it went back to when the Mannings had lived in the great mansion known as The Hall, where a certain room would in fact be set aside to be used only in the first part of the day while the drawing-room was being buffed up and hoovered.

The morning-room at Ranelagh House was smaller than the drawing-room but had the same plaster moulding and graceful lines. There was a good though very old and faded wallpaper in a rich greyish-green. The furniture too was all very dated: a *chaise-longue*, button-back wing chairs, a circular table with a pair of spoon-backs nearby, another dominant fireplace in marble and the usual ornate chandeliers.

'I've decided that this will be my future office,' Polly told him. 'All to be state-of-the-art. The fireplace will go and I'll have a desk against that window, a wall of bookshelves for reference books, a large baize-board on this wall that I can display designs on for clients. A bright decor, this table French polished and which can be used for meetings or light lunches. A parquet-tiled floor, I think.'

'Sounds great. And with the view over the back garden.'

'What an appalling state *that* was in. *Ah Wilderness*! I used to exclaim on drawing back the curtains in the morning, but Jane is working wonders on it. She really is a little slogger.'

'You're going to make an excellent team.'

'Do sit down. Where's your drink?'

'I finished it in the drawing-room.'

'Let me get you another.'

'Thanks, no. I'd better keep my brain clear for the next half-hour.'

'That could be difficult,' Polly said, with a faint smile. 'That could be very difficult ... Frank ...'

Crane felt as if his heart had been given a sudden squeeze.

Pam couldn't settle to anything. She'd tried reading the paper but had been unable to concentrate on the words, tried watching the television but had rapidly lost the thread of a play that was being transmitted. She was in a very nervy state. She'd had bad dreams last night, all to do with the party she'd gone to with Frank, but with Polly and Jane behaving in a sinister way and making enigmatic remarks. When Frank had come home for the dinner she'd prepared she'd tried to get him to postpone the meeting with Polly but he'd talked again of one last possibility of pinning down some part of the truth, especially when the object of the meeting was to be a discussion of the investing of money fraudulently obtained.

Pam had felt she couldn't push it. He was a clever man, quite capable of calculating the risks of the situation, assuming there could be any. She was really in no position to tell him how to do his job. She'd been subdued as they'd eaten, filled with a peculiar and persistent sense of dread, unable to respond easily to the pleasant hour of inconsequential chat Crane allowed himself as a break from his relentless work schedule.

The house phone rang, making her jump as it sounded so loud in the calm silence of a summer night 'Hello.'

'Oh ... hello. I think I may have misdialled, madam. I was trying to get a Mr Frank Crane.'

'This is Mr Crane's number. I'm ... I'm a guest in his house.'

'Ah, then I'm Detective Inspector Terry Jones. Perhaps you'd be kind enough to tell Frank I called.'

'This is Pam Draper, Mr Jones. We spoke in connection with the death of Lydia Glover and ... the whereabouts of Ken Glover that night.'

'I remember, Mrs Draper—'

'Is Frank in some kind of trouble?'

'Not that I know of. What makes you think he might be?'

'He's going to Ranelagh House about now. Polly Manning's place.'

There was a brief silence. 'You ... know about Frank's involvement with Polly Manning?'

'Only because of my involvement with Ken.'

'Why do you think he might be in some sort of trouble?'

'I think Polly Manning could be dangerous.'

'Frank is a very competent investigator.'

'I wish you'd send one of your people to Ranelagh House. To make sure Frank's all right.'

'I really couldn't do that. Frank's a private man doing a private job. He's working under an assumed name and identity. He really wouldn't want a DC sent to hold his hand.'

'I ... I suppose you're right,' she said disconsolately. 'It's just that with Ken being murdered in the Queensbury house—'

'We have our own views about who might be involved there, Mrs Draper, but Miss Manning doesn't figure in our enquiries.'

'I just feel certain Frank might be in some kind of danger.'

'He really is a very capable PI.'

'And ... and he just might be up against someone who's just as capable.'

'We can forget about an investment plan, Frank Crane, private investigator.'

Crane made to get up but she said, 'I'd not think of making a rush for it. The doors are all secured with deadlocks and the keys removed.'

'I can smash my way out.'

'You can't, you know. I'm sure you've heard of a Mickey Finn. Not a term much used these days but I popped the equivalent in your G and T, which was a generous measure as you probably noticed. Quite soon you'll be out of it.'

Crane sank back in his chair, cursing himself inwardly. How had she found out and how had he underestimated her so badly?

'Big mistake,' Polly said, in her usual collected drawl, sitting across from him at the round table, 'asking Jane had she been to mass the morning after the party. And being a good deal less than explicit about your background. And eschewing a roll in the hay with either of we two very fit and willing girls. In fact you could have had a threesome, we've done it before for chaps who've been really useful. I had thought of letting Ralph be the filling in a gorgeous Polly and Jane layer-cake, with him having been such a star about the Ripon connection. The trouble is he does get *so* excited and I wouldn't want an ambulance clanging up through the estate, if not a hearse, and his wife proving tiresome.'

He stared at her. How could she be so casually jokey when she'd spiked his gin? He'd always known about her clever brain, had never guessed it could be quite so formidable. How long, he wondered, before the narcotic could be expected to kick in, as she smiled her calm smile and sipped the inevitable gin and Dubonnet? 'Pinning down who you really are wasn't too easy,' she told him, 'but I knew your car and its number. Remember a couple of nights ago when you and the chaps were here and I went off to my room saying I'd developed a bad migraine? Well, I crept out of the house and drove to Heaton. I'd gone easy on the booze. I guessed your route to Toller Lane would take you up Oak Lane and Lilycroft Road so I waited in Mannheim Drive for your car to go past. The roads were quite clear and when I spotted your Renault I followed you. I saw you turn off Toller Lane and I drove on a little way, parked, and walked back to the side road you'd taken. I was disguised, of course. You *could* have put your car in a garage and that would have taken me longer to get a fix on you. But no, you were parked in the drive of what was clearly your house. So then I had your address. I got your name from the electoral rolls.'

He watched her across the table, his mind in a turmoil. She needn't have told him any of that. She'd done so because she was pleased with herself for thinking it through as she had done. He wondered again how long he could give the drug. She was watching him closely now, obviously thinking the same thing.

'Your house phone is unlisted but I was pretty sure by now you were some kind of a detective. Yellow Pages to the rescue. Quite a nice little spread about the discreet investigations you undertook: divorce matters, legatee searches, fraud, bad debt, life-style checks. So why is Frank checking *me* out, I asked myself? The question being rhetorical; by this time I knew.'

'The insurers ... they hired me to check why Lydia Glover had taken out such ... such a lot of term assurance cover. It ... it all seems ... quite straightforward. I'm ... I'm going to tell them that. There ... there was no point in doing this to me. Just ... just let me sleep ... sleep it off and I'll ... I'll get out ... your hair.' He was beginning to speak very slowly.

'I don't believe you, Frank. You used to be in the police and you've been involved in one or two big cases. I suspect you've learnt a lot more about the Lydia Glover affair than I'd really want you to know.'

'Let me ... sleep it off and ... and go home. I'll not take any ... anything any further,' he said, unable to keep a note of desperation out of his voice.

'But you wouldn't, would you, Frank? Not take it any further? Once you were away from here you'd keep on with it. That's the sort of chap you are. I recognize things in you that are similar to things in me.' There was a slight note of approval in her voice.

'Polly ... trust me.' He closed his eyes for a moment, as if simply trying to speak was an effort. 'I'll drop ... the case tomorrow.'

'Sorry, Frank, I made it an absolute rule years ago never to trust men who called themselves Jim and were economical with the truth about being police-trained PIs.'

'What ... what are you aiming to ... to do with me ... then?'

'Bury you. Beneath the trees at the bottom of the back garden. We have a trench all ready.'

Pam could no longer sit doing nothing. She put on a jacket over her T-shirt and jeans and went to the garage to get her car. She then began the drive over to Eccleshill. It wasn't an area she knew well and she took two wrong turnings. She wished now she had the sat-nav she'd once thought of installing. She glanced at the dashboard clock. He might still be at the Mayfield. It was somewhere in the area, she'd no idea where. She might be able to stop him going back to Ranelagh House, or at least insist that she went too. She knew she might be being very silly but she also knew she couldn't stop herself trying to find him. It wasn't just Polly and the bad dreams and the dreadful things that had been happening, it was simply some kind of powerful instinct that he might be in danger that she'd stopped trying to rationalize.

She drew into the kerb and asked an elderly couple walking a dog if they could direct her to the Mayfield. They weren't too sure and it took some time before they could agree on a route. She lost her way once more but finally spotted the hotel with its façade lit up. She parked and hurried inside. The main room was a bar lounge and she crossed to the bar. There were two men serving, both busy with orders. Even when these were completed they continued to ignore her and attended to regulars first. Frustration made her stomach feel as if it was producing pure acid. She couldn't see Frank, Polly or Jane anywhere. Perhaps they were in one of the other rooms.

'Madam?'

'I'm looking for someone called Frank ... er Jim Parry. He'd be with a woman called Polly Manning.'

'Polly was in earlier. She and the other lady went, what, about half an hour ago.'

'With Jim? Mr Parry?'

'There was a man with them. Tall, well-built.'

'Could you tell me where Ranelagh House is from here? It's very important.'

The barman looked harassed, it was a busy night. But one of the men in a group that stood about a yard from the bar said, 'You go back to the main Harrogate Road, miss, and turn left. It's less than half a mile along the road. It's part of the Ranelagh estate, a big house at the end.'

'Thank you so much. I do know how to locate the house once I find the estate.'

The man looked at her more closely. 'Weren't you at Polly and Jane's party last Saturday with Jim?'

'That's me. I'm Pam. I really must rush.'

'If it's Jim you're looking for I think he's gone home.'

'Gone ... home?' His words gave her a sudden surge of relief.

'I believe he *was* going back to Polly's, to help with her finances, but she told me she'd decided to leave it till next week as she's very busy on one of her projects.'

For a few seconds her body felt weak with the absence of tension. 'But ... but they all left together according to the barman.'

'To go their separate ways, I suppose. Can you not raise Jim on your mobile?'

'He's switched his off.'

'I can't say I blame him. Some people seem to think you should be on duty twenty-four seven.'

'Thank you so much.'

She went out into the night. She checked the car-park again. Frank's car was definitely not there. He'd told her he normally left his car at the hotel and walked with the group who were going back to the house for more drinks and picked it up later.

She rang Frank's house, hoping and praying he'd be there. But there was no response. She sat in the car wondering what was the best thing to do. If he wasn't at home at this time of night and Polly had postponed her meeting with him about her finances, where could he be?

'What … what are you … talking about?' Crane was slurring his words now and speaking with an obvious effort.

'Don't fight it, Frank,' Polly said. 'It'll get you anyway. You'll very soon now go off into a nice sleep, in fact what Chandler called the big sleep. We'll give you a tasteful burial in our big back garden and the skilful Jane will be able to call on her expertise to make the ground look totally undisturbed within a few days.'

For the first time in his life Crane knew what it really meant when the skin was said to crawl. The skin of his entire body seemed to be crawling at the ghastliness of it. 'People … people … know … I'm … here,' he croaked.

'Actually they don't. I've told the chaps at the Mayfield I've put off having you back tonight. You could be anywhere.'

'My … car …'

'I shall drive it to somewhere like Skipton or Ilkley and abandon it. Jane will follow me in our car and bring me back. You were never here. They are going to search for you carefully but they'll have to give up in the end. You'll be quite famous as a latter-day Lord Lucan.'

'Kill me?' Crane gasped. 'Like … like you killed Ken Glover?'

She gave a dismissive shrug. 'Oh, Glover was a useful idiot, as Lenin said, I believe, of Arthur Ransome. You know about the money, of course. It really doesn't matter now just how much you do know. Glover wanted too much for the little bit he did, though only he could do it, admittedly.'

She was totally composed, her calm drawl always in place. He'd known men who were capable of doing the frightful things she was outlining, never a woman. But she had nothing in common with other women.

'I'm genuinely sorry you have to go, Frank. You're very good. Made an excellent job of infiltrating my fan club at the Mayfield. You're nearly as good as me. Had me totally taken in by your FA act. No hard feelings, old chap, but I've got this rather obsessive ambition to have the family name mean something again. A couple of million is buttons really, in the noughties, but it's a start.'

'You ... can't ... think ... you'll get ... away ... with it.'

'I'm quite sure I shall. People may suspect things but they'll have no proof.'

'Glover...?'

'We never left the house that afternoon. My car was in the drive throughout. And Jane and I are each other's alibi, not that it'll come to the local plod cottoning on. Quite apart from anything else they know to watch their step around a Manning.'

Crane closed his eyes. She'd thought of everything, of course.

'Do let yourself go, Frank. Forcing yourself to stay conscious can only prolong the disappointment of knowing I've got away wit it.'

Pam rang Crane's home number again. Still no reply. She'd tried his mobile but that was still switched off. She even tried his car phone but that was on the answering service. She drove out of the Mayfield car-park and along Harrogate Road to the Ranelagh estate. The street lights and the lights that glowed through the curtained squares of the house windows on the estate gave a sense of the comforting and the ordinary. She would just have to accept that she was being a silly, panicky woman and that eventually she would track him down and find he'd come to no harm. He would surely be all right in these perfectly normal surroundings, even if he had in fact gone back to Polly's house. There could have been another change of mind on Polly's part. There was only one lit window at the front of Ranelagh House, from memory that would be the drawing-room. She parked her car on one of the estate's side roads and continued on foot. Frank's car was in the drive! Polly *had* gone back to the original plan. Again she felt great relief. She glanced about her then walked quietly along the path that ran by the side of the house to the immense back garden. As she came to the rear of the house a security light was triggered, making her heart lurch. But she stood still and a few seconds later the light was extinguished. It seemed not to have attracted any attention. She knew the light would be activated by anything that moved, even a fox or a cat. It was unlikely to alert anyone in the house.

A second room of the house was in use. This one had a french window, with the curtains undrawn. She crept up to this and looked carefully through it but any people inside must have been sitting out of range. She could hear voices but couldn't make out what was being said. One was a woman's, one a man's. It had to be Polly and Frank discussing the investment plan. She could go home, Frank would be along later.

But having come this far she felt she had to see him leave the house safely. He'd said he'd not be staying too long. She was being silly again but she'd had a drawn out worrying evening. She decided that the best thing would be to stand among the trees of the copse at the end of the back garden. She walked across one of the lawns, triggering the security light again. She was glad of it this time and its powerful beam, otherwise she might have fallen into a trench that had been dug in a small clearing beneath the trees, the earth from the trench carted off and tidily piled some yards away.

Another shock! What could it be for? What could it possibly be *for*?

Crane's eyes still opened now and then but were mainly closed and his breath was slow and stertorous. Polly got up and came round to him. 'I've got to hand it to you for willpower, old son. I couldn't have imagined you'd hang on to your marbles as long as this. Of course you are a big man. But I think this is it now. I'm sorry about it but I'm sure you do know too much. I rather think I'll miss you. Like Whistler, I'll remember you as a warm personal enemy.'

Crane suddenly leapt to his feet. 'No need to say goodbye quite yet, Polly. The spiked gin was a shrewd move and it's just a pity I never drank it. I decided it might just put me over the limit after all. Piece of bloody good luck for me, don't you agree? You'll have a vaseful of dead flowers in the morning.'

He guessed that shock was something Polly simply didn't do, had probably never done it in her life; she did it now. Her mouth fell open, her eyes were so wide the whites flared round the pupils. Knowing how very strong she was he allowed her no chance to strike, he gave her a single blow across the side of her face which sent her reeling into her chair, over which she lost her footing and went crashing to the ground. Crane only heard the soft footsteps behind him when it was too late. The blow he received to the side of his head knocked him unconscious. Genuinely this time.

FOURTEEN

Benson sat down on the other side of the desk. He looked grey with fatigue.

'Ted, you must get off home early tonight. A worn-out copper is no good to himself or the department. We'll all be meeting in the morning. We'll go through everything we've got and we'll brain-storm, the usual razzmatazz.'

Benson gave a weary sigh. 'I can't honestly see much new coming out of it, boss. The trouble is, the hooker was a closed book. We can't pin down any of her clients, or at least any who'll admit to giving her one. And Glover, well he was with Pam Draper for quite a time and since then there hasn't been any new totty. That youngster at the estate agent's, he's quite a knowing little sod. He could always figure out who was Glover's latest bonk. We've followed them all up. Nothing.'

Jones was silent for a few seconds. 'I've given it a lot of thought, Ted. And Frank's given it a hell of a lot more. He's convinced it all comes back to Polly Manning. He's dreamt up this idea that she might have been in the car with Lydia Glover, driven the car to the edge of the gully and threw herself out before she went over with it.'

'For Christ's *sake*, Terry!'

Jones nodded. 'My first reaction too. And there was a lot more that seemed well over the top. But the thing is, Ted, Frank's got to know Polly, believes he knows what she's capable of. And, well, you know how Frank kicks things round endlessly in his head. He *might* be on to something. Just.'

Jones knew Benson didn't really want to hear this. He also knew that when Frank had tampered with some evidence when he was in the CID Benson had been in it with him, though Benson didn't know he'd guessed. Frank Crane had carried the can for the lot because of Benson having a family to support.

It had left Benson with a debt he could never return and he'd resented Frank, once his best friend, ever since. Even so, Benson was a good hard-working officer, if never in Frank's league.

Benson said, 'I thought Polly was an untouchable. All those relations who know the law backwards and close ranks round her.'

'She is, you're right. But somehow, Ted, I think we've got to find a way of getting her in for questioning. We just need a peg to hang our jackets on.'

Crane wasn't out for very long. He came round with a headache so bad he could hardly think straight. He tried to get up from the floor but found he was in handcuffs and with his legs tightly bound with cord at the ankles. The two women stood looking down at him. Polly's face was becoming swollen and discoloured with the blow he'd given her but now wore its usual look of total self-possession. Jane looked very scared and her lips trembled.

'Nice try, Frank,' Polly said, her drawl only slightly affected by the muffled note her injury had induced. 'What a strong man you are. I thought you'd be out for some time yet. Had I had just one strong man like you in my life things might have been very different. I really shall be sorry to see you go. However I'm certain that in your case it's a matter of once a policeman always a policeman.'

'Some people need to be,' he grated, 'with scum like you about.'

Jane gave a sudden sob. Polly turned to her. 'Oh, do try to pull yourself together, Jane,' she said briskly. 'This man is our very last obstacle, even though I hold him in such high personal regard. When he goes we'll have a completely clear run at last.'

'What do you mean?' Jane said uneasily. 'When he goes? What do you *mean*?'

'You *know* what I mean. You did after all not long ago bean him with the baseball bat.'

'That ... that was because of *you*! I couldn't let him hurt *you*. But why have you put those handcuffs on him and tied his legs?'

'Someone had to, with you rushing off to throw up as usual. I could have done with a hand frankly.'

'But *why* have you tied him up like this? What are you going to do with him?'

'Give him a decent burial in the trench we dug.'

'But that ... that was just for the baseball bat and any clothes that might—' She suddenly realized what she was saying and clapped a hand to her mouth, staring down at Crane.

'Oh, Frank knows about Glover,' Polly said calmly in her muffled drawl. 'He knows far too much about everything. You know perfectly well I could smell a rat some time ago. There's a curious phrase, thinking outside the box. Well, Frank was born thinking outside the blessed box.'

'Why do you call him *Frank*?' Jane said, in a tone of bemused anguish. 'His name's Jim.'

'He was rather coy about using his real name, which is Frank Crane. He's a private detective who used to be a policeman.'

'You can't ... we can't do anything to *him*! He's not ... he's not—'

'If this man leaves this house to go anywhere beyond our back garden the next time *we* leave would be in a car with blue flashing lights. You must get a grip on things.'

'I *can't* ... *we* can't ... have any more dreadful ... I couldn't *stand* it!'

'These things happen,' Polly said patiently, as if explaining simple facts to a backward child. 'However carefully one plans, and we planned very carefully, one can never quite guard against a wild card being dealt. Frank is a wild card. If we let him hang about everything else will go for nothing. You do see that, don't you?'

'Oh, *Polly!*' Jane's protest was almost a wail.

'We need to get him to the trench. Will you get that trolley affair or shall I?'

But Jane stood in a state of what looked to be a catatonic daze, and Polly, with a pained glance, opened a leaf of the french window and stepped out into the night. Crane struggled to get himself into a sitting position without success. He felt as if his head had split in two. He'd never known a fear of such intensity. She'd bury him, he had no illusions. She set and re-set her objectives like a First World War general; what price the size of the butcher's bill if they gained a hundred yards of terrain?

Jane stood with her back to him, shoulders bowed, as if unable to bring herself to look at him. 'You can't let her do this to me, Jane,' he said, striving to keep his voice evenly controlled. 'I'm simply doing a job. The insurers were puzzled about someone in Lydia's position taking out so much cover. I've told Polly I'm prepared to forget everything I've found out if you'll just let me go.'

She gave another sob, her shoulders shaking. Crane felt that if he had the remotest chance of survival it had to be through this woman, who still seemed to be hanging by her fingernails to something that resembled a conscience. 'Come on, Jane,' he said gently. 'You're not like Polly. She can do these things but you find it impossibly hard, don't you? If Polly wants something she really doesn't care about what she does to get it, including killing people.'

'Shut up!' she cried. 'Don't *talk* to me. I don't want to know anything about it. There's nothing I can *do*!'

'But there is, you see. You'll have a mobile. You can tell Polly you have to go off and be sick again and ring the police.'

'I can't. I can't do that. Just shut up, *shut up*! I can't *stand* it!'

'That's because you're a decent woman beneath it all, aren't you? You've always wanted to be one of Polly's people, yes? It must have seemed like a dream come true to be Polly's best friend, going into partnership together, going to the Mayfield every evening and learning to manipulate the chaps like Polly does. But it comes with a price-tag, Jane, doesn't it? It always does with Polly and it seems to get bigger by the hour.'

'Shut up, shut up, *shut up*!' she screamed, clapping her hands to her ears. She was clearly close to hysteria. At that point both leaves of the french window were opened and Polly wheeled over the threshold the sort of sturdy garden trolley that could be used for moving heavy loads. 'Come along, old girl, the sooner this is over the sooner we can have a drink and call it a day. There's a fair amount of earth to be replaced. You take his legs and I'll take his shoulders.'

'I *can't*, Polly. I can't do any more of these hideous *things*!'

'Oh, come on, Janey.' Polly's voice had taken on a cajoling note. 'Just one more, which I assure you will be the last, the very last. Then everything will be fine, marvellous. A couple of days and we'll be back to normal. In fact, next week I think we might have a few days in Town. Stay at Claridges and see a couple of shows. Dinner at the Ivy. I'll only need to mention Mama's maiden name and they'll be able to find a table. You'll like that, won't you? We'll gear ourselves up for the Ripon work. My card will cover it till the money comes through. Oh, do come along, none of it would have worked without you. I'm so very grateful.'

The pain in his head intensified the wave of nausea that swept over him. He looked on with a feeling of helplessness he'd never known before. It was Polly in siren mode again, her compelling song drifting over scented water, to captivate men who'd not stopped up their ears and a woman called Jane, who'd adored her for half a life-time. Jane was gazing at Polly with that look of almost abject veneration he'd seen at the Mayfield. Seeming to be in a trance, eyes turned away, she grasped at his legs. It couldn't have been easy for them to lift and transfer him to the trolley but both women were strong and managed it without undue difficulty. About two thirds of his body lay on the trolley, his legs, from the knees down, trailing on the floor. The women then took hold of the pram-type handle of the trolley, pulled it across the room and over the threshold of the french window.

'Jane,' he said, striving to keep the gentle note in his voice that was now coming from a constricted throat, 'I'm not something to get rid of like a dead cat, I'm a human being. I've got a right to go on living just like you have. What would your mother and father think if they could see you now, preparing to bury a man, who's done you not the slightest harm, in a hole in the garden?'

'Take no notice, Jane,' Polly said evenly. 'Frank, I've got absolutely nothing against you, in fact I'm quite sorry about this. You were simply in the way. I wish we *could* buy you off with a hundred grand, but it's crucial one knows the calibre of the buyee and I know yours only too well.'

'Oh, *do* let's buy him off, Polly!' Jane burst out. '*Please* let's buy him off. He promised he'd forget all this if we let him go. And if we gave him some money—'

'He'd promise to go to Tasmania if we set him free. But the only place he'd actually go to would be the nearest police station.'

Crane made no attempt to promise anything as the trolley was dragged across the patio area, past the little pool and over the lawn to the tall forest trees at the foot of the garden, briefly lit up by the glare of the security lamp. He knew there was nothing to say to Polly that would make the slightest difference. She was the end result of her illustrious breeding: gifted, nerveless, focused and totally self-absorbed.

His only hope still lay in Jane.

'You can't do this to me, Jane,' he said. 'Polly will be fine in the morning, but you won t. You'll *never* get it off your mind, you know you won't. Our lives are the only things we've got that really belong to us. You can't take mine away. You've already taken Ken Glover's away. You can't go on like this.'

'Frank,' Polly said, her drawl slightly uneven with the effect of pulling the trolley. 'Pack it in now, old chap. You must know that nothing you can say will make the slightest difference to anything.'

The women gave the trolley a final tug, so that it lay alongside the trench, which he could just make out in the darkness. Polly fiddled with some object at the end of the trench, then lit a cigarette lighter and ignited a small lamp that operated on canister gas. Head pounding, Crane brought himself to glance to his right. He could see that the trench was almost his length exactly.

Pam stood trembling beneath the trees. As she watched, the french window was opened and Polly came out and walked across the patio area. The security lamp flared as she came into range and Pam saw that she was dressed in black: black shirt, black trousers, black mules. The clothes deepened her sense of unease. She shrank into herself like a small animal seeing a predator. Polly halted in front of what looked to be a garden cart or trolley. There were some heavy stones stacked in it which she moved aside quite easily. Then she wheeled the trolley to the french window, opened both leaves and pushed the trolley inside. What on earth had she done that for? Pam couldn't begin to guess but her unease intensified.

She was soon to know. In a short time the leaves of the french window were reopened and the trolley dragged out and towards the trees by Polly and Jane. There was something bundled on the trolley but it was only when the security lamp came on again that she could see what it was.

Her stomach felt as if it was filling with iced water. Dear *God*! It was *Frank*! Frank handcuffed and with his ankles bound! She was hardly able to breathe with the shock. The women dragged the trolley, with Frank's legs trailing on the ground, over to the trench, which was only a few yards from where Pam cowered. What were they going to do? What were they going to *do* with him? They couldn't, could they, they couldn't possibly be, they were never going to put him in the *trench*?

What could *she* do, what could she *do*? Beyond the great square house that sealed off the back garden stood the houses of a modern estate. She must alert people there, bring some of the men back here, to see with their own eyes what was going on. But the two women stood between her and any way out. She'd be seen, heard.

She scrabbled in a pocket for her mobile, dropped it because her hands shook so badly, had to feel for it as quietly as possible in the grass and earth at her feet. Fortunately she could hear voices from the vicinity of the trench and they covered the sounds she was making. She keyed 999.

'Which service do you require, caller?'

'The police,' she whispered hurriedly. 'The police ... Detective Inspector Jones.'

'Please speak up, caller, I'm having difficulty hearing you.'

She raised her voice slightly. 'I need Detective Inspector Jones. My name's Pam Draper. I'm at Ranelagh House and Polly Manning is going to bury Frank Crane in a hole in the ground.'

'Try to speak slowly and clearly, Pam. DI Jones won't be on duty now. Please give me your full address and exactly what the problem is and I'll connect you to an appropriate person.'

Pam had the mobile clamped to her ear so that the crackle of the operator's voice wouldn't carry. 'Please tell Inspector Jones, he'll understand. It's Ranelagh House on the Ranelagh estate in Harrogate Road and Polly Manning has Frank Crane tied up and she's going to bury him in a hole she's dug in the back garden....'

She couldn't stop her voice rising a little and in the light of the small gas-lamp that stood near the trench she now saw Polly's head suddenly swivel in her direction. She closed her mobile and crouched close to the ground, heart beating wildly, breath coming in gasps she fought to control. Polly walked slowly among the trees until she stood barely a yard from Pam, curled up behind the wide trunk of an oak. Both then were very still for seconds that to Pam seemed like minutes. Polly moved away at last. 'I thought I heard something,' she said over her shoulder. 'It must have been a fox.'

Pam had to fight an urge to lie full length on the ground, she felt so weak with relief.

'Come along, Janey, do buck up. It'll take us an hour at the very least to fill in the trench,' Polly said quietly but firmly.

'You can't do this, Jane.' Crane strove to keep the desperation out of his tone. 'You need to own up. You need to own up and atone. If you don't do it now you'll not have an easy mind for the rest of your life. You'll be fine during the day when Polly's jollying you along, or you're with the chaps at the Mayfield, but when you're in bed and can't sleep ... *that's* when it'll keep going through your mind, all the ghastly things you've involved yourself in.'

'I should have gagged you, Frank,' Polly said, with her indestructible composure. 'Can't imagine why I didn't with Jane feeling a little jumpy. When this is all over, Janey, I'll give you the best years of your life. We'll not confine ourselves to the UK. The sort of people we'll be cultivating buy properties abroad: Provence, Tuscany, the Greek Isles. They'll want the renovations done and the gardens sorted by people they can trust. Mama's connections will be incredibly useful. We'll be able to spend entire winters in the sun. And this lovely old house to come home to. Looked after by a live-in cook-housekeeper. I'll not want you to do any more cooking or cleaning the moment we can afford staff.'

Crane said, 'But there'll be a body in the back garden, Jane, won't there? You'd never forget it was there. There'll always be a fear that will never go away, that one day the police will come along and dig it all up.'

'They'll only dig it up if they know about it,' Polly said. 'And they never will know as neither of us will let anything slip. Come along, Jane.'

Jane stood hunched between Polly and where Crane lay on the trolley. She looked to have a mind at the end of its tether, a mind struggling to cope with being wrenched in two directions by forces almost equally powerful. Crane willed her to pretend she was going to be sick again with every fibre of his being, to rush off into the house and phone the police. He said, 'Polly was born without a conscience, Jane, so you'll have to have enough conscience for the two of you. You can't do this, you know you can't.'

'For heaven's *sake*, Jane, let's get him in, so we can start our new life without any more hitches.'

'Why do we keep calling her Jane?' Crane asked politely. 'Your real name's Lydia, isn't it? Lydia Glover.'

FIFTEEN

'He *knows*!' Jane screamed. 'He knows who I really am!'

'Not that it matters,' Polly said, her drawl intact. 'Not where he's going. I did warn you he thought outside the box.'

'No, Polly,' Crane said, 'I thought the unthinkable. If Lydia could *seem* to be dead that absurd amount of money she'd insured herself for would actually be paid out. Nothing else in the end fitted the facts. The entire plan was yours, of course.'

'Of course.'

'Jane, you must wish you'd never met up again with Polly. I suppose I should call you Lydia but I can only think of you under your assumed name. You've idolized Polly ever since you first saw her, yes, at Bradford Girls? I've done quite a bit of research into Lydia Glover's background.'

'Oh, Polly, he knows everything, *everything*!' Jane whimpered, sobbing again.

'Yes, he's done a great deal of premium-grade thinking,' Polly admitted, unable to keep a note of admiration out of her voice.

Crane's head had never stopped throbbing from the blow it had had in the morning-room, his skin never stopped crawling at the appalling death Polly was determined to inflict on him. His one idea was simply to keep them talking until Jane might crack. She was shaking now as if in the throes of a tropical fever.

'You were the tract woman, Polly, and you needed to find someone of about the same age as Lydia and had roughly the same looks and build. You found that in the street-girl called Libby and you were lucky in that Libby was a lapsed Catholic, open to accepting one of your tracts and your powers of persuasion. She even invited you to her flat so you could help her regain her faith.'

'She served her purpose,' Polly agreed dismissively. 'Like Glover, she was another useful idiot.'

Crane, distracted as he was by the trench at his side and a head that felt it was going to explode, could sense all the same that she was taking a certain pleasure in the way he was outlining that incredibly well-thought-out and executed scheme. 'You went to her flat and talked religion to her. You took her for a nice drive in Lydia's car. You got her to have two or three drinks to relax her, one of which you doctored. And then, when she was out of it, you drove the car to the Royds Cliff Gully very fast and at the last moment jumped out before you went with it.'

'Always been very athletic,' she said, with a faint smile of pride, 'in bed or out.'

'Please don't let him talk about it any more, Polly,' Jane pleaded, her agonized voice almost a whisper. 'Please don't let him talk about it. I can't bear it, I can't *bear* it.'

'But that's how it happened, Jane, isn't it? A harmless street-girl died in your place and your husband Ken identified the body as yours, didn't he?'

'And for that necessary but trifling contribution to the affair he wanted a half-share of the pay-out,' Polly put in.

'I know,' he told her, 'I was in hiding at the side of the house when Glover was demanding his million.'

'If only I'd known you ten years ago,' Polly said, in a tone of what seemed to be genuine regret, 'before I got mixed up with Brain-dead.'

'It wouldn't have made any difference if you had. I've only ever gone out with women I could actually like.'

'Oh, I can do likeable. You'd be surprised how incredibly likeable I can be when I put my mind to it.'

'I wouldn't, you know. I can quite imagine the pitch your like-ability must have reached to be able to get Jane-stroke-Lydia here to agree to letting someone else die in her place.'

'Please, please, *please!*' Jane cried, hands clutching her head as if hers too was filled with scarcely endurable pain. 'Polly, stop him *talking!*'

Crane said, 'But we must talk about it, Jane, mustn't we? Because, you see, it wasn't just Libby Dawson who lost her life but also her closest friend Tracey Sharp. Polly had found out that Libby had this friend she told everything to and she suddenly realized that Tracey might contact the police and report Libby as a missing person. She might pass on details of the tract woman and the fact that she drove a blue Clio, the one she still has. She might even have clocked the registration number that day Polly called on Libby in her flat. And Libby might have told Tracey how very well-spoken Polly was. So Polly took no chances. Well, as it turned out Tracey passed on to me what details she had and it took me a long, long time to work out why anyone should want to kill her. I also couldn't get a fix on this woman called Jane. She seemed to have no background, lived with Polly and wore a very good wig and heavy glasses and had had something done to her face just in case anyone saw her who'd known her in a previous existence. She gave herself a month off work just before the car crash to attend to these changes.'

'Two dead harlots,' Polly said with an indifferent shrug. 'A pair of five-pound fannies. Death was the best career move they ever made.'

'Oh God!' Jane moaned. 'Oh God, oh God, oh *God!*'

'But they weren't five-pound fannies,' Crane went on doggedly, nausea coming in waves from the pounding in his skull. 'Tracey was a fine young woman who genuinely wanted to get out of the game. They both did. They wanted jobs in the straight world and Tracey had enough money to buy a house they could share. And what's more I was able to arrange an interview for Tracey, for a job she was certain to get, but Polly battered her to death the day before she was to have it. So two decent young women lost their lives just as they were on the point of making the most of them.'

Jane was keening like a wounded animal while Polly looked disdainfully on in the small pool of light thrown by the gas-lamp. She said, 'Enough now, Frank, full marks for sorting it out so brilliantly but we'll take the rest as read.'

Yet even now he could tell she was still not entirely reluctant to have him recount what in her relaxed way she clearly regarded as a masterpiece of organization and nerve.

'And then there was the final death, Jane, wasn't there, apart from mine, of course: your husband Ken? He womanized and gambled and he once beat you so badly that you told Mrs Peel at Airedale Books you could have killed him. And so you could just about go along with him actually *being* killed. When Polly divorced her husband and returned north and became your best friend it seemed like the nicest thing that had ever happened to the sort of shy retiring woman you were and if Ken could be tricked out of the money he'd been promised to identify a dead prostitute as you, you felt he deserved it. But he turned so nasty about the con that Polly insisted *he* had to go too. I've no doubt you weren't quite so sure.'

'It was only meant to be one wretch of a *street walker*!' Jane screamed. 'Polly said she'd be better out of it, we'd be doing her a favour and she'd die happy with Polly reading from the Bible and giving her drinks. I didn't want any other deaths, I never even *knew* about Tracey. I never knew about Tracey till *now*! I didn't *want* any more deaths!'

'But *one* death was one too many, Jane. You know that, don't you? You always knew it, you've not got a blank space where your soul should be, like Polly. Polly just swept you along with her incredible powers of persuasion, didn't she? And there was the Mayfield and all the chaps making a fuss of you and wanting to sleep with you. But you always knew, didn't you, in your heart, that that wonderful life simply wasn't worth it against the life of one poor prostitute, not even if the pay-out had been a *hundred* million.'

'Oh *God*,' she cried. 'Oh God, I'm going to be sick again. I'll have to go inside.'

A tide of hope swept through him. She was going inside to alert the police. He was certain of it. She'd reached breaking point, was barely holding on to her sanity by a thread. But then Polly caught hold of her. 'No need for these middle-class manners, Janey, you can puke anywhere round here. In fact you can puke in the trench if you feel like it. Frank won't mind. He won't be in a position to once he's in it.'

Crane closed his eyes. There was nothing more he could say or do. There was nowhere else to go.

Pam felt herself to be in a state of near-paralysis by what she'd heard behind the oak tree. Her entire body felt chilled despite the warmth of the summer night. She'd caught every word spoken near the trench in quivering horror. All those killings! And Jane being Lydia! And Polly now prepared to bury Frank!

She tried to control her panicky feelings so she could decide what to do. It was obvious nothing was going to happen about the 999 call. The operator would have thought she was a crazy woman. She wondered if she could creep further away from the vicinity of the trench without being detected. Somewhere where she could talk a little more clearly and report the situation in a way that made some kind of sense. Voices sounded again out by the trench.

Polly said, 'Well, are you going to puke or not?'

'I want to go *inside*. I want to be *alone*.'

'Oh, come on, Jane, let's get this business finished. It'll pass off, the feeling you want to be sick, when we start filling the trench.'

'I can't do that, I can't *do* it!'

'You helped me with Ken.'

'This is Frank, he's a *decent* man.'

'You can't do it, Jane, can you?' Crane's voice was hollow with the desperation he could no longer keep out of it. 'You've been involved in too many deaths, haven't you? You were a decent woman too, weren't you, once? You'd never have been involved in killing *anyone* but for Polly.'

'We can't stand about here all night,' Polly said, the slightest note of asperity in her drawl. 'Look, I'll do it myself, but you'll *have* to help with refilling the trench.'

With that, she grasped the edge of the trolley and tilted it so that Crane crashed down into the trench that was to be his grave.

Pam had to clasp a hand to her mouth to stifle the scream that almost forced its way through her lips of its own volition. He was in the trench! Very soon they'd start moving the earth back. She would have to do something, anything, *have* to. She wondered if, when they began moving back the earth, she could creep away from the sheltering trees a few yards at a time and work her way down the back garden, staying close to the boundary hedge to her left. There was the security light to consider but hopefully its lateral range didn't extend as far as the hedge. She had to draw on an almost depleted store of courage to move at all. Her legs had stiffened with the crouched motionless position she'd had to adopt for so long. She hoped it wouldn't be a handicap. Oh, Frank, Frank, lying at the bottom of that frightful hole in the ground. She'd have to do *something*.

Crane, face down, lay in a state of distilled terror at the bottom of the trench, his heart banging in his chest. He moved his arms as much as he could, afraid they might be sprained or even broken with being handcuffed in front of him. They felt all right, though aching. He began to shrug himself with shoulders and hips so that he was lying on his back. It took some time but he had to be able to use his voice. He tried to force out of his mind the thought of soil raining down on him to the point where he'd not be able to breathe. He'd be desperately holding his cuffed hands to his face to keep the soil from his nose and mouth but it would very soon be of no avail.

He had to suspend his imagination, that's what Hemingway had said you had to do when you were in a dangerous situation, and this is what he strove to do now, even though there was no way out of his grave, even though if the police caught up with these women it would be too late for him. He'd be dead.

'*Another* death, Jane,' he shouted. 'You'll be spending the best years of your life in prison when the police catch up with you. They'll never give up on me because I used to be one of them. Your only chance of any kind of leniency is to keep me alive.'

It had gone very quiet in the area of the trench. She'd heard Frank shouting, his voice muffled so that she couldn't make out the words. With great caution she dared to take a look at the women. Jane stood there alone weeping, her shoulders bowed and shaking. As Pam looked on, Polly came into the light of the little lamp, holding a spade.

'Come on, Jane, it's got to be done. He's in there now.'

'I feel so *sick*. I just want to go in the house for a few minutes. My insides are upset. It's not just wanting to be sick, it's the other end too.'

'Just go under a *tree*, for heaven's sake. But be *quick*.'

'No. I want the bathroom, and paper and hot water....'

The women bickered on, Jane doggedly insisting she be allowed to go in the house. Pam straightened up, forcing herself to silence her groans at the cramping pains in her legs. Then she began to make her way, a few feet at a time, towards the boundary hedge. The voices became fainter and she was encouraged to make faster progress. She could hardly believe she was contriving to get clear of that dreadful place. She felt she'd be out of danger once she reached the house. She could skirt the house and make her way rapidly through the front garden and out on to the estate. Once there she could go to the first house where lighted windows indicated that people were still up, doing normal things like reading the papers, or sipping cocoa, or watching the late film.

'Hold on, Frank,' she whispered, 'I'll have you out of there in fifteen minutes.'

She was halfway along the back garden, staying close to the hedge, when the security lamp flared. Jane, walking across the lawn, had triggered it. She must have got her way. She saw Pam and gave a short, shocked scream. The two women stared at each other open-mouthed, both equally frightened. Then Pam began to run towards the house and the flagged path that led to the front garden. But Polly, alerted by the noise and reacting in part of a second, like the security lamp itself, raced across the lawn and clutched Pam in her arms before she could reach the house and began dragging her back, kicking and struggling.

'It appears to be the Draper woman,' she told Jane in her collected tone, as if Pam running across the back garden was simply another small irritation on a night turning out to be rather tiresome. 'God knows how long she's been here. I *thought* I'd heard something a while back. Don't worry, I'll sort it out.'

'What are you going to do now?' Jane asked, in an odd, flat monotone that was a complete contrast to her hysterical tone of earlier. 'She must have seen you push him in the trench.'

They were now back beneath the trees and Pam had stopped struggling. Polly seemed to have the strength of a man.

'There's only one thing we can do with her. She goes in the trench with her boyfriend. Quite a romantic way to go.'

'Frank!' Pam cried through trembling lips. 'It's *me*. I came here thinking I could help you. I couldn't. They ... they've caught me. I'm sorry.'

'*Another* death, Jane!' Crane's muffled shout came from the trench.' They are going to put you both inside for the rest of your lives. You'll *die* in prison!'

'Come along, Jane,' Polly said, 'we deal with this complication exactly like we dealt with the others. It's simply a matter of getting shot of two cars instead of one. It might be an idea to drive them to the coast and leave the cars on the cliff tops. They've had a suicide swim together in the North Sea. I just need the woman's car keys. I got Frank's earlier. Ah, here they are.' She drew the keys from Pams jacket pocket.

Rigid with fear, Pam had never heard anything as chilling as Polly explaining in her calm, matter-of-fact tones how their slow terrifying deaths in this hole in the ground would be covered up.

'Please don't put me in there,' she gasped. 'Please don't put me in there.'

'Let her go, Polly,' Jane said quietly. 'I'm going to give myself up. I could never live with myself if I went on with any more of this. And as for Libby ... that poor woman who died in my car, it *was* one too many.'

'Oh, come on, Janey.' Polly's voice now held the old, warm, coaxing note. 'This has been a very difficult night for you, I realize that. But tomorrow, with the trench filled in and the cars disposed of, it'll be the first day of our new life, and what a life it's going to be.'

'No,' Jane said, in a voice as calm as Polly's. 'I shall give myself up. I could never have believed I could have involved myself in such evil things. We've killed three people and now you're wanting to kill two more.'

'We've been through all this, Janey. Three of those people were worthless and in the case of Frank and the woman it's jolly bad luck, but they got in the way and it's either them or us.'

Crane lay on the uneven earth, holding his breath in case he missed any of the words spoken above. Jane now sounded so completely different he'd thought for a few seconds it was someone else. Her voice was both controlled and held a peculiarly authoritative note.

Jane said, 'Frank had it right, if it hadn't been for you I'd never have let myself be talked into these dreadful things. You once told me you hardly noticed me at school, but you did. Clever extroverts like you are *always* aware of shy nonentities like me. It gives you a special thrill to be able to tell how much we yearn to be one of your friends, how much we'd *give* to be one. And I had nothing to give then that would let me into your circle: I wasn't funny or talented or well off. But with that memory of yours you never forgot how very unhappy it made me to be outside the big tent. And when we met again all those years later you found nothing had changed, the shy, colourless teenager was now a shy colourless woman who still idolized you. Idolized you to the point of being ready to do anything to please you, even to going along with a scheme to rob the insurers of two million and letting a prostitute die. A prostitute who was desperate to regain her faith and lead a better life. Well, I'm going no further and I'm prepared to go to prison. I *want* to go to prison. I've got a lot of atoning to do.'

'I think we can probably help there, Mrs Glover.' A heavy man in chinos and a fawn linen jacket moved out of the darkness into the dim light of the gas-lamp. 'Release Mrs Draper, Polly Manning. I am Detective Inspector Jones and I'm arresting both you and Lydia Glover on suspicion of causing the death of Libby Dawson. There'll be other deaths to take into account, but that will do to be going on with. Don't try anything foolish, I've got DS Benson here and several constables.'

Ted Benson stepped into the light with four PCs – three men and a woman.

'Please get off my land,' Polly said assertively, 'and take these people with you. You are intruding into our private affairs. Matters you wouldn't understand.'

'There's quite a lot I don't understand, Miss Manning, but I'm getting there with Frank Crane's help. He's convinced Tracey Sharp's murder and Ken Glover's are also down to you and Mrs Glover and once we have samples of your DNA I daresay they'll make an interesting match with those our forensic people took at the scene.'

'Don't say anything, Jane,' Polly said firmly. 'No comment to any of the absurdities they throw at us. My cousin Godfrey will sort it all out. He only takes defence cases and he rarely loses one.'

'I'm quite prepared to admit my guilt,' Jane said, in an equally firm voice. 'I shall confess to everything to make it slightly easier to live with myself.'

'Very wise, Mrs Glover,' Jones said heavily. 'Ted, give them the full caution just to preserve the legal niceties and get them down the station.'

Benson took hold of Jane's arm and with simple dignity she allowed herself to be led away. A well-built PC grasped Polly's arm. 'Take your hands off me, my man,' she said briskly, 'and show a little respect for your betters. I can walk unaided.'

The PC looked to Jones for guidance, clearly reacting to a sort of confidence he'd not experienced before in these circumstances.

'Keep a firm grip on her, lad,' Jones told him, 'or she'll pull a fast one, that's guaranteed.'

'You'll live to regret this,' she said to Jones, 'when my people sort this out and you've been demoted to dog-handler.'

'For the first time in your life, Miss Manning,' he said, 'you've managed to do something that none of your people will be able to sort out.'

'I'd not count on that,' she said. She turned away and held out her arm to the PC and flashed him one of her sexy smiles. It left him even further confused. Jones watched her go pensively, as if wondering if she really would, even now, be able to work the usual Manning sleight of hand, get herself released on bail and vanish overnight.

'Thank God you came,' Pam said shakily. 'Oh, thank God you came.'

'They were worried when your line went dead,' Jones told her, 'and with you giving them Frank's name and mine they rang me at home. It was a garbled story but having spoken to you earlier I decided to get some people together and come here. Where *is* Frank?'

'He's in the trench! She pushed him in. She was going to push me in too. Oh, thank God you *came.*'

'I've got a torch, sir,' one of the PCs said. He switched it on and shone it into the trench. Crane lay staring up at them, dirty and dishevelled.

Jones said, 'Are you quite comfortable down there, Frank, or were you aiming to come and join us?'

Crane was still lightheaded and almost breathless with relief but he managed a twisted grin. It was like being back in the CID. However much danger you'd been in, however traumatic the circumstances, it was *de rigueur* to take a light-hearted approach, the unspoken attitude being that it sorted the men from the boys. 'I have to admit I'm strongly tempted to stay. A summer night under the stars, be quite like my days as a boy scout.'

'I'm sure we could find the time to join you in a short sing-song.'

'Can any of you hum the tune to *I'm riding along on the crest of a wave?*'

Another of the PCs, grinning, spoke into the trench. 'If you were able to manoeuvre yourself into a sitting position, sir, I could get in and untie your legs. I'll give you a push and my colleague here will give you a pull. We'll soon have you out.'

The PC eased himself down into one end of the trench and cut the cords on Crane's ankles with a pocket-knife. He then held his hands together like a sling into which Crane put one of his feet. With his handcuffed arms held by Jones and the other PC they yanked him up on to the side of the trench, where they brushed the loose soil from his clothes and wiped his face with a handkerchief.

Pointing at the handcuffs, Jones said, 'I could have sworn I'd heard you say not long ago you'd packed it in, the bondage.'

'Two years abstinence gone for nothing. Polly made it sound so incredibly exciting I couldn't resist.'

He sat at the side of the trench, instinctively drawing in great lungfuls of the air he'd thought he'd soon be cut off from and feeling the circulation return fully to his feet with a pain he revelled in.

'I've got some keys in the car, sir, I'm sure we'll get the cuffs off, they're a standard design,' the PC said, who'd also produced the torch. He was back in minutes and had the handcuffs off in a few more. Crane gave a sigh of relief and began to massage his wrists.

'Oh, Frank, you poor man,' Pam said, putting a hand on his arm. 'How could she believe she'd get away with this frightful business?'

'She's had a lifetime of getting away with things. She'd have got away with burying me if it hadn't been for you.'

Crane was suddenly overwhelmed by a sensation of utter fatigue. It was the reaction to lying in a trench and waiting for the spade-fuls of earth to slowly extinguish his life, even though he'd striven to suspend his imagination. 'You can't begin to guess how it feels,' he said in a low voice, 'to know you're not going to be buried alive.'

Jones gently patted his back. 'All right, Frank, joking aside, we'll get you home. If you're not up to driving your car one of these lads can drive it. Come down in the morning and we'll go through the whole thing.'

The young woman constable, who'd been quietly talking to Pam earlier now came forward. 'Would you like me to arrange coun-selling for you, sir?' she asked.

He gave a faint smile. 'I feel I've handled this badly. Could you ask them what would be the best line to take the *next* time I'm tied up and find myself at the bottom of a trench?'

'Oh, I'll arrange for them to talk it all through with you, sir,' she said solicitously, a woman it seemed who'd been born with an irony bypass.

Crane, fresh from the shower, sat in pyjamas and dressing-gown, sipping a large brandy. Pam said, 'I'll have nightmares for a month. The thought of the two of us buried in that *trench!*'

'I was certain I was a goner. I've got to know that woman, know what she was capable of. If it hadn't been for you ... what made you come after me?'

She shook her head. 'I simply can't explain it. I'd been thinking over all the things that had happened: the car crash, Tracey being killed and then Ken. It always came back to Polly and Jane. And then when I thought of you being alone with them, well, I just couldn't control the urge to make sure you were all right. It was like a strange force, pushing me along.'

'Thank God for a woman's intuition. I was sure I'd not be in any danger, in spite of everything I suspected. But she'd outflanked me. Pinned down who I really was with her usual flair. What a waste of an incredible talent.'

'You may think you owe me, Frank, but I certainly owe you.' She sipped some of the brandy she'd also decided to have, to calm her nerves. 'What if I'd gone on with Ken, decided to live with him? Polly murdered him because of the money. What if she'd murdered me because she thought I might know too much, just like she murdered poor Tracey?' She gave a shudder at the thought.

'Well,' he said, 'it's all over bar an extremely drawn out and complicated court case. The men in the jury will be drooling over Polly, quite unable to believe this elegant, self-assured and incredibly attractive woman could possibly have done such dreadful things, whatever the evidence. And the distaff side of the family will gather round her. People like them always do whether she's guilty or not. She'll certainly give the state a run for the taxpayers' money.'

They sat without speaking for a time in the early hours' silence. Then Crane said, 'Are you still aiming to go home over the weekend? You know you can stay as long as you like.'

'I really must go. I've enjoyed being here so very much. Too much. I've got to get back to work and make a start on sorting out my life. And it's all behind me at last, the fear and the worry. But I'll never forget these days here with you and I'll always wake up glad I'm still alive....'

'John Gillis.'

'It's Frank Crane, John.'

'Ah, Frank, hello there. Any news?'

'There'll be a great deal of news about this particular case in the papers before very long.'

'Do go on.'

'The crucial part as far as you and the insurers are concerned is that Lydia Glover isn't dead. She's alive and well and sitting in a remand cell in Bradford nick. Polly Manning is sitting in another.'

'How can she possibly not be dead, Frank?'

'It's a long story.'

'I can find the time.'

Crane gave him the details as succinctly as possible, broken off now and then by Gillis's astounded exclamations.

'My *God!*' he said, when Crane had finished, 'I've never known anything like it.'

'It's not quite in the same league as those blokes who set fire to their business premises to graft a few bob, is it?'

'Well done, Frank, you've done a marvellous job. The insurers told me only yesterday they'd have to pay out next week if nothing came up. As you no doubt remember there were two insurers involved.'

'For a million each. The original plan was a million to Glover and a million to Polly and Lydia. But they decided Glover wasn't worth a million as all he'd done was identify a dead prostitute as his wife.'

'The insurers will be delighted. I'm sure they'll want to express their gratitude in some kind of a bonus. I'll suggest they think in terms of a percentage of the insured amount. You have after all saved them a considerable sum.'

'That's good of you, John.'

Crane was comfortably off these days, but the money could be invested to cushion his old age. Not that he even wanted to consider being old, however well-cushioned, however slight the risk of being buried alive in someone's back garden.

Crane said, 'They'd have a recording of the call?'

'They played it back to me at home. It didn't make much sense but she came over as very frightened and she was someone I felt I could trust. Ted got the uniforms together and we drove up through the estate without the blues and twos going.'

'How did you get across the back garden without triggering the security light?'

'Good question. It just so happened we'd gathered at the side of the house when the Lydia woman came across the lawn and set off the light, and then there was the kerfuffle when Polly dragged Mrs Draper back to the trees. I was ready to go in mob-handed, but that bright young uniform who was good with torches and pocket-knives and keys for handcuffs, well, he suggested we all crept along by the hedge as Mrs Draper had done. It would be outside the range of the lamp and would be a better surprise tactic. And it was; we got to hear Lydia banging on about the killings and being ready to turn herself in.'

'He is a bright young chap.'

'A born CID man, I reckon. Can you just run through the entire farrago for us, Frank, from the kick-off.'

For the second time that day Crane recounted the full story, as Jones made notes. He sat once more in front of Jones's desk with Ted Benson to one side. When he'd finished, Jones said, 'How do you reckon the three of them got together on this?'

'I'm not sure, but I should think Jane stroke Lydia will fill you in as she's in the mood for putting her hand up. What I do know is that Ken Glover was the agent for the Ranelagh House sale. I think we can take it as read that Polly would take off her knickers for him as long as he screwed the vendors into the lowest possible price. I daresay he mentioned at some point that Lydia had been at Bradford Girls' round about the time Polly had been there and Polly could remember how badly Lydia had wanted to be a Polly friend. Maybe Glover fixed it so that Polly appeared to meet Lydia by chance in town. When Polly twigged that Lydia still thought she was Lady Wonderful I reckon that was when she thought the scheme would work. She had this fantastic knack of manipulating people, no doubt about it. I saw her in action at the Mayfield.'

Ted Benson said, 'And it took a year to sort the thing out?'

'Yes, the cover had to be in place for twelve months before the insurers would cough up on suicide, if that's what it was deemed to be. As it turned out the coroner brought in an open verdict.'

'The premiums must have been hefty.'

'Not for term assurance. There's no endowment involved and the cover's only in place for say twenty, twenty-five years.'

'But still, for all that cover ...'

'Polly screwed a good divorce settlement out of her ex-husband and Lydia was earning reasonable money and bonuses. Between them they'd have been able to cover the premiums for one year.'

Jones said, 'But if Jane was Lydia and Lydia was supposed to be dead she'd be a non-person. She'd have no NI number, no driving licence or passport. It could have led to big problems later.'

'I think Polly just swept her along, Terry, saying the money would sort everything out. I reckon she kept her topped up with booze and there was the Mayfield every night with Polly's new circle. I'm sure Lydia must have had misgivings but her feelings for Polly blotted them out.'

Benson said, 'Well, we know how it happened now so we have to assume that's how it was between Polly and Lydia, but Ken Glover, Frank. I mean there's no doubt he was a bit of an arsehole but he didn't actually murder anyone and he led a basically decent life. How do you think he could bring himself to get involved in a murder?'

'Because Polly had promised to do all the dirty work. I'm certain he'd not have wanted to know had there been any question of him having to be in at the sharp end. As we know, he was flat broke with his gambling addiction. I reckon that the idea of a bunch of loot like that and all he had to do was identify a body was a no-brainer to a weak character like him.'

'This Polly: she gives an impression of being normal but she's got to be wrong in the head, like all these people who think they can get away with murder.'

'You're wrong, Ted,' Crane said, 'she's one of the most intelligent women I've ever met. If the scam had worked she'd have built up a successful business very fast. She was gifted and driven and knew how to network. Arendt wrote about the banality of evil but it doesn't somehow apply to Polly. With her it was like that old film *The Godfather* where the killings were always very precisely defined: they were either business or personal. If they were business there was no emotion involved, they were just carried out to improve the market share of the family in question.

'And that was how Polly operated. She needed seed-corn capital so she killed a prostitute. She decided Tracey Sharp might know too much so she killed her. Glover was demanding too big a share so he had to go, and me and Pam just had the bad luck to get in the way. There were no hard feelings involved. Believe me,' he said feelingly, 'I know.'

'Frank,' Jones said, 'how could an intelligent, well-bred, well-educated woman like her *do* these things? Year in, year out we deal with people in the nick who do do banal things: killing their woman in the kitchen because she seems too friendly with the bloke next door, kicking a bloke's head in because he tries to stop his motor being nicked, giving an old lady a fatal stroke by breaking in and stealing nine quid. I just can't get Polly's carry on together.'

Crane got up and crossed to the window, where he turned and stood with his back to it. He'd been very restless since his session in the trench. 'I've given it a lot of thought. Her line on her mother's side goes back five or six hundred years. It was a noble line and I have a feeling Polly inherited the genes intact. In those days the upper classes tended to regard the commoners as either cannon fodder, servants or toilers on the land. They were a sub-species, their lives and deaths of absolutely no account. I doubt Polly lost a minute's sleep over the deaths, they were just necessary so she could bring the family name back to the prominence it once had. When she got her business going I'd not have been surprised if she'd let herself have a couple of kids by some healthy boyfriend or other so she could give them the best education and groom them for the best spheres of influence. I think the family thing's bred in the bone too.'

He grinned widely. 'But that's just my theorizing. It could be a load of old cobblers. All I know for certain is that I'd not want to meet another woman like Polly on a dark night.'

'There'll have to be psychiatrists' reports, all that expensive rubbish,' Jones said dourly. 'They'll have a field day with the odd couple.'

'You're going to have a tough fight on your hands,' Crane said. 'Polly will never stop thinking it all through and she's got those very formidable relations behind her on her mother's side. They'd not lend her money when she needed it, but they'll rally round if it's going to reflect badly.'

'They'll have their work cut out with you and Pam as chief prosecution witnesses. This relationship the women had, it was kind of, what do you call it, sym ... sym—?'

'Symbiosis. Let's say there are two people and each have something the other needs or wants, so even if they're totally different types they make allowances for each other and accept the differences and both benefit.'

'How do you think they feel about each other now?'

'They'll not be able to stand the sight of each other. Polly being Polly I'm pretty sure she always regarded Lydia as a total wimp, and as for Lydia, she finally saw Polly for the monster she is.'

'Pity we got shot of capital punishment in the sixties. Those two deserve it.'

Benson said, 'I wish when they go in the slammer we could

arrange to have them banged up in the same cell. I reckon that would have the edge on capital punishment.'

Crane said, 'You've hit the nail, Ted. I'm sure they'd sooner be hanged.'